Brigade

urther Adventures of Lestrade

Volume II in the Sholto Lestrade Mystery Series

M.J. Trow

A Gateway Mystery

REGNERY
PUBLISHING, INC.
Since 1947 • An Eagle Publishing Company

Published in the United States by
Regnery Publishing, Inc.
An Eagle Publishing Company
One Massachusetts Avenue, NW
Washington, DC 20001

Distributed to the trade by
National Book Network
4720-A Boston Way
Lanham, MD 20706

Printed on acid-free paper.
Manufactured in the United States of America

10 9 8 7 6 5 4 3 2 1

Books are available in quantity for promotional or premium use. Write to Director of Special Sales, Regnery Publishing, Inc., One Massachusetts Avenue, NW, Washington, DC 20001, for information on discounts and terms or call (202) 216-0600.

International Standard Book Number:
0-89526-342-4

They that had fought so well
Came thro' the jaws of Death,
Back from the mouth of Hell,
All that was left of them,
Left of six hundred.

Alfred, Lord Tennyson

A Day To Remember

Alex Dunn took Edwin Cook's hard-boiled egg and peeled it carefully. He watched the pieces fall away beyond his stirrup leather and munched the egg gratefully. He'd had no breakfast, nor indeed any dinner the night before. His stomach was telling him loudly that his throat had been cut. Then, suddenly, there was a stir right front and he wished he hadn't made that mental analogy. A staff officer – Lewis Nolan, wasn't it? – galloped past the waiting lines to where Lucan sat his horse. He was the fourth galloper that morning, but Lewis Nolan usually meant business. Dunn finished his egg and turned in the saddle. Away to his left Roger Palmer was scribbling a note on the smooth surface of his sabretache.

Dear Father, Palmer's pencil was a stub and his hands were cold, *Just a hurried note* . . . His pencil snapped. He tucked the paper in his sabretache and followed Dunn's gaze along the line. Harrington Trevelyan was wrapping his sword knot around his wrist. Palmer did not approve of Trevelyan's forage cap. It was not regulation and Palmer was ever a man for regulations.

Henry Wilkin was delighted. He'd never really known why he'd become a surgeon. Up to the armpits in other people all day, what sort of life was that? A serving officer now, that was different. Mind you, if Yates hadn't reported sick, he wouldn't have been here this morning. If Nolan's gallop meant action he'd have to rely on his sword because his bullet pouch was full of laudanum – the legacy of a medical man. He really must quit the medical service. As if to take the first steps in that direction, he urged his horse forward to the front of F Troop. Cook glared at him, snorting something about damned quacks, and Wilkin backed up a little. George Loy Smith was too old a hand to let a horse's arse in his face bother him. He was adjusting his stirrup leather when Wilkin attempted his backward manoeuvre. He straightened up and tilted his busby back into position, tucking the chain under his great auburn beard, and snarled at Bill Bentley to spit out his tobacco. No soldier of his troop was going into action with black spittle on his chin. Bentley hadn't really heard him, until he felt the sergeant-major's hand sting him smartly on the shoulder. He had been day-dreaming. Today was his Emma's birthday. She was eleven. And Bentley had been remembering the day of her baptism at Kilmainham. He had been a private soldier then, but proud in his regimentals carrying the baby to the font. She had been the most gorgeous baby in the world, snuggling into her dad's pelisse.

Seth Bond sat on the wing of C Troop. He was shivering from cholera and couldn't keep his horse still. He tried to keep his mind occupied by watching the altercation at the front. The staff officer was waving his hand behind him, scarlet in the face and defiant. Lord Look-On seemed bemused, uncomprehending. The staff officer wheeled away to join the 17th to the left. It was the first time Bond had seen the generals actually talking to each other – Look-On and the Noble Yachtsman. He couldn't catch more than a muffled conversation, what with the champ of bits and the muttering of the men behind him.

John Kilvert on his right was wondering why he had enlisted at all. He too had spent most of the night throwing up over his boots and was glad no one had offered him any breakfast. He wished he was back in Nottingham, selling wines and spirits. He wasn't likely to become mayor now, and the chance faded by the moment as he saw Cardigan walk his chestnut to the centre of the brigade.

It was not Cardigan's appearance that worried William Perkins, unless of course His Lordship were to place a beady blue eye down his trumpet that morning. He had traded some of his French photographs for Bentley's tobacco, but was dismayed to find that Bentley had used the photographs to fix a gap in his tent. He was even more dismayed to find that someone – he thought immediately of Jim Hodges – had wedged a plug into his mouthpiece. Still, Joseph Keates was trumpet-major for the 11th. If called upon to sound, he would have to hope Keates would cover for him. In the noise of an advance, no one could tell.

William Pennington was new to all this. Was the Mercantile Marine, he mused now as he sat his horse in B Troop, so awful that he should have left them? Perhaps it was the porter in Dublin that day in January, perhaps it was the glittering uniform of the Bringer, perhaps the bounty of £9, perhaps . . . but the moment for self-doubt had gone. John Parkinson nudged him in the elbow and nodded to the front. Cardigan nodded stiffly to John Douglas, tall and silent in the saddle in the centre of the 11th. They were going. Alex Dunn slid his sword upwards so that its extra three inches flashed in the sun breaking weakly on the tattered brigade below. Loy Smith barked as he saw that idiot Hope gallop into place to his right. The cripple was riding a troophorse of the Greys. Where the bloody hell had he been? Having a fit somewhere, he supposed. Well, he'd give him hell for it when this was over.

Stillnesses and sudden hushes don't really happen, Pennington was telling himself. But he was sitting in the middle of one anyway. Ahead stretched a long valley, parchment-coloured sand and rubble. On the hills to the right, a line of guns. Russian guns. On the left, more of the same. What was ahead? He couldn't see, but he felt panic grip his heart. Loy Smith turned in the saddle.

'All set, Mr Pennington?' and he gave a fatherly glance to Edwin Hughes, sixteen years old and less than regulation height. He'll outlive us all, the sergeant-major thought to himself.

'The Brigade will advance,' came Cardigan's hoarse, chesty bark; 'first squadron of the 17th Lancers direct.'

And the shrill notes of the trumpet drowned his words. For a second, three, perhaps four, the 11th, Prince Albert's Own Hussars sat motionless, each man a prisoner of his private thoughts and fears. Then they broke forward, shifting position as on the parade ground at Maidstone at Lucan's order for the 11th to fall back and the 17th to take the lead. The dark-coated lancers fronted the brigade, their pennons snapping in the wind that crossed the valley. It was the noise that Pennington remembered most, the snorting of horses and the jingle of bits and from time to time above the

incessant sound of hoofs, the growling of Loy Smith to his
men.

'Draw swords.' It was Colonel Douglas, freeing his own
weapon as Cardigan increased the pace. He could see the
leaders – Mayow and FitzMaxse – beyond the line of the 17th.
The swords of the 11th shot clear.

'At the slope,' Loy Smith reminded his troop. Bentley
cradled the blade against his shoulder and tightened his rein.
They were at the trot now, rising and falling as a man. Still
the lances were upright. Still Cardigan was leading. Like a
church, thought Palmer. He moved neither to left, nor right,
the sun flashing on the gold lace of his pelisse. He felt the line
quicken, following the last of the Brudenells.

Loy Smith saw it first, as his wise old eyes saw any
irregular movement in the line. The staff officer, the one who
had brought the last order, was spurring ahead, out from the
left wing of the 17th, chasing Cardigan, but cutting across to
the right. He was waving his sword arm and yelling, but Loy
Smith couldn't catch the words. The 17th began to waver.
They were turning. Douglas checked his horse, Dunn began
to pull his charger to the right. Was the Brigade turning?
There was no trumpet call. Why wasn't there a trumpet call?

A whistle, moaning high above the wind. Louder. Louder.
A crash and a burst of flame and smoke. The staff officer
crumpled, hooked over like a crab in the saddle, but his right
arm was still upright. The terrified horse swerved, wheeled
round, reins hanging loose, and charged back through the
lines. The 17th negotiated the mêlée and the line re-formed.
One by one the serrefiles and troop sergeants and the centre
men saw it and heard the unearthly scream. What was left of
Lewis Nolan flashed past them all. His face was a livid white,
his eyes sightless and his lungs and ribs visible where his
gold-laced jacket had been.

'Look to your dressing,' Loy Smith reminded his troop,
knowing the damage that sight could do to his callow boys.
The moment was past. Nolan had gone and the 13th saw him
fall under their hoofs.

The trumpet sounded the gallop. Swords came up from the
slope, ready and vertical in men's fists. The crash of artillery
fire increased, drifting along the lines of horsemen. And those

lines were less steady now. Dunn held his sword arm out to his side to correct the pace of the horsemen behind him. Was Cardigan mad? he found himself wondering. The enemy was visible now, despite the smoke – a row, perhaps a double row of reeking guns ahead, more on the hills on each side. It was a trap. A valley with a closed end. The 17th's lances came down, level, thrusting, twelve feet of ash and steel slicing through the air. The wind cut through the horsemen, each man now bracing himself for the impact. The roar of cantering horses moving into a gallop drowned the noise of the guns. But in the centre, where Pennington and Parkinson were riding knee to knee, the guns were evident. Charles Allured, on Parkinson's right, went down, his horse bucking and screaming. On Loy Smith's flank Joseph Bruton slumped over the neck of his troophorse. Isaac Middleton caught him momentarily, but lost his grip and the soldier fell.

'Mend your pace. Watch your dressing.' Loy Smith's calming words rang out above the slaughter. A shot smashed into a horse's head at Bond's elbow, and the blood spattered over his jacket and face. He could hear Robert Bubb to his left crying as his horse went down.

How long, thought Douglas, how long can we endure this? The 17th were closing ranks in front of him, as the murderous shot tore into them.

'Keep together, Eleventh!' he shouted, but knew as always it was his troop sergeants who were the steadying influence, the backbone. The roar of hoofs and cannon was unbearable. Horses were racing now, vying with the riderless mounts to get to the Russian guns and silence them. Cardigan had vanished into the smoke, the lances of the 17th jabbing the blackness ahead. Behind Bentley, Pennington's horse staggered, reeling to the left. Pennington struggled to keep him upright, but couldn't see where he was going. Men were standing in their stirrups, sword arms extended, yelling themselves hoarse in the confusion and noise. Loy Smith swore he heard Hope, that mad Welsh bastard, singing 'Men of Harlech', but it could have been Keates' trumpet notes, lost in the din. David Purcell was blown out of the saddle on his right, and he saw Tom Roberts fall back, clutching his leg.

Then, for Douglas at least, the smoke cleared. He was on

the guns. To all sides, grey-coated Russians were scattering. There were horses and men heaped around the cannon, blackened and hot with rapidity of fire. The remaining 17th were leaping over them and Douglas leapt with them. A knot of the 11th, led by Loy Smith, were behind him. All semblance of order was lost, the lines so beloved of Maidstone and the Curragh gone in the frantic rush for the guns. Dunn was scything about him, hacking at the gunners. Palmer and Trevelyan rammed their spurs into their chargers' flecked flanks and leapt into the battery smoke. Flames and screams were all about them. Will Spring felt a searing pain in his shoulder and his horse dragged him for several yards before his foot fell free of the stirrup. Gregory Jowett tried to reach him, but was beaten back by the weight of numbers.

In the mill beyond the guns, Bond and Bentley found themselves together. Neither man could believe his eyes. Cavalry. Russian Cavalry. Perhaps four or five times their own number were advancing along the sand towards them. What was left of the 17th and 11th were fighting in tiny knots, steel flashing and ringing in the sun. There wasn't time for a word, or a glance, before the two sergeants were parrying for their lives. Bond wheeled his horse, hacking behind him in the most difficult cut of the 1796 Manual. Bentley did likewise, but his opponents were lancers. He felt a lance tip jab through his busby, parting his hair for a second time that morning. Another thudded into the saddle, an inch or so from his groin. He was turning in the air like a man possessed, snapping off one lance pole, then another. As he hacked, he prayed. But it wasn't Almighty God who cantered to his side, but Lieutenant Alexander Dunn, scything down one Russian, then two. He wheeled his charger across Bentley's.

'"Rear protect" never was a sensible guard.' He grinned and batting aside another lance jab with his bridle arm drove his blade through the teeth of its owner.

Pennington's mare had fallen, sending her rider sprawling under the wheels of the guns. By the time he scrambled to his feet, the first line of the 8th Hussars swept past him. Pennington caught sight of the Old Woman leading his men in, clearing the guns with a thud and a spray of dust.

'Grab the rein, man,' the bark of a sergeant-major snapped him back to reality. He snatched the leather, somehow found the saddle and found himself charging the Russians with the 8th. The field was now a mass of individual duels. Gregory Jowett was laying about him alongside Roger Palmer. To his fury, his blade was bouncing off the Russian greatcoats around him and he cursed the Birmingham cutlers who had made such useless weapons. In the end he used the hilt like a knuckle-duster, aiming for the moustachioed faces under the fur caps. Lieutenant Palmer, swinging at his side, having given up the neat cuts of the Manual, was unaware of the Russian carbine aimed at his head. Jowett saw it and for a split second remembered that Palmer had upbraided him days before for being asleep at his post. The split second passed and Jowett's sword sliced down through neck and collarbone, the carbine shot flying wide. After all, he reasoned with himself, Palmer had not had him flogged. He owed him that at least.

Douglas, at the head of D Troop, had outflanked the guns on the left. His was the only unit marginally intact and he pointed his sword at the Russian squadrons advancing to meet him. 'Right Engage.' Stragglers of the 17th, bleeding, their lance caps gone, wheeled in behind him.

'Rally men!' Douglas shouted. 'Rally men of the Seventeenth.' But in the dust and smoke the majority of the lancers were not the 17th. Palmer saw it first.

'That's the enemy!' he said and swung in to the attack again. A rifle exploded near him, bringing down a soldier of the 4th Lights who had swept past the guns. For a moment he caught sight of Lord George Paget, a bedraggled cigar in his mouth, and then he turned to look for his own regiment.

Alex Dunn saw a remarkable sight he would remember for the rest of his days. Through the choking smoke he saw Cardigan, unhurt and upright, facing a mass of Russian lancers. The officer in their centre seemed to know Cardigan and the two men saluted each other with their swords. The general of Hussars wheeled away to another part of the field.

Paget had lost his own 4ths and was busy directing an aimless mass of the 11th. Loy Smith was doing the same thing beyond the furthermost guns. Instinctively, knots of survivors were breaking away, hurling tired insults at the hesitating Russians. Without cohesion or any real leadership, the enemy dithered at the end of the valley, allowing the British cavalry to pull back. Still the firing went on: Loy Smith's horse was now swinging a broken leg. The sergeant-major kicked himself free of the stirrups and ran as soon as his feet touched the ground. Bullets were kicking up the dust at his heels as he caught a riderless mount and clinging on for dear life, rode back up the valley. He saw Pennington running back too, but hadn't time to reach him before he fell, blood spurting from his leg. Undaunted, the soldier rolled upright, unbuckling his equipment to give him extra speed and hobbled onwards as Russian swordsmen swung at him. A soldier of the 8th lifted him awkwardly behind him and they galloped to cover.

To his right, Trevelyan saw the flashing sabres of the Chasseurs D'Afrique, briskly silencing the guns on the heights. The next moment, he felt a crippling pain as riderless horses, terrified by the noise and lack of weight, crowded in against his legs. Their staring eyes and foam-flecked nostrils were as painful to him as his legs, but he found himself using his sword to cut himself free of them.

Slowly, in ones and twos, the remnants of Cardigan's brigade limped back up the valley. They rode or stumbled over the debris of battle – horses with their intestines steaming on the ground – men with smashed limbs and unrecognisable faces. Here and there, a wounded man dragged between comrades. And as the bullets lessened and the shots died away, an eerie calm fell over the field.

Alex Dunn sheathed his sword, dark brown with the blood of Russians. He took his position at the head of D Troop and waited in the numbed silence as the stragglers came back through the smoke. Medical orderlies were everywhere and amid the cries for stretchers and the shots of farriers going about their grisly business, the solemn roll call was taken. In his own regiment the gaps were cruel – Lieutenants Cook and Houghton were unable to answer, Sergeants Jones and Jordan dead, Corporals France and Williams. And as the list increased, Dunn found himself counting the dead and felt the tears trickle down his cheeks.

Sergeant Bentley saw Dunn with his head in his hands and

thought that this was not the moment to thank him for saving his life. Jim the Bear was cantering on his blown chestnut along the line, still as steady as a church. Bentley caught only part of it . . .

'It was a mad-brained trick, men, but it was no fault of mine.'

Behind him, the sergeant heard a voice. 'Never mind, My Lord, ready to go again.' Bentley prayed that Cardigan had not heard.

'No, no, you have done enough.' And he rode away from his old regiment.

In the silence of his tent that night John Douglas wrote to his wife. *My Dearest Rosa* . . . but he could not find the words. Of the 142 officers and men of the 11th Hussars on parade that morning, 25 were dead, 31 were wounded, 8 were missing and over half the regiment's horses lay rotting in the biting night wind out there in the valley. Alex Dunn walked the cavalry lines, cradling for a moment the head of his charger as he passed. He patted the animal's neck and pulling his cloak around him went into his tent. His orderly had laid out the writing case as he had asked. He forced his numbed fingers around the quill and began to write. *Darling Rosa* . . . and the lamplight flickered on the canvas walls . . .

It was October 25th, 1854. A day to remember.

The fire crackled as the logs fell. Joseph Lestrade straightened up and looked behind him.

'Time that boy was in bed, Martha.'

'Let's try him again before he goes, Joe, one last time.'

Lestrade looked at the woman kneeling on the hearthrug and the round, curly-headed boy on her lap.

'All right, Sholto. Come on, come on. Come to your dad.' The little boy gurgled and his eyes flashed, but he made no move. Joseph Lestrade knelt down, arms outstretched across the rug.

'Come on, lad. You can do it.' The boy's eyes caught sight of something flashing silver in the firelight. His father saw it too.

'What's that, Sholto? My coat? The numbers, isn't it? The

numbers on the collar.' And the proud father spelt them out. 'PC one-six-five,' he whispered.

With a gabble of nonsense, Baby Lestrade struggled to his feet. For a moment he swayed back against the comforting breasts of his mother. She held him to her and then he was gone, staggering now to the left, now to the right. His eyes were flashing in the firelight as he advanced on his father and his father's coat.

'That's it. That's it. Good lad. Come and get it. Come on.'

And Baby Lestrade collapsed into his father's arms, his fingers grabbing at the buttons. 'He did it, Martha. How about that? Nine months old and his first step. How about that?'

But Martha's eyes were wet with tears. She whirled away to fetch her house-book and snatching up the quill wrote:

Little Sholto took his first step today, October 25th, 1854. A day to remember.

The New Broom

Sholto Lestrade's walking had come on admirably. But then he was nearly forty years old. He found himself looking at his feet particularly hard that morning. That silly magazine *Punch* had been caricaturing Her Majesty's Metropolitan Police again, and inevitably most of the humour was of the street and at gutter level – tortuous jokes about 'A Policeman's Boot is not a Happy One.' Nothing outsize there, Lestrade thought to himself.

'Mornin', sir.' Dixon's hearty greeting brought his eyes up to the usual level.

'Sergeant,' acknowledged Lestrade. 'Anything for me today?'

''Is nibs,' Sergeant Dixon motioned heavenwards, 'would like to see you when you can spare a moment.'

''Is nibs?' queried Lestrade.

'Assistant Commissioner 'isself, sir. Proper gent 'e looks.'

Lestrade made for the stairs, then remembered the possible effect on his feet and took the lift instead. It whirred and clanked in the time-honoured tradition of a contraption less than three years old to the second floor, where Lestrade had his palatial office, wedged between a broom cupboard and a latrine. Constable Dew was waiting for him, mug of tea in hand.

'Not this morning, Dew, I've had the call.'

'What could it be, sir? Mrs Manchester's tart?'

But Lestrade had gone, leaving Walter Dew with one of those inevitable silences to which his humour usually entitled him.

The door, which Lestrade always thought of as McNaghten's, stood square and solid before him.

'Enter.'

It was not McNaghten. He had retired a month ago, lost and bewildered over the death of his daughter, and in his place stood one of the largest men Lestrade had ever seen. He weighed, Lestrade guessed, nearly nineteen stones and most of that lay somewhere between his chest and his knees. He had the look of a bulldog on heat, red-rimmed eyes and loose, quivering lips.

'Inspector Lestrade, sir. You wished to see me?'

'Yes.' The bulldog came snarling out from behind his desk. 'My name is Frost. Nimrod Frost.' The bulldog circled Lestrade, swinging his girth ahead of him like a coster-monger's cart in Covent Garden. 'Assistant Commissioner. The new Head of the Criminal Investigation Department.' Each word was delivered with precision and relish. Lestrade tried to place it. Dixon was wrong; wherever the bulldog came from, he was no gentleman. The voice was worked, moulded, hammered into shape by a man who had waited, watched, come up the hard way. There was no tougher policeman. 'You'll hear a lot of me in the days ahead.' The bulldog completed the circuit and regained his seat.

'Sholto Joseph Lestrade.' Frost's eyes narrowed over the stub that was his nose. 'Bachelor.' The word sounded like an accusation. Frost seemed to be waiting for some kind of admission. 'Born – Pimlico. January eighteen fifty-four. Father, Police Constable Joseph Lestrade, Metropolitan Police. Mother, Martha Jane Appleyard, laundress.' The bulldog waited again for some sort of statement. There was none. 'Eldest of three children, the others dying in infancy. Education. . .' Frost paused. 'Hmmm. School at Blackheath. Right, let's stop there.' The bulldog was padding round the room again. Occasionally he let his eyes wander to the window and the sun gilding the statuary of the Houses of Parliament. 'Lestrade,' he suddenly said; 'that's a foreign name, isn't it?'

'Huguenot French, sir. Or so I've always believed.'

'Frog?'

'Some time ago, sir. One of the things I picked up at Mr Coulson's Academy at Blackheath was that large numbers of Huguenot weavers came to this country in the late seven-teenth century. My grandfather used to say the Lestrades came from La Rochelle and settled in Spitalfields where—'

'Thank you for the history lesson, Lestrade.' The bulldog appeared to have bitten off more than he could chew. 'Why did you become a policeman?' He turned again to the file on Lestrade.

'It seemed like a good idea at the time.'

'Quite. Regrets?'

'About the Force? No, sir. It's always with you.'

'Quite. McNaghten spoke highly of you. You've got some good collars.'

Lestrade was surprised momentarily by the compliment. 'I think smartness and efficiency go together, sir,' and as he said it, he realised Frost was referring to arrests, not his sartorial elegance.

'What I don't like in detective inspectors,' growled the bulldog, 'is a sense of humour. It doesn't become them.' A weighty pause, then a new tack. 'Are you familiar with the latest Home Office paper on the Metropolitan Police, Inspector?'

Blank.

'I thought not. Junior policemen, good, bad, or indifferent tend not to read such things. A pity. An awareness of the views of the hands that feed us is no bad thing.' Lestrade was vaguely aware of a mixed metaphor, but let it pass.

Frost produced a welter of official-looking documents, cleared his throat and read aloud: '"An inspector is looked upon as a guide, guardian and referee by those whose unpleasant business causes them to seek police aid. In contrast with bygone days an inspector must be a man of education' – the bulldog paused pregnantly – 'and capable judgement; the public must feel a firm reliance in him as such." Well, Lestrade, are *you* that man?' A dramatic finger stabbed the air inches from the inspector's face. 'Good God, man.' Frost was suddenly astounded. 'You've got no tip to your nose!'

'Some of it is probably still lying on a pavement in Cambridge, sir. In the line of duty. Still more of it is interred in Highgate Cemetery. That was a private matter.'

'Very cryptic,' scowled the bulldog, but Lestrade knew it wasn't a joke. 'This department,' Frost went on, 'is in for a shake-up. People haven't forgotten the Ripper.' Neither had

Lestrade. 'Or the *Struwwelpeter* murders,' Nor had Lestrade.
'The magazine *Punch*' – it was as though Frost had been
reading his mind on the way to the Yard – 'persists in calling
us the Defective Force. It's not funny, Lestrade, not funny at
all.' His voice fell from the crescendo he had been building to
all morning. 'Sir Melville McNaghten spoke of you as his
best man.'

'That's very flattering, sir.'

'Yes, isn't it? But I want to know if he's right. I don't want
prima donnas on my Force, Lestrade. I want a team of
dedicated, trustworthy officers.' He began his perambu-
lations again, 'So I've got a little job for you . . . .'

To Sergeant Dixon the new Head of the Criminal Investigation Department quickly became, behind his back and always
in hushed tones, 'His Nims', on account of his name. The
new broom swept through the stuffy corridors of New
Scotland Yard, kicked out the infestation of sergeants which
had lurked for nearly three years in the basement, insisted that
Inspector Athelney Jones replace the ill-fitting patrol jacket he
had worn man and boy for sixteen years, and generally made
his presence felt. If anything, communication within the great
building was slowed down as the lifts, built to carry eight
men, now carried five and Assistant Commissioner Frost. It
did the other three good to run up and down stairs. After all,
exercise was next to Godliness.

But Inspector Lestrade knew little of this. On the day after
his first meeting with Nimrod Frost he was Swindon-bound.
The last time he had taken this route he had had to change
because of Brunel's blasted wide gauge. Now at last the
railway companies had seen sense and demolished it. He still
had to change at Swindon however because of track works,
and the tea and sandwiches at the Great Western buffet were
as nauseating as he remembered them. Mrs Manchester had
begged him to take some of her pasties, but making for
Cornwall as he was there was something of coals and
Newcastle about the whole thing. He browsed through the
periodicals on the shelves of the W.H. Smith bookstall and he
shuddered as his fingers alighted on a copy of the *Strand
Magazine*. For a moment, he wondered if that idiot Watson

was still feeding Conan Doyle those ludicrous stories about Sherlock Holmes, even though the man had been dead these eighteen months. He had no time to ponder as the whistle was blowing and he dashed through the steam to catch the twenty past two for Exeter.

He spent the night, warm for April, within the sound of the cathedral bells. Lestrade was not a romantic in the conventional sense, but the great grey stones and the solemn bell had a haunting quality all of their own. Supper was modest enough on the expenses Frost had been meagre enough to allow him and he dozed fitfully.

The following afternoon found Inspector Lestrade flanked by a sergeant and two constables of the Cornwall Constabulary overlooking the Helford River. Behind them was the huge, silent earthwork which surrounded the little church of Mawnan. Through the strange, stunted trees below them, the policemen could see the sea, shifting in its greyness, rolling in its quest for the coast. There was a stillness Lestrade found odd. He was still happiest in the clutter of the city, even if he hadn't actually been able to hear Bow Bells when he was born.

'You say it was sighted here?'

The sergeant nodded and, attempting to modify his broad Cornish for Lestrade's benefit, replied, 'Three times, sir. Once there, in the woods. Once on the banks behind us and the parson seen it in the crypt.'

'In the crypt?' Lestrade was incredulous.

''Ere's parson now.' The sergeant indicated an elderly gentleman striding manfully with the aid of a stick over the earthworks.

'Neolithic,' shouted the vicar.

'Lestrade,' the inspector answered.

'Ah yes. My name is Ashburton.' Lestrade must have misheard earlier. 'Yes, this earthwork,' the vicar went on; 'it's neolithic, you know. Where the church stands now was probably part of a Celtic fortress, of prodigious size, wouldn't you say?'

Lestrade would.

'If you've finished with the constables, Inspector, I can show you around. And then you're very welcome to partake of some supper. My good lady wife makes a marvellous

Cornish pasty.'

Marvellous it was, but the Reverend Ashburton's brandy was better. In the mellow study of the parsonage that evening, Lestrade found himself becoming mellower with each moment. But he did have a job to do.

'Can we go over it again, sir?'

'Certainly, Inspector, but tell me, are you familiar with Gilbert White of Selborne?'

'Gilbert White the forger?'

The vicar chuckled. 'Well, he may have been, but he is best remembered as a naturalist. A long time before all this nonsense of Darwin's and Huxley's, the Reverend White collected specimens and made drawings of all the flora and fauna of his native Selborne. With far less skill, I have attempted to do much the same here in Mawnan. Around you, you see the fruits of these labours.'

Lestrade had thought the plethora of birds' eggs, stuffed newts and mounted butterflies a little zoological for an Anglican priest, but it took all sorts.

'I am familiar with all the animals native to Cornwall and Devon, Inspector, but I have never seen anything like the creature I saw in my churchyard last week.'

'Which was?'

'As I said, it was dusk. I had just finished bell practice. Are you a campanologist?'

'Politics aren't encouraged on the Force, sir.'

Ashburton gave Lestrade an odd look. 'Anyway, I was crossing the South Gateway – the entrance to the Old Fort, that is – when I hear this . . . well, unearthly scream. Fortified by the fact that the Lord was with me, I went to investigate. I was carrying a stout walking stick at the time. I heard noises in the shrubbery and saw a shape – huge.' The vicar swigged his brandy. 'It *was* a lion, Lestrade.'

'Have you had a travelling circus pass this way?'

'Er . . . I don't know. I don't follow such things. If there was a circus, I assume Exeter would be its likely venue. You think the beast escaped from a circus?'

'Unless you or Gilbert White know of Mawnan or Selborne lions, sir, I am forced to that conclusion. What I cannot understand is why I should be sent here.'

'Inspector,' the Reverend Ashburton refilled Lestrade's glass, 'although I would not wish you to repeat this to a living soul, I do not have the greatest respect for the County Constabulary. It was I who contacted Scotland Yard, although, I must admit, I did not think anyone would come. Over thirty sheep have been slaughtered, Inspector. Most of my parishioners are farmers. Their life blood is being drained away on the moors.'

A commotion in the hall brought the two men to their feet. Sergeant Winch of the Cornwall Constabulary almost fell in through the door.

'Sorry, sir, Mr Ashburton, to disturb you, sir. Inspector. You'd better come. The thing's attacked again, over at Constantine.'

Lestrade looked at the vicar. 'A village about four miles away. We can take my trap.'

'No need, sir. I've got the station wagon,' offered the sergeant.

The night had chilled. April was like that. Winch, Lestrade and the vicar found themselves bouncing off each other in the cheerless interior of the Maria. They jolted past midnight through the sleeping Cornish countryside, through the deserted main street of the curiously named Constantine, to the scene of the slaughter.

'I hope you've got a strong stomach, Inspector,' was Winch's parting shot as he jumped out of the Maria. With the aid of bull's-eyes, the little party stumbled and cursed – apologising to the vicar all the way.

'Over here!' a voice called in the darkness.

Lestrade and his party scrambled over the ling to a crouching figure.

'Good God,' the vicar crossed himself. Rather a Papist gesture, Lestrade thought.

Spreadeagled on the escarpment lay the body of a man. In the wavering light of the bull's-eyes it was obvious his throat had been torn out. There was blood everywhere, from the chin to the waist.

'I thought you told me lambs had been killed.' The sergeant rounded on the crouching figure. 'You didn't say nothing 'bout a man.'

'No, no, you blitherin' idiot,' the other riposted. 'I told you Lamb was killed. William Lamb, my shepherd.'

'Who are you?' asked Lestrade, content to leave the body until later. William Lamb was going nowhere by himself.

'Who are you?' The other man was equally straight-forward.

'Inspector Lestrade, Scotland Yard.'

'Oh,' the attitude changed, 'I'm John Pemberton. I own this farm. William Lamb, 'e works . . . worked for me.'

'What happened?'

'I was on my rounds. Lambin' time is always busy. Most of 'em have borned now, but it pays to watch, crows and foxes an' all. Well, I was just goin' home, when I heard this snarling and snapping, then a scream. My pony shied and by the time I got up here, William was lyin' like this.'

'Dead?'

'No. But 'e were goin'.'

'Did he say anything?'

'Well, it were difficult to hear . . . but . . .'

'But? Come on, man. Out with it.'

''E said one word, Inspector. Tiger.'

Lestrade looked at the assembled company one by one, as if for confirmation of what he had heard.

'"Tyger! Tyger! burning bright,"' the Reverend Ashburton was soliloquising,

'"In the forests of the night,
What immortal hand or eye
Could frame thy fearful symmetry?"'

'A tiger?' repeated Lestrade.

'It could have been,' the vicar answered.

Instinctively, the men on the hillside had huddled closer together. The bull's-eyes threw shafts of light over the ling and tufts of grass.

'Whatever it was, it's gone now.' Pemberton motioned to the ghostly grey shapes of sheep, munching, calm and oblivious in the distance.

'Even so, we'd better not risk spending a night in the open.' Lestrade longed for the claustrophobia of the city. 'Sergeant, get the blanket from the Maria. We'll take him back to your

station. Mr Pemberton, we shall need a statement. And
Sergeant—'

'Sir?'

'By morning I shall have a note for your chief constable.
We'll need guns issued to your men.'

They laid William Lamb out, appropriately enough, on the
slab in the local butcher's shop. The Sanitary Inspector was a
rare enough visitor and as it was Sunday, no one was buying
their viands that day. As the bell of Mawnan Church
summoned the faithful to prayer, under the solemn auspices
of the Reverend Ashburton, Lestrade stood alongside the
deceased.

He was used to the sights. A hardened copper like him,
he'd seen it all. Forget it's human, he told himself for the
umpteenth time. It's a job. That's all. Do it. Have done. He
laid his bowler down on the throat wound. It just fitted.
Pretty massive jaws must have done that. Tiger? Perhaps.
Lion? Perhaps. There were scratches, deep, parallel on the
chest and face. There was something else. Hairs. Not Lamb's.
Too coarse, too light in colour. Sort of tan. He held them up
to the light. Tan colour with a hint of darker brown at one
end. He put his nose to the corpse. A smell of wet grass, of
sheep (the smell which had haunted Lestrade since he arrived)
and something else. Was he sniffing tiger? Lion? Always the
same vicious circle. The plain truth was the men of the Yard
were not well equipped to deal with big cat spoors. Their
training did not give them the edge against the call of the
wild. Dead lurkers in Seven Dials. Gonophs in Whitechapel.
All that was in a day's work, but tigers in Cornwall? No, that
strained credulity. It just didn't fit.

He folded Lamb's arms, limp now after rigor mortis,
across what was left of his chest. He looked briefly at his face.
He was an old man. Small, weak. A curious scar ran across
his forehead and dipped across his left eye. Not a recent
wound. Not the mark of the beast. That was old. Years old.

There was no camera available at Mawnan police station.
Lestrade doubted if there was room in the place to set up a
tripod. He had sent for one from Falmouth. A photographer

would chronicle the injuries later that day.

Lestrade had a mug of tea with Sergeant Winch before returning to the parsonage. He left word with the station to send a message to the Yard to tell Frost of the developments. His return would be delayed. On the way, the inspector met the faithful returning, shocked and gabbling, from church.

'Inspector,' Ashburton hailed him. 'Have you made any headway since last night?'

'A little sir.'

'May I introduce my brother, Percival?'

Lestrade found himself blinking in disbelief. The two men before him were virtually identical. Percival was a little taller, leaner, certainly more tanned.

'Sir.' Lestrade collected himself.

'Yes, it has that effect on most people. Percival is recently back from Australia. Sheep farming.'

Lestrade did not really have time for pleasantries.

'Did I see a microscope in your study, Mr Ashburton?'

'Yes, you did, Inspector. Do you wish to use it? Have you a clue?'

'We have those gadgets at the Yard, sir. Unfortunately I do not know quite how they operate . . .'

'That doesn't present a problem, Inspector. Be my guest. But do tell me. What have you found?'

Lestrade produced the tuft of hairs from the paper bag in his pocket.

'These.'

The brothers Ashburton peered closer. Percival broke away, a little sharply, Lestrade thought. 'Must be going, Thomas. Inspector,' and he tipped his hat.

'Oh, really? Well, don't forget tonight. Dinner after evensong. The inspector will be there, won't you, Inspector?'

'That's very kind of you, sir, but I could not impose—'

'Nonsense. Come on. Modern Science awaits,' and linking his arm with Lestrade's, the vicar led the way beyond the Neolithic earthwork, striding for the parsonage.

Over the vicar's brandy that night, Percival Ashburton became decidedly morose. Apparently, although there was few sharp years of drought and endless attacks by dingoes had taken their toll. It took Lestrade a while to realise that the Alice Springs Ashburton had left behind was not an old flame. But the night was drawing on and the conversation was moving to the altar, how Cardinal Manning had gone too far, and the significance of the ivy in Holman Hunt's *The Light of the World*, all of which sailed sublimely over the inspector's head.

He made his excuses and decided to walk to the inn where he was staying. It was a chill night after a warm day, but the moon was bright and shone silver on the ribbon of road ahead of him. Dogs barked in the distance, answered as in a dream by the remote call of the curlews and the sibilance of the sea. Of these, Lestrade recognised only the dogs, and he didn't like dogs. The Reverend Ashburton's microscope had not proved very helpful. It showed what Lestrade had thought it would – a very large tuft of hairs. But he was absolutely no nearer tracing the animal from which it came, still less catching it. And what had possessed Nimrod Frost to send him on this wild goose chase? It couldn't *be* a wild goose, could it?

Lost in thought, it was a little while before Lestrade noticed him. It was only the moon that betrayed his presence, for he made no sound. A wizened little figure, small, like a monkey, was moving at a trot along the road towards him. As he neared, Lestrade saw that he wore no shoes. He also saw he had loose, straggly hair and a bone through his nose. Hardly a native of Cornwall, Lestrade mused and hailed him. The little man stopped and straightened up, his flat nose level with Lestrade's tie-knot. He grinned broadly, a row of yellow teeth appearing in the burnt umber of his face.

"Ello, boss.'

Lestrade had never heard an accent like it.

'Who are you?' he asked.

'Uku, boss. Mis' Ashburton's abo.'

'Abo?' Lestrade was lost.

'I 'is man, boss. 'Is slave.'

'Slave?'

'Yes, boss. I do work for Mis' Ashburton.'

The light of realisation began to dawn on Lestrade's knitted brow.

'You are an Aborigine? From Australia?'

'Australia. Yes, boss. I come back with Mis' Ashburton. I was hunter in bush.'

'Were you now?' Lestrade was interested. 'Can you track for me?'

'Track? Track what, boss?'

'I don't know,' Lestrade admitted.

'You crazy, boss?'

'Probably. Where are you going now?'

'Message for Mis' Ashburton, boss. I take to brother's house.'

'All right – er – Uku, is it? If you come here tomorrow early – at dawn, I want you to track for me – I will give you . . .' he fumbled in his pocket, 'a shilling.'

The abo snatched the coin, bit it and slipped it into his pocket.

'All right, boss. Sunarise. 'Ere. But you crazy, boss. No dingo 'ere,' and he padded off into the night as silently as he had come.

No dingo, eh? From the conversation earlier in the evening, it seemed as though the Australian wild dogs could easily bring down a sheep. And a man? Particularly an old man, slow, weak, a little deaf, maybe? Yes, it was possible. But first, he must get back to the parsonage. That library of the vicar's. There was some research he had to do. The vicar was bound to have a book on it.

'My dear Inspector, charity may begin at home but it is nearly' – the Reverend checked his half-hunter – 'two-thirty. Contrary to popular belief, I do work on other days than the Sabbath, you know.'

'Forgive me, sir. I have imposed on your hospitality too long,' Lestrade snapped shut the last of several tomes, 'but I think I have what I require.'

'A solution to the death of Lamb?'

'Perhaps.' Lestrade raised a solemn hand to the start from Ashburton. 'As you say, sir, it is late. And at the moment what I have is circumstantial and speculation. And even to say that at two-thirty in the morning is no mean achievement.'

* * *

It had been a long time since Lestrade had seen a country
sunrise. He was tired and cold and the bed at the inn had been
far from comfortable. The abo was waiting for him as he
turned the corner, crouching, sniffing the wind.

''Ello, boss.' The same inane grin.

Lestrade found himself staring at the bone which ran
through the elongated fleshy part of his nose between the
nostrils. 'What we track?'

'What?' Lestrade came to. 'Ah, yes. Can you find me a
dingo?'

The abo laughed, a short, sharp cackle, rather like the
kookaburra Lestrade had been reading about in the vicar's
library the night before.

'Dingo, boss. 'Ere? You crazy all right.'

'Look at this.' Lestrade produced the tuft of hair. 'Dingo,
Uku?'

The abo looked, felt between his fingers, smelt the strands.
He looked puzzled. 'No, boss, no dingo.' Then his face
cracked into a wide grin. 'No dingo, boss. Tammanwool.'

'Tammanwool?' Lestrade was back to his usual repetition.

'You lucky, boss. I been Tamman. No abos there now. I
seen tammanwool.'

The conversation had left Lestrade behind, which was
exactly what the abo was about to do. 'Can you find the
tammanwool for me?'

'Sure, boss. We go now,' and he took to his heels, moving
off at a low run down the road, Lestrade staggering in his
wake. Probably, thought Lestrade, the wake of the long
white cloud. Or was that somewhere else? The sun began to
climb as the abo took to the moors, padding silently through
the yellow fields of mustard around the village and up on to
the greyness of the hills, splashed here and there with the
white of the heather and the yellow and green of the gorse.
Lestrade prided himself on being a fit man, but his temples
and lungs felt as if they were going to burst. Always, the
retreating figure of the abo ahead was like a needle in his flesh,
forcing him on. God, thought Lestrade, the black bastard's
going all the way to Constantine. Four miles. God, he
thought again, perhaps he's going all the way to Australia?
His shirt was hanging out in an undignified flapping at his

waist. He had long since lost his bowler and his collar stood out at an angle from his neck. He hoped to God he didn't meet anyone who knew he was an inspector of detectives from Scotland Yard, as his image would never recover.

Then he realised the abo had stopped. He was crouching, like a coiled spring, in the low, twisted trunks below Mawnan Church, where the vicar had seen his lion weeks earlier. The bastard wasn't even out of breath and Lestrade was on his hands and knees, fighting to keep the pain out of his tortured lungs.

'There, boss. Tammanwool hole.' The abo pointed ahead, to an overgrown outcrop of Neolithic earthwork. Lestrade saw nothing but an overgrown outcrop of Neolithic earthwork, but the abo was adamant, and Lestrade followed him through the undergrowth to a concealed opening. Even the nostrils of a city copper, unused to the country airs, and wide now with the exertion of the run, could not fail to notice the stench. Lestrade pulled back, almost gagging. The abo chuckled, seemingly revelling in it. 'Tammanwool,' he said triumphantly.

'Well, where is it?'

'Not 'ere now, boss. Gone away. We find 'im,' and he sprang to his feet. Lestrade caught the dark, sinewy arm.

'Will it come back, the tammanwool?'

'Oh, yes, boss. Tonight, late. 'E come back 'ere.'

'Then we'll wait.' Lestrade was emphatic. 'You go home now, Uku. Don't tell anyone about our hunt this morning. Do you understand? Anyone.' It couldn't have sounded very authoritative, even though Lestrade was recovering his composure. A wreck of a man sprawled in the undergrowth hardly inspired confidence. But the abo had gone.

Lestrade had gone alone. Ordinarily, he would have taken constables with him. Sergeant Winch would have been at his elbow. But the whole thing was too bizarre. Too untried. He was aware always of Nimrod Frost – 'People haven't forgotten the Ripper. Or the *Struwwelpeter* murders.' Lestrade was McNaghten's best man and somehow his whole career was on the line, hunting dingoes in the outback of Cornwall.

So he was alone. The moon wasn't there to help him

tonight. Or at least, the clouds were hiding it, scudding, conspirator-like across the sky. Lestrade didn't like dogs. Big ones, little ones, it didn't matter. And here he was crouching in the thickets below Mawnan Church, waiting to catch one. True to the speed of the Cornwall Constabulary, the chief constable had not yet responded to the urgent appeal for firearms sent by Lestrade. Fortunately, the inspector had been able to borrow a 12-bore from Farmer Pemberton and it was crooked in his arm now. Lestrade was never *very* happy with a gun this size. He had seen the result of too many careless loadings and he even carried the scars of a rogue shot on his own shoulder. He fumbled with the cartridges. One. Two. Click up the barrels. Now to wait.

Behind him reared the blackness of the Mawnan earthwork, silent as the graves that lay beyond it. William Lamb was to be buried the next day. If Lestrade was lucky tonight, his killer might be buried before him. The owls were flying, hooting as they swooped over field and forest. Lestrade had seen one at dusk, an eerie white in a ghostly silence, winging its way over the heather in search of prey.

Policemen – those who become detective inspectors any-way – have a sixth sense. Not that Lestrade felt at one with Nature. Yet it was *something* which made him turn, gun levelled. There had been no noise, no warning. But there it was. Above him on the earthwork, an animal he had never seen before, and never would again. In the split second before he fired, he saw its teeth gleaming, its tongue hanging out, its eyes small and piggy in the fox-like head. His fingers squeezed on both triggers and the roar lit up the bushes. He fell backwards, unprepared for the recoil and rolled through the trees before struggling upright. Had he hit it? Was it coming for him? Could he outrun it? After this morning, out of the question. Could it climb trees? Could he? But the panic within him subsided. There was no movement, no sound. He fumbled in the leaves for the gun and reloaded. He must have killed it. Both barrels, at almost point-blank range. He must have killed it.

He hadn't.

There was nothing on the crest of the earthwork but leaves and grass. Damn. Lestrade whirled round, now in this direction, now in that. Nothing. For a long time, nothing. Then a crack. A twig snapping? Over there, down in the trees. The inspector crawled forward, his fingers sweating now on the trigger. Please don't let me blow my foot off, he thought. The awful smell came to him again, and for the first time a snuffling whine, then a snarl. There was a hiss above his head, then another. He crouched lower, trying to focus his sights on something ahead. But it was so dark. He couldn't see anything.

'Tammanwool, boss.' A voice sounded behind him. It was the abo, grinning as ever. Even Lestrade's twin barrels pointing at him didn't seem to lessen the grin. Lestrade momentarily flopped back, his heart descending from his mouth. He'd nearly shot the man.

'Dis way, boss,' the abo was calling from beyond the earthwork. On the far side of the parapet lay the body of an animal. It was about five feet long, with the head of a wolf and a cunning, cruel mouth. Its fur was tawny, with broad, dark stripes across its back and less obvious ones on its tail. Two barbed arrows lay embedded in its flanks. The stench was strong.

The abo retrieved his arrows and slung the animal over his shoulders.

'We'll *walk* back.' Lestrade was insistent.

Percival Ashburton was not pleased to be brought from his bed at that hour. In fact, he was about to summon pen and paper to dash off an angry letter to Lestrade's superiors when the abo dropped the dead animal on his feet.

'Yours?' asked Lestrade.

'What the bloody hell do you mean?'

'Your abo calls it a tammanwool. What do you call it?'

'Is this some sort of joke, copper?'

The colloquialism when ascribed to an officer of Lestrade's rank sounded a little odd, but perhaps it was an Australian commonplace, the inspector mused.

'I'll tell you what *I* call it, Mr Ashburton. I call it murder,' he said.

'Murder?' Ashburton kicked the animal off his slippered

feet and strode for a brandy. 'You'll forgive me if, under the circumstances, I don't offer you one?'

'You brought this . . . thing . . . back with you, didn't you? A souvenir of the Antipodes. But it got out, didn't it? What I don't understand is how your abo here didn't know about it.'

'Well, he'll be looking for another job come the morning,' Ashburton snapped and roared something at the little brown man, who scuttled out of the room.

'What did you say to him?' asked Lestrade.

Ashburton slammed the stopper onto his decanter. 'If you must know, I threatened to point a bone at him.'

Lestrade looked bemused.

'The abos are a superstitious people, Lestrade. Backward. He believes bones can kill.'

'And I believe these things can too,' said Lestrade, crouching to peel back the animal's lips to reveal a row of razor teeth. 'All right when it was a few sheep, wasn't it? Some stray dog, no problem with that. But a man. When Shepherd Lamb died, that was different. That was why you were offhand when we met. It wasn't just your outback taciturnness. You were afraid.'

'I've faced mad abos, dingoes, drought, swollen rivers and plagues of everything from boils to rabbits. There's nothing I'm afraid of.'

'Except imprisonment for life.'

'What?' Ashburton's knuckles whitened round the glass.

'Unless you trained that thing to kill Lamb—'

'That's not possible.' Ashburton's assertion was too quick.

'—In which case you'd get the drop. As it is, you are an accessory to the fact of murder.' Lestrade circled his man, watching him closely, but painfully aware of the corpse, grotesque and evil-smelling at his feet. 'Take Pentonville,' he went on; 'five hundred and twenty cells. Each one is seven feet square. You will wear a brown cloth mask. No one will recognise you. You will recognise no one. Once a day, you will walk in a circle with a hundred or so others of your kind, the sweepings of society.' Lestrade was becoming lyrical. 'You will eat ten ounces of bread and three-quarters of a pint of cocoa for breakfast. For dinner you will have half a pint of soup, five ounces of bread and one pound of potatoes—'

'For God's sake!' Ashburton broke in.

'You will be a number, working on a treadmill all day, every day, climbing eight thousand, six hundred and forty feet into nothing. And you know the worst thing, Mr Ashburton,' he leaned close to his ear, 'me ol' cobber, you'll never see the sky again.'

Lestrade walked to the door. 'Now let's see if your brother can identify this,' pointing to the corpse.

'All right,' Ashburton sat heavily down in the nearest chair, 'All right, Lestrade.' He sat with his head in his hand for a moment, then looked at the animal. 'It's a thylacine, better known as a Tasmanian wolf or Tasmanian tiger. As my brother would tell you, it's actually neither. It's a marsupial, Lestrade. Do you know what that is?'

Lestrade did not.

'A pouched animal, like the kangaroo. It carries its young in a pouch on its belly. This one is a female, a species, I can tell you, more deadly than the male. The Tasmanian wolf is very rare, Lestrade. There may be a handful in the wild. Nobody knows. I went out on a hunting trip there recently and caught it. A miracle. A bloody miracle, it was.'

Ashburton prowled his study, an odd figure, his face tanned and furrowed under the ridiculous nightcap. He chuckled. 'It was supposed to be a present for Thomas. I'd thought he might appreciate it. But before I could tell him about it, the flaming thing escaped. They're unpredictable, Lestrade. It was used to killing to survive. Sheep went. One here, a couple there. Then people began to see it. Thomas saw it. He thought it was a lion.'

'Why didn't you tell him?'

'Oh, I was going to. On several occasions, I was going to. I don't know why. I went out myself, a number of times, with a gun. No luck.'

'I used your abo to track it. Why didn't you?'

'The same reason I didn't tell him I'd brought it over. I told you, Inspector, abos are superstitious people. I thought if he knew I'd brought the Tasmanian wolf he'd go berserk. They can, you know. They've got a sixth sense when it comes to animals. They're part of them, almost. When Lamb was killed, I guessed what had happened. He was probably tending a ewe at lambing time. A new-born lamb and its mother are easy meat. Lamb must have got in the way, somehow. I never thought it would kill a man. God.' He buried his face in his hands again. 'Then there's rabies,' he suddenly remembered.

'What?'

Ashburton was pacing again. 'I don't know if it's likely, Lestrade. Dogs get it. So do other animals.'

'I do know the word, sir. One day they'll muzzle all dogs. Not to mention Tasmanian wolves.'

'What happens now?'

Lestrade looked into Ashburton's eyes. 'Now, I go to bed,' he said.

'What about . . . Pentonville?'

Lestrade allowed himself to smile. 'Don't worry, Mr Ashburton, we're not going to take away your sky. The wide-open spaces are important to you, aren't they?'

Ashburton nodded.

'Being in the Outback as long as you have has dulled your sense of British law, sir. I shall, of course, report my findings to my superiors and the Cornwall Constabulary will require a statement from you. I should think the most you'll get is a fine for not declaring a wolf at customs.'

'But there's a man dead,' said Ashburton.

'Such is life,' said Lestrade – and vaguely wished he hadn't.

Inspector Lestrade climbed the parapet again where the abo had killed the Tasmanian wolf. It was raining as the little funeral cortège wound its way through the trees below him. He took off his hat and nodded to John Pemberton. He noticed the coffin was of the finest oak, resplendent with gleaming brass fittings, by courtesy of Mr Percival Ashburton. Momentarily, the vicar stopped as the party went on to the place.

'He's a good man, Lestrade,' he said, motioning towards his brother, 'but the Outback has coarsened him. We've all learned a lesson.'

'Amen to that,' said Lestrade and he walked away. As he crossed the churchyard, graves leaning aslant in the drizzle, he heard the vicar's voice. 'William Lamb, late of Her Majesty's . . .—' and the wind in the trees drowned the rest. As he reached the road and the waiting trap, he saw a lone figure on the parapet. A little brown man stood, almost silhouetted against the skyline. He waved his bow and arrows at Lestrade and then was gone.

'Gooday,' Lestrade found himself saying softly. 'Good hunting,' and he cleared his throat and straightened up as he noticed the cabman was looking at him strangely. It was, of course, entirely the cabman's fault therefore that as Lestrade climbed into the trap he caught his hand in the door and broke his little finger. He didn't remember much about the journey home. Except that his hand was about a foot across and every image in his brain was curiously finger-shaped and throbbing.

Beastie

Benjamin Beeson, ex-sergeant of the Metropolitan Police, sat in Lestrade's office with his massive fist around the inevitable mug of tea. Walter Dew, constable of the Metropolitan Police, lounged on Lestrade's desk in front of him, until the inspector swept in, whereon the aforesaid Dew swept away to busy himself with filing. Beeson stood to attention as his old guv'nor came in.

'Hello, Beastie,' grinned Lestrade. 'I'd shake your hand, only . . .' and he held up his bandaged finger.

'Oh, dear,' growled Beeson in the familiar old way. 'Nothing trivial I hope, sir?'

Lestrade had forgotten, momentarily, the sense of humour. He motioned to Dew to pour him some tea and offered Beeson a cigar.

'No, thank you, sir. I don't any more . . .'

Lestrade sensed the man's discomfort and noticed the frayed cuffs and shabby shoes. The pension didn't go far, he mused to himself and stuffed two cigars into Beeson's top pocket.

'Well,' he said, negotiating the steaming mug with his moustache. Shaving wasn't what it had been before he'd broken his finger. And all in all, he'd thought he'd better decline Mrs Manchester's offer of help with the cut-throat razor. 'Well, how is it, Ben?'

'Not good, sir.'

Lestrade's grin faded. 'The pension?'

'Love you, no, sir. I can get by on that. No, it's my old mate Joe Towers. He's dead.'

'I'm sorry to hear that, Ben. What was it? Accident?'

'No, sir. I think it was murder.'

Lestrade leaned forward in his chair. 'So this isn't exactly a social call?'

'No, sir, not exactly. I don't like coming to you, sir, but I thought perhaps twenty-six years on the Force counts for something.'

Lestrade nodded. He had been here before. 'Dew, get more tea for the sergeant. You'd better tell me about it, Beastie.'

Had Beastie Beeson been an ordinary member of the public, it might have been different. Had his description of the corpse and the manner of death been more unusual. Had Joe Towers not been sixty-two years old. If all this had been so, or not been so, Lestrade would have applied for an exhumation order in the usual way. Triplicate. Forms. Hours bashing away on the upright Remington on the first floor.

As it was, Lestrade trusted to Beastie's sixth sense. To the 'nose' he knew this old sergeant possessed. After all, the man was right – twenty-six years on the Force must count for something. And he laid his career on the line.

Kensal Green had never been Lestrade's favourite part of London. Especially at night. Amazing, isn't it, he thought to himself as the wrought-iron gates chinked and shook under the heavy pincers he carried, amazing how sounds carry at night. Breaking and entering. He swung the gate back. He could get ten years for that before a pious beak, out to prove that the law was harsher on bent coppers than on bent civilians. His breath wisped out before him and wreathed back around his face.

'This way, sir.' Beeson crunched with all the weight of his twenty-six years' service on the gravel. Without the aid of lights, the going was hard. The two men stumbled through the undergrowth and tangle of rhododendron bushes, making for the grave they wanted. Around them, in rows neat and clipped, the tombs of deceased Londoners bore silent witness to their intrusion. Tailors from Pimlico rubbed dusty shoulders with bank clerks from Norwood and the odd retired admiral, aptly enough from Gravesend. Beeson collided with a weeping angel, but only his hat brim was dented. In the flitting moon, the smooth white of the draped urns and the grooved columns, broken to the sky, threw shadows across the grass, crisp in the frost of the early hours.

'Here.' Lestrade dropped to his knees beside the fresh grave

Beeson indicated. A single wreath on the wet, brown earth. Lestrade checked his watch. In the moonlight, he caught glimpses of the hands. Nearly quarter to two. They set to work, each man with his spade, slicing through the earth. Beeson, for all his strength, was past his best. A man retired for three years is not in peak condition. Lestrade's contribution was also limited, digging as he was with hand and elbow, to minimise the pain in his finger. Beeson was concerned, in fact something of a mother hen, as, with every other stroke, he apologised again to Lestrade for putting him through this. For a thousand reasons, Lestrade breathed a sigh of relief as his spade struck wood. Getting the coffin to the surface, even with the ropes Beeson had brought, was no mean feat and both men were cursing and panting as Joe Towers flopped limply into the waiting canvas and Beeson trussed him up.

'Sorry, Joe,' he muttered, 'but it's for the best. You know, Inspector, I feel like old Ben Crouch, the Resurrection Man.'

'Before my time,' hissed Lestrade, lowering the coffin as best he could. 'Let's cover this up.'

A casual observer, at dead of night, would have noticed little difference in the appearance of the grave now that the wreath and temporary marker were back in place. Lestrade wondered if the same lack of critical observation was likely to apply to an astute grave-digger in the broad daylight of the following morning. But it was too late to worry about that now. That same morning was showing signs of breaking through to the east, lending an eerie light to the hoar frost on tomb and vault. Between them they carried their tragic bundle down the hill, quickening their pace as they reached the gate. They steadied Towers against a pillar, where he rested his sack-covered head on Beeson's shoulder, while Lestrade deftly replaced the snapped chain with another from his pocket. He clicked the padlock into place, flattering himself on the skills he had learned from dozens of bettys, now mouldering no doubt as surely as Joe Towers, but in the living graves of Pentonville or the Scrubs.

'Remember, Dew,' Lestrade called to the hooded figure sitting atop the Maria, 'you've seen nothing. Heard nothing.'

'I shall be as silent as the grave, sir.' Lestrade and Beeson looked at the constable, now feeling rather silly and small on his high perch. At a signal from Lestrade, he slapped the reins and the wagon lurched forward, Croydon-bound.

It was nearly dawn as Joe Towers lay on the kitchen table at 20 Sanderstead Road. The gaslight flickered green on the walls.

'I never got on with post-mortems,' Beeson was saying, 'but there's something don't sit right with old Joe.'

'Tell me again,' said Lestrade, as he undid the linen shroud. 'From the beginning.'

Beeson sat back in the chair and lit his pipe.

'Like I said, sir. Me and Joe was mates, from way back. Went through the army together, India. Then I was transferred to the Twelfth Lancers and he stayed with the old mob. We lost touch for a while, and I joined the Force. That would be in' – he paused to count his fingers – 'early 'sixty-seven. Well, I was a copper on the beat for years, and one day – I'll tell you when it was, it was the day old Dizzy died in 'eighty-one – one day I was patrolling along the Ratcliffe Highway.' (Lestrade was grateful the sergeant had not used the immortal 'Proceeding in an easterly direction in the execution of my duty'.) 'And I saw Joe Towers, me ol' mate. Well, we had a jar aplenty that night, I can tell you – after my duty hours, of course, sir.'

Lestrade smiled mechanically, loosening the funeral tie of Joseph Towers and unfastening the collar stud. There was a mild smell of putrefaction. Not bad. Lestrade had smelt worse, but he must remember to tell Beeson to open his kitchen window once this was over.

'Joe was working in the Royal Albert. Stevedore, he was. Well, we saw a lot of each other after that. 'Is missus was a good sort and she gave us breakfast many a time after a session. He did like 'is pongolo, did Joe.'

''Is missus still with us?' asked Lestrade, checking the blackened, numb fingers for signs of a struggle.

'No, guv'nor. She went of the diptheria four years back. Salt of the earth, she was.'

'How did Joe die?'

Beeson began to prowl the length of his meagre kitchen, glancing sadly every now and again at the yellow-black face of 'is 'ol mate, staring sightlessly up from the kitchen table at the bowl of the gas light.

''E was the fittest man of 'is age I knew. 'E'd work all the hours God and Ben Tillet sent. Never missed a day.'

'Ben Tillet?' As he opened the striped shirt, Lestrade's nostrils quivered. There was something else.

'Joe was 'is right-hand man in the Dock strike. "Tanner" Towers, they used to call him. Course, that was a bit awkward. You know how we used to be called out then, truncheons, cutlasses an' all.' Lestrade knew.

'I found 'im, in 'is parlour. Sittin' in 'is armchair, 'e was. I thought 'e was 'aving me on, at first, you know. Then I realised. 'E was dead.'

'How long do you think it had been, Ben?'

'Well, 'e was as rigid as a board,' offered the sergeant.

'Rigor mortis,' mused Lestrade, quietly enjoying the role of coroner as he lifted Towers' eyelids. 'About twelve hours, then.'

'If you say so, sir. I was never very good at that scientific sort of thing – leave that to the jacks. Oh, beggin' your pardon, sir – the detectives.'

Lestrade looked at Beeson under his eyebrows. 'Come here, Ben.' The sergeant dumbly obeyed. 'What do you smell?'

'Death, sir,' came the answer.

'Yes, that's what I smelt too, at first. But sniff deeper. Here, under the shirt especially. Something else.'

Beeson virtually buried his nose in 'is 'ol mate's chest. 'No, sir. Nothing.'

'Bitter almonds, Beastie. Can't you smell it?'

Beeson shook his head.

'And I'll lay you five to one the coroner couldn't, either. Nor the doctor who signed the death certificate.' Lestrade paused. 'Was there one?'

'Oh, yes, sir. Poor Law doctor, name of ... I can't remember.'

'It doesn't matter.' Lestrade plunged his hands into the water bowl on the draining board. The water was freezing to the touch.

'You were right, Beastie. You didn't know why, did you? What was it you said? "Something didn't sit right." Well, it's paid off. Joe Towers was murdered, Ben. Cyanide.'

'Straight up?' exclaimed Ben.

'I don't know how it was administered,' answered Lestrade. 'When you found him, did you notice any foam or spittle around his mouth?'

Beeson hadn't.

'Signs of a struggle? Convulsions?'

No.

Lestrade realised after the first flush of triumph that he had saturated the bandage on his finger. It would take hours to dry.

'What happens now, sir?'

'Now, we put him back, Beastie. It'll have to be tonight. And Beastie . . .'

'Sir?'

'We'll get him. Make no mistake about that. But because of the . . . er . . . unorthodox way we lifted old Joe, there'll be too many questions asked. I've got a new guv'nor myself now, one Nimrod Frost. He's very much a man who does things by the book. We'll have to tread softly, softly.'

That night, with the same ease as before, Lestrade and Beeson reburied 'Tanner' Towers. It was so smooth, so simple, that Lestrade felt vaguely uncomfortable. Perhaps he'd joined the wrong side after all.

So Lestrade trod softly, softly. And before he could tread at all, he had a visit from one John Watson MD, of Baker Street.

'But it's here in black and white, Lestrade. In *The London Charivari* for April eighth – "The Adventures of Picklock Holes". *And* they've the nerve to make a pun on Conan Doyle's name – Cunnin Toil! Pathetic!'

'So what has you miffed, Doctor, is that they haven't mentioned you?'

'Nonsense! In fact, they have.' Watson drew himself up to his full height. 'I am referred to as "Potson". Puerile nonsense!'

'Your Sherlock Holmes stories?'

'No. The *Charivari*'s plagiarism. Damn you, Lestrade, you are deliberately goading me.'

The inspector chuckled. 'No, no, my dear Watson. Dew. Tea,' he shouted through to the corridor, waving his bandaged hand by way of explanation of his own inactivity. 'Tell me, do I appear in this plagiarism?'

'No,' Watson snorted, as he subsided into Lestrade's other chair.

'Well, that's a relief,' said Lestrade. 'At least I won't have to charge the editors of *Punch* with libel.'

'What do you mean?'

'For the past two years, you and Dr Conan Doyle have been taking my name in vain. You have done your best to undermine the confidence of the people in Scotland Yard. And in particular, me.'

Watson blustered, sweeping his grey whiskers from side to side in embarrassment. 'But it's all done in the best possible taste, Lestrade. Holmes and I . . .'

'Sherlock Holmes is dead, Dr Watson. As I recall, he hurtled over the Reichenbach Falls eighteen months ago, struggling with an innocent bystander whom he mistook for you.'

'Ssssshh!' Watson spun round in all directions in case of Ears.

'It's all right. Dew is deaf and dumb. Isn't that so, constable?'

Dew placed the tea on Lestrade's desk and went about his business as though he hadn't heard. 'See what I mean?'

'Good God, Lestrade. It's terrible that a man so depleted as that in natural functions should be allowed in the Metropolitan Police!'

Lestrade's resigned look would have withered a brighter man.

'Lestrade. Sholto. You promised . . .'

Lestrade waved aside the doctor's mute protestations.

'In all seriousness though, Dr Watson. I cannot take any action against *Punch*. They have their little jibes at the Yard, too, you know. In any case, there are more pressing matters.'

'Oh?' Watson examined his tea carefully before taking his first sip.

'Are you living now in Baker Street?'

'Yes,' said Watson. '221B. I . . . I've tried somehow to keep Holmes' spirit alive. I'm afraid Mycroft was no help.'

'Mycroft?'

'The Great Detective's brother, at the Foreign Office.'

Lestrade winced at the description of the dead addict.

'And Mrs Hudson?'

'It's all lies, I tell you.' Watson realised he had been a little too vehement. He checked his pulse, momentarily. Lestrade sensed the raw nerve and took a different tack.

'You have a surgery in Butcher Row, off Ratcliffe Highway?'

'I have.' Watson began to feel uneasy.

'You are what is known as a Poor Law doctor?'

'I believe it is my Christian duty to—'

'Quite. Quite. And did you attend a death at eighteen Havering Court on March the seventeenth last?'

'March the seventeenth? Er . . .'

'A docker named Joseph Towers.'

'Oh, yes, now I remember. Natural causes.'

'Cyanide poisoning.'

'What?' Watson was on his feet again.

'Can you smell almonds, Doctor?'

Watson looked around him, sniffing manically.

'Not at the moment,' said Lestrade, 'In the natural course of things.'

'Almonds? Of course.'

'But you can't smell them on a corpse, evidently. What about the pupils?'

'Whose pupils?'

'The deceased's pupils.'

'Er . . . God, Lestrade. You're talking about three weeks ago.'

'I'm talking about murder, Doctor. Were the pupils dilated?'

'No.' Watson was as emphatic as he could be, bearing in mind he hadn't the faintest recollection. 'But how do you know it's murder?'

Lestrade wasn't going to compromise his career before the good doctor, so he resorted to all the subtlety at his command. 'We'll ask the questions, sir.' Lestrade began to wander the confines of his office. He had time again to glimpse the grandeur of Norman Shaw's architectural style as the view of the blank wall from his window met him. If he craned his neck a little and stood on Dew's shoulders and then stooped, he could catch a flash of the water in the morning sun on the river. But he had seen the river before and it wasn't really worth the contortions.

'So there was nothing about the case that led you to suspect foul play?'

'I'm afraid not.' Watson was doubting not only his many years as a medical practitioner, but his many years in association with the Great Detective.

Lestrade decided to let the matter drop. Watson sensed it and pursued a new tack.

'I read about your West Country adventure, Inspector. How you found the . . . er . . .'

'Tasmanian wolf.'

'Yes.' Watson thumped his knee and strode to the door. 'Er . . . I hesitate to mention it, Lestrade. Especially in view of the *Charivari*, but . . . well, I've been' – another glance round to see that Dew was still deaf – 'I've been thinking that I might resurrect Holmes, give him a new case. How about . . . "The Wolf of the Ashburtons"?'

'You're going to give Holmes *my* case?' snarled Lestrade, even his bandaged knuckle turning white.

'Well, no, not exactly. But . . .' Watson was edging through the door, 'how about "The Beast of the Aborigines"?' and he dodged out as Lestrade threw his bowler at him. The inspector called out as the doctor fled the building, 'You may as well call it the Hound of the Baskervilles.'

Ben Tillet sat as though in a studio portrait, in his waistcoat, sleeves rolled up, flanked by two heavies from the Dock, Wharf, Riverside and General Workers' Union, who Lestrade thought he recognised from innumerable editions of the *Police Gazette*. Either of them, Lestrade surmised, could have cracked walnuts with his elbows.

'I'd lost touch with him, Mr Lestrade,' Tillet was saying, never a man to acknowledge titles. 'The last time I saw Joe Towers was – oh – three years ago.'

'You've moved on to higher things?' ventured Lestrade.

'I don't consider being an alderman of the City of London, a member of the Parliamentary Committee of the Trades Union Congress and a prospective Member of Parliament "higher things". No, I'm still a man of the people, as I was in 'eighty-nine. Aren't I, boys?'

'Yes, Mr Tillett,' chorused the heavies, as though he had pressed the switches on two automata.

'And what of your work with the Independent Labour Party?' Lestrade thought he might as well get in a bit of fishing while he was there.

'Forgive me, Mr Lestrade. I thought you were enquiring into the death of Joe Towers, not my political affinities. If I am wrong, then of course I must have my lawyer present.'

'Towers, then.' Lestrade returned to the point. 'The man worked closely with you. How well did you know him? Did he have any enemies?'

'We all had enemies in 'eighty-nine, Mr Lestrade – the pillars of society, the wealthy, the bourgeoisie in their smug middle-class houses – not to mention, of course, the boys in blue.' Lestrade ignored the jibe. 'But we had friends too – thousands of dockers in the Port of London, engineers like Tommy Mann and John Burns. We even got thirty thousand pounds for our cause from our brothers in Australia. Now that's working class solidarity, Mr Lestrade. Something I'm proud of. Joe Towers was part of all that. I remember the first time I met him in the main yard at the West India. He was a casual, Mr Lestrade, one of those countless numbers who drifted to work each day until 'eighty-nine, hoping for a ship to unload. He told me he hadn't worked for four days and hadn't eaten for three. It's funny, but Joe Towers, as much as anybody, is why I called the Dock Strike. It was for men like him we fought for the "Tanner". I can see him now, standing in the Committee Room alongside Cardinal Manning, his face a picture of rapt attention to the great man speaking on our behalf.'

'But he didn't have any specific enemies?'

'No, he was a mild man. Everybody liked Joe.'

Lestrade felt Tillett could help him no longer and rose to go.

'Of course,' the Alderman went on, 'we are all mild men

and there are thousands of us. There is a Union of Clerks and Teachers, of Shop Assistants, a Miners' Federation with two hundred thousand members this year. Altogether we number over one and a half million. How many Metropolitan Policemen are there, Inspector Lestrade?'

'Enough, Mr Tillett.'

'Of course,' the alderman began again, 'if you can't beat us, you could join us. Think of it, a Police Federation. Full pension rights, sick benefits, funeral expenses, strike pay. It's got to come.'

But Lestrade was already on the stairs whence he had come, out into the warm sunlight, where the air was fresh.

Walter Dew was a copper of very average ability. There was nothing disparaging in that. Wasn't it a fact, regularly voiced by the *Charivari* itself, that the vast bulk of the Metropolitan Police were of average ability? But on the subject of vast bulk, Nimrod Frost, the Head of the Criminal Investigation Department, was anxious to weed out the weak ones in his department. So it was that Constable Dew, hair macassared to perfection, moustaches combed just so, stood in Frost's office that day at the end of April, unusually for a plainclothesman, bedecked in his full uniform, helmet glittering in the crook of his arm. Perhaps crook wasn't the right term and he shifted it as the thought struck him. Lestrade had told him to box clever, to be circumspect (something which Dew thought only happened to Jews) in that the evidence pointing to foul play in connection with the death of Joe Towers *without* Lestrade's unofficial post-mortem findings was thin indeed. Even so, Frost was as impressed with Beeson's suspicions, based on long service within the arm of the law, as Lestrade had been, and so sanctioned Dew's depositions taken from all and sundry who had known Joe Towers and who were among the last to see him alive.

'All right, Dew, let's have the last of them.' Frost rested his podgy hands on the enormous velvet area of his waistcoat.

Dew flipped the page of his notepad and began, 'On the twenty-fourth instant I had reason to attend a public house—'

'A public house, Dew?' Frost interrupted him.

'In the pursuance of my duty, sir.' Dew was quick to reassure him. 'A public house called, appropriately, the Pig and Helmet—'

'Appropriately, Dew?'

Dew cleared his throat to cover his failure at levity and went on: '... where at twelve-thirty p.m. I met one Abel Seaman—'

'Abel Seaman, Dew? Are you trying to be funny?'

Dew noted that Nimrod Frost's face was slowly turning the purple of his waistcoat.

'I'm sorry, sir, that was the man's name – or so he claimed.' Frost's eyebrows disappeared under what was left of his hairline, but he said nothing. '—Who told me that he had seen the deceased Joseph Towers at approximately three-thirty on the day of his death and accompanied him some little distance towards his destination, viz and to wit—'

'To wit, Dew?' repeated Frost, doing a passable impression of a barn owl.

'Er ... Mr Lestrade told me to put that in, sir.'

'Go on.'

'This Abel Seaman is known to us, sir. He was a one-time cash carrier, known to be a bug hunter and cly faker, who—'

'Dew!' Frost rose with all the speed and majesty his paunch would permit. 'Could we have this in English, please? It is, after all, the language of the Queen.'

Dew looked a little shamefaced. 'Of course, sir. He was a one-time prostitutes' manager, who has done a little bit of pickpocketing and stealing from drunks.'

'Not a man whose word is reliable?' Frost took a pinch of snuff from the elaborate silver box on his desk. Dew could read, upside down (in fact, rather better than the right way up), the inscription 'From the grateful people of Grantham' before Frost snapped shut the lid and proceeded to inhale violently the orange-coloured powder from the back of his hand.

'I rather think in this instance, yes, sir.'

Frost waited for him to go on.

'Seaman talked with Towers about this and that and Towers had told him that he was expecting someone that afternoon and declined his offer of a gatter ... er ... beer.

Seaman was on his way to the penny gaff . . . er . . . Punch and Judy Show, and spent perhaps five minutes in Towers' company.'

'A grown man attending a Punch and Judy Show, Dew?' Frost was incredulous.

'Well, if you ask me, sir, it was probably an Under and Over,' and as Frost spun round with the speed of a laden sloth, Dew corrected himself, 'a fairground swindling game, sir.'

'Did Seaman learn more of Towers' visitor?'

'No, sir, except that he was Trasseno.'

'An Italian?' Frost felt he was learning the lingo quite well.

'No sir, a bad person.'

Frost humphed his indignation at being wrong and continued to strut round his office.

'So it is likely that Seaman – if we can accept his word at all – was the last person to see Towers alive and that the . . . er . . . Trasseno was the murderer – if indeed he was murdered at all, and of course we only have ex-Sergeant Beeson's sixth sense on that.'

Dew felt the ground shifting beneath him. Box clever, Lestrade had said, box clever.

'Yes, sir,' was the height of Dew's wit and repartee.

Frost took Dew's notepad and thumbed through the pages. The man was barely literate, he thought. The lines could be the work of a deranged chimpanzee.

'Tell me, Dew, what do you want to be when you grow up?'

'Sir?' Dew frowned at the unusual levity from the Head of the Criminal Investigation Department.

'What are your ambitions, Dew?' he said by way of an explanation for the feeble-minded.

'Well, sir,' Dew was grinning at the prospect, 'I'd like to be a chief inspector one day, sir . . . and . . .'

There was an 'and' Frost realised. As if the first hope wasn't forlorn enough.

'And?' He leaned over towards Dew's right ear.

'And I want to write a book, sir, a biographical account of my greatest case. It will be called "I Caught . . ." and then the name of the arch-criminal.'

Frost sat silently down in the folds of his leather armchair, whence he only ever rose with difficulty.

'That will be all, Dew,' he said, and as the ambitious young constable turned to go, he said, with all the sympathy and encouragement at his disposal, 'I think you'd have difficulty catching a cold.'

To the Lighthouse

Joseph Towers had been dead for exactly one month. He had been buried for three weeks. And reburied for nearly two. Lestrade reflected again, as he had so often in the past, how difficult it was to reconstruct the last hours of a man's life. Particularly an old man, a man with few real friends. And in a way, Joe Towers had been lucky. He had a good friend in Ben Beeson, whose nose had smelt a rat, if not bitter almonds. How many more old men, and young ones too, and women, mouldered in paupers' graves or the elegance of Abney Park, apparently dead of natural causes, precisely because they did not have Ben Beeson for a friend?

And had one such case now landed on Lestrade's desk, in the form of a plea from the Norfolk Constabulary? It was Sergeant Edgar Bradstreet who brought it to Lestrade's attention – Gregson's blue-eyed boy.

'The inspector thinks it's anarchists, sir,' Bradstreet was saying. 'He suspects the Russians, perhaps using Irish *agents provocateurs.*'

'Inspector Gregson always suspects Russians, Sergeant, and he usually throws in an Irishman or two, for good measure. After all, he does help run the Special Irish Branch. What would we do without Irishmen, eh?'

'Do I detect a note of cynicism, sir?'

Well, thought Lestrade, Gregson had chosen a bright one this time.

'Realism is, I think, a better word, Bradstreet. Do I understand I am to have the pleasure of your company on this little visit?'

'I have been seconded to your division, sir.'

'Not enough anarchy in London at the moment, hmm? Well, never mind. If you're right, we'll smoke a few out in the fleshpots and opium hells of Cromer, eh?'

Lestrade was suffering from a superfluity of sergeants. In addition to Bradstreet, a new boy was thrust upon him – one Hector Charlo, by special recommendation of His Nims. 'He has friends in high places,' Frost had said. 'He looks to be a good boy, Lestrade. I think you can rely on him in a crisis.'

In the event, Lestrade couldn't. Sergeant Charlo stood before the inspector in the angle of the Yard's plumbing system that passed as Lestrade's office, a cherry nose swathed in a muffler, and eyes swimming with all the signs of terminal pneumonia.

'I'b sorry, sir,' he mumbled. 'Not good forb, I know, and by first assignbent with you, but I'b afraid I . . . I . . .,' and his whole body shook with the violence of his sneezing.

'You don't fancy the Norfolk air then, Charlo?' Lestrade proffered.

'With respect, Inspector, the odly place I fancy dow is by bed.'

'All right,' sighed Lestrade, never impressed by physical illness. 'Get your head under a towel and dose yourself up. You'd have thought they could haved cured the common cold by now.'

'There's nothing common about by cold, sir,' said Charlo, with a brave stab at some dignity. 'It's probably turning to bronchitis as we speak.'

'We should be back in a day or two,' Lestrade went on. 'Report bright and early Monday morning.'

Bradstreet hoped that Lestrade had been joking about the fleshpots and opium hells, but he had never been to Norfolk before and he didn't know *quite* what a hell-hole Cromer was. The representatives of Her Majesty's Detective Force caught the train from Liverpool Street, Lestrade having made some quip about Bradstreet's railway guide, which fell on professionally deaf ears, and they journeyed without incident to Norwich. Thence by another train to Cromer, where they found, with surprising difficulty for two men trained to know their way around, the Police Station.

The chief constable, no less, informed them that the body was still *in situ*. Lestrade allowed a whimsy to enter his mind that had Dew been with him he would have been searching his gazetteer of Norfolk to find the village of Situ. He was grateful that Bradstreet seemed to have a smattering of Latin, or perhaps it was just that he hid his naïvety better than Dew. The deceased was one William Bentley, lighthouse keeper, and the cause of death was natural. The only reason that the Yard had been called in was one of mere formality since one of Her Majesty's lighthouses constituted an area of strategic importance. Should a French or even a German fleet appear in the Wash, Cromer Lighthouse could be instrumental in their landing. As such, and as a matter of course, an officer of the rank of inspector or above from the Metropolitan Police was duty-bound to carry out the aforesaid formalities. In view of the threat from possible espionage, that some dastardly foreign power was eliminating lighthouse keepers one by one, presumably before starting on the garrisons of the Martello Towers and Palmerston's Follies around the south coast, it was natural that the Special Irish Branch and its most noted bloodhound, Tobias Gregson, should be involved. Gregson however had larger problems. It was rumoured that William F Cody was staging another British visit at the closing phase of his Continental tour and if there was a nation other than the Russians whom Gregson suspected, it was the Americans. So Bradstreet had been sent instead. Lestrade wondered why he too had been sent. The reason that appealed most was that he hoped Nimrod Frost shared his suspicion of the Special Branch and daren't let Bradstreet out alone.

The little party of policemen picked their way across the cliffs that evening. The dying sun lent a magical glow to the small town clustered below them, gilding the great grey tower of St Peter and St Paul. Below to their right stretched the sand and shingle of Foulness, nearly dry now at low tide. The light flashed with its inevitable regularity above the whitewashed building. No one spoke. They were greeted at the door by the head keeper, Nathaniel Blogg, whose family, the Yard were told, had for years been rescuing sailors and fishermen from the jaws of the sea. The skin of his weathered face was the colour of the crab shells which littered the rocks. There was no trace of humour, no trace of warmth. It was the face, thought Lestrade, of a man who had looked too often on death. It was like looking into a mirror. Shifting the metaphor mentally, it was the face that saved a thousand ships.

Blogg led the way, with a series of grunts and rustic growls, to one of the upper rooms. On a makeshift bunk inside lay the body of William Bentley, dead these four days. The sea air through the window had removed the smell of death. Lestrade looked at the body, checked the eyes, having removed Blogg's pennies first. Something. What?

'Bradstreet,' he motioned to the sergeant. 'Your views?'

The sergeant looked carefully. He was not used to whole bodies. Most of the corpses he saw in his current line of duty had been eviscerated by explosives. Cause of death seemed a little academic after that.

'Age about seventy, sir. Height, five feet eight inches or so. Colour of eyes, hazel. Not much hair. I would have to remove his clothes for distinguishing marks. Dead about four days.'

'Hmm.' Lestrade looked at the chief constable for confirmation. He nodded. 'Cause of death?'

'Natural, sir. Old age?'

'Mr Blogg, you found the body?'

'Ar.'

'What?'

'Ar,' said Blogg louder, assuming the moustachioed Londoner with his distinctly inland pea-jacket to be deaf.

'Who else has been in this room?'

'Er – until today only me, young Emma and 'er fella and Jem.'

'Who are these people?'

'Jeremiah Rook is the local constable who Mr Blogg sensibly summoned,' offered the chief constable. 'Emma Hopkins, née Bentley, is the daughter of the deceased. She arrived from York yesterday with her husband. Is any of this relevant, Inspector?'

'Yes, sir, it is. You see, my sergeant's description of the corpse is admirable, but he did get one thing wrong.'

'Oh?' Bradstreet thought it best to straighten himself so that he was a full inch taller than Lestrade.

'Your lighthouse keeper was murdered.'

'Murdered?' The word was echoed round the octagonal room, chorused by all but Lestrade and the corpse.

'Who has examined the body?'

'Er ... only me and Jem,' Blogg answered, as the one-most-likely-to-be-in-possession-of-that-information.

'No doctor? No death certificate?'

The chief constable blustered. 'A matter of security, Lestrade. You know as well as I do that lighthouses are of strategic importance.'

Yes, Lestrade knew that.

'Look here.' Lestrade lifted Bentley's eyelids, first the left, then the right. 'You see these tiny specks of blood? Mr Bentley was suffocated. Oh, expertly, certainly. One of the neatest I've seen. Normally you'd expect blood at the lips and nose and more discolouration of the face.'

Lestrade mechanically sniffed the various cups and glasses in the room. 'He was probably drugged first. Quite a painless way to go, actually; if you must go at all, that is.'

'I want to go at sea,' Blogg informed the company, 'with a good nor' easter blowin'.'

The chief constable looked at him curiously. 'Well, each according to his taste, I suppose.'

'You and Bentley took turns about on duty here?' Lestrade put the question to Blogg, still gazing into the middle-distance of his vision of a viking's funeral.

'Ar.' He recollected himself.

'So you wouldn't know if he had any visitors, say, within the last five days?'

'No, I ... Although ...'

'Yes?' The word was chorused by the policemen assembled. They all looked at each other a little sheepishly.

'Well, it's probably nothin' really.'

'We'll be the judges of that, Mr Blogg,' said Lestrade.

'Well, I did see a ship moored 'ere. Must of been last Sunday.'

'The day before Bentley died,' Bradstreet said aloud.

Lestrade ignored him. 'Was that usual, Mr Blogg?'

'No, not really. Oh, boats come alongside now and then. Nosey parkers from Lunnun, mostly.' He scrutinised the present company.

'Was it a supply boat?' Bradstreet was getting above himself.

'Of course not,' Blogg said flatly. 'What do we need with a supply boat when you can walk to the bloody lighthouse?'

The chief constable and Lestrade turned to Bradstreet with an I-told-you-so expression on their faces. The sergeant had an inclination to follow this up by asking Blogg if the craft had been a submersible, for it had been rumoured for some months at the Yard that such an infernal machine was being manufactured for a forthcoming invasion. In view of his superiors' faces, he decided against it.

'Did you see anyone in the boat?' the chief constable asked, desperate to prove that the weight of silver braid had not diminished the incisiveness of his enquiry-making.

'No,' said Blogg.

'What sort of craft was it?' Lestrade asked.

'A ketch.'

'Did you see a name?'

'Ar.'

The company waited.

'Well, out with it, man. What was it?' Lestrade's patience only extended so far.

'Furrin.'

'Furrin?' the inspector repeated.

'Ar. You won't find it registered in an English port, I'll wager.'

'So,' mused Bradstreet, 'Gregson and I were right. It *is* a foreign power, bent on eroding British manpower gradually, here and there, whittling away the watchful eyes on the coast, ready for the great onslaught when there were no watchers left. Diabolically cunning.'

'Bradstreet.' Lestrade's voice snapped the sergeant back to reality. 'Mr Blogg is about to tell us the name of the boat, aren't you, Mr Blogg?'

'No,' said Blogg, being as obtuse as possible, 'but I'll tell you the name of the ship. As near as I can, anyhow. It was somewhat like . . . like . . . "Ora Rosa".'

'Spanish,' said Lestrade.

'Italian,' said Bradstreet.

They had spoken simultaneously.

'Bradstreet,' said Lestrade. 'Wear out some leather along the coast here. Check all the boats,' he glanced at Blogg, ' – and ships – in harbour.'

'You won't find it 'ere. I never seen it roun' before or since.'

'We shall need to talk further, Mr Blogg,' said Lestrade.

And so it was with Nathaniel Blogg that Lestrade and Bradstreet began their enquiries. Unfortunately for them both, Blogg was only a part-time lighthouse keeper. The rest of the time he was a fisherman, when he wasn't manning the lifeboat, that was, saving souls from the deep. And Bradstreet in particular, looking every inch the city gent in his bowler and Donegal, kept hearing that word 'deep' each time the boat took a plunge into the grey of the North Sea. Looking back at the land was worse. The line of cliffs at Cromer yawed up and down like a demented seesaw, the spire of the church leaning at a rakish angle. It wasn't long before Bradstreet had turned the colour of the sail creaking tautly overhead – the colour of old parchment.

True, Lestrade was more suitably attired. Whenever his job took him to maritime areas, he tried to dress the part, but the jaunty black sailor's peaked cap and the matching pea-jacket could not disguise the landlubber's inability to roll with the ship. Most of the time, in fact, he rolled against it, barking his shins on lobster creels and smearing his sleeve with tar and foul-smelling bait. The smack bellied and plunged on the roaring surf, making interrogation of a crucial witness well nigh impossible.

Bradstreet's task was to commit the vital deposition of

Blogg the fisherman to his notebook, but when he looked at the page of jottings, he realised that it would do justice to Mr Isaac Pitman, except that it wasn't shorthand. When Lestrade saw it later, in the relatively tranquil surroundings of the Fisherman's Arms, he pronounced it unintelligible. As well, then, that Lestrade's memory served to record the conversation. William Bentley, it transpired, was a native of Yorkshire, had served some time in the Army, and had been a lighthouse keeper for eight years. He was past retiring age really, but nobody else wanted the job. It didn't pay well and most of the younger men were either fishing or moving into the new profitable tourist trade that was becoming the vogue along the coast. Folk from Lunnun mostly and it was the railway that brought 'em there. Blogg spat volubly and contemptuously into the hurtling waters in scorn of both institutions. The act alone was enough to send Bradstreet over the edge, not literally, but metaphorically, and he vomited copiously over the side.

Friends? Only one really – a royal coachman from Sandringham, the Prince of Wales' estate, who came over once a month to play chess with Bentley. Enemies? Well, there was the Tuddenhams. Tough bunch they were. Bentley had fell foul of 'em almost as soon as he arrived. Blogg didn't rightly know why. The Tuddenhams, it transpired, were a family of fishermen from nearby Mundsley whose names were well known to the local constabulary as trouble makers, drunkards and shifters. Jem Rook had had his nose broken by one of them only last year, simply because the constable had smiled at him funny one morning. Yes, the Tuddenhams were the boys. If anybody had murderous inclinations in the area and bore Bill Bentley a grudge, it was them.

The conversation ended there, as nets were cast and hands dashed here and there, flinging ropes, hauling weights. Bradstreet was quietly wishing he was dead. Even Lestrade felt a little green round the gills, much like the wet, flapping mackerel that flopped down on the slippery deck. There were shouts and laughter and it was well into the afternoon before

Bradstreet's prayers were answered and Blogg turned his smack for home.

Another magic evening, the sun casting long shadows across the shingle. Lestrade's legs had returned to his body and leaving Bradstreet flat on his back in his room at the Fisherman's, the inspector walked the beach with Bill Bentley's daughter. Emma Hopkins, as she now was, was a middle-aged woman who still retained much of the striking good looks of her youth. She spoke fondly of her father, but was not surprised that he had enemies.

'Always in trouble, that was Dad,' she was saying with her soft-spoken Yorkshire accent. 'If there was a family like that here that didn't like him, you can bet – mind you, 'e weren't a betting man – but you can bet 'e'd put up a fight.'

'Liked a scrap, did he, your dad?' Lestrade asked.

'Aye, 'e did.' Emma Hopkins chuckled. 'Eeh, there were times Ma didn't know what to do wi' 'im, but 'is heart was in't right place. Y'know, I've seen that man take on't bare-knuckle champion of Bradford just to buy me a dolly I'd seen in Mr Althorpe's toy shop. He damn near won, too. I can see 'im now, Mr Lestrade, smilin' as 'e give me the doll, 'is knuckles all red and raw and 'is face a mass of cuts. I loved 'im, Inspector. 'E was a darling old man,' and she brushed a single tear from her cheek. 'No,' she breathed in the sea air sharply to recover herself, 'I'm not surprised 'e died the way 'e did, though I'll wager – not that I do wager, y'understand – they didn't give 'im a fighting chance.'

Lestrade ignored the fact that Mrs Hopkins was contradicting herself. It was one of the more controlled manifestations of grief. He'd seen it before, countless times. Why was it, he mused to himself, that even before the season began, they exercised donkeys on these beaches? And he shook his trouser leg with the resignation of a man who did not always look where he was going.

'I 'adn't seen 'im in, oh, five or six years,' Mrs Hopkins was going on. 'Well, you know 'ow it is when you've a family. My own children are nearly full grown now and there's John, my 'usband. Have you a family, Inspector?'

Lestrade hadn't.

The couple turned for the cheap hotel in the wrong part of town where the Hopkinses were staying. Lestrade watched the darkness settle over the sea before he began his journey back.

'Can we take 'im 'ome, soon, Inspector? The old man, to York. 'E'd want that. We'll bury 'im in 'is native peat. 'E'd like that,' Lestrade heard Emma Hopkins say again, in his mind.

'Yes, you can take him back,' Lestrade found himself saying aloud, hoping suddenly that there was no one nearby. He picked himself up from the sand of the cliff walk and made his way back to the town, the great perpendicular tower of the church black and silent now in the gathering gloom. Beyond that, the sibilance of the sea, a band of mauve-grey under a purpling sky. But Lestrade, as ever, had other things on his mind.

Blogg had told him that the Tuddenham tribe could usually be found in Cromer of a Friday night, in the tap room of the Cuttlefish, a far less salubrious hostelry than the one in which Bradstreet still lay, trying, no doubt, to make the bed lie still under him. It was one of the last refuges of the old Cromer, local Cromer, the Cromer that was the fishing village before the well-to-do began to spend their summers there. The place was crowded enough, with brawny good-natured fishermen and labourers, the smell of the salt and the brackish beaches lost in the all-consuming ether of Norfolk beer – a pint of which Lestrade ordered and took to one of the quieter corners, with his crab supper.

The girl who served him didn't seem too anxious to help him by pointing out the Tuddenhams, but in a few minutes it became obvious that Lestrade had found his quarry. He recognised the signs, the hurried glances in his direction, the lips moving silently behind cupped hands, the emptying of the bar and the tables around. And the final signal, the abrupt end of the fiddle music in the corner. Lestrade summed up the situation. His back was to the wall, a crackling log fire to his right. He had one good hand, but the other would not serve him well in a fight.

He transferred the pewter mug to his left hand and noiselessly slipped his right into the pocket of his Donegal draped over the settle behind him. He felt warm brass and waited. Four men, rough seafaring types, stood before him, all bearing a vague resemblance to one another, watching him in silence.

'Mr Tuddenham?' Lestrade ventured.

'Yes,' the four chorused.

'Who wants to know?' The eldest of them edged forward, elbowing aside the rest.

'Inspector Lestrade, Scotland Yard.'

'Where?'

A growl and a ripple of laughter. The fiddler flashed his bow suddenly across his instrument, as though to punctuate the joke.

'I would like to ask you a few questions,' Lestrade went on, as the merriment subsided.

'Oh, ar? What about?' The older man hurled his tobacco plug around his mouth and spat it with unerring accuracy into a spittoon some yards away.

'The death of William Bentley.'

A murmur and a rumble this time. If Lestrade had been asked to swear on oath what had been said, he would have been bound to say it sounded like 'rhubarb'.

'What be that to do wi' us?' one of the younger Tuddenhams asked.

'Stow it,' snapped Tuddenham the Elder; then, fixing his beady eye on Lestrade, 'What be that to do wi' us?'

'Mr Bentley was murdered.'

Another ripple of rhubarb.

'Ay, we'd heard that. So?'

'So, how did you kill him?' Lestrade always tried the direct approach with the lower orders. It wasted less time, and there was less chance of a charge of wrongful arrest.

The murmur ran to positive allotments of rhubarb.

'What be you accusing us of?' another Tuddenham asked.

'Murder,' said Lestrade.

'And how are we supposed to have done it?' the eldest

62   M.J. TROW

Tuddenham enquired.

'You tell me,' goaded Lestrade.

'Better yet,' snarled the biggest Tuddenham, 'I'll show you.' And he lunged at Lestrade with both massive hands outstretched.

It was one of those pieces of pure poetry of which inspectors of Scotland Yard are occasionally capable in moments of stress and which would be talked about in Cromer for years to come. Lestrade brought up both forearms simultaneously, spreadeagling his opponent's arms so that Tuddenham's chin crunched down on the table, narrowly missing the shell of Lestrade's crab. As he landed, Lestrade brought both his fists together on Tuddenham's temples, which would have been painful enough had they been fists, but in his left hand Lestrade still held the pewter mug and in his right the brass knuckle-duster without which he never ventured far. The assaulted Tuddenham knelt on the flagstones with his tousled head in Lestrade's supper, groaning. Apart from that, the tap room was silent and Lestrade had not left his seat.

After what seemed like an eternity, the two other Tuddenham children broke forward, but Papa restrained them, forcing them back with his scarred, burly arms.

The tension was broken.

'That's Matthew,' he said, pointing to the prostrate Tuddenham, 'this be Luke, this be Mark,' to the other sons; 'I be John.'

'I thought you might be,' said Lestrade. 'Landlord.' A figure answering that description appeared from behind the bar. 'A pint of your best ale for the Messrs Tuddenham – and some butter for the head of this one.'

Lestrade proffered a chair to John Tuddenham and as he took it, slowly, uncertainly, the whole tap room unfroze and returned to life. The fiddle struck up, even the fire crackled anew. The Tuddenham boys carried off their fallen brother like some tragic hero in a play.

'Did 'im good, that,' mused Tuddenham Senior over his pint, 'I 'ope 'e didn't spoil your supper, sir.'

Lestrade shook his head. The new-found submission he

could do without. 'Now,' he said, 'about Bill Bentley.'

'I'm not sorry 'e's gone. I won't say that I am. Whatever else I am, I bain't be no 'ypocrit.'

'I've heard of your feud. That's what brought me to you. What caused it?'

'That's no secret.' Tuddenham gazed obviously into the abyss of his tankard and continued only when Lestrade had signalled mine host to refill it. 'When 'e first come 'ere – upstart 'e were. From Yorkshire. What did 'e know of the sea? Landlubber, 'e were. We don't cotton to strangers here. Saving your pardon. We don't mix wi' them Lunnuners wi' their airs and graces.'

'The feud,' Lestrade reminded him.

'Oh, ar. Well, 'e accused us Tuddenhams o' wrecking. I be a fisherman, Inspector. All me life. Man and boy. And my father before me. Why, there's been no wrecking on this coast for years. Not since I . . . not for years.'

'So you hated each other.'

'We did.' Tuddenham Senior quaffed off his second half pint. Lestrade signalled for a third. He promised himself it would be the last. He didn't yet know how Nimrod Frost reacted to 'expenses'.

'Mind you, we didn't kill 'im. Matthew there, 'e's always been a bit hasty, but in a way 'e was right. If we wanted to do in old Bill Bentley, I'd 'ave gone round there and wrung his neck like a chicken.'

Looking at Tuddenham's fist around his mug, Lestrade was in no doubt that that was so, but he wasn't letting the old fisherman off the hook just yet.

'So it was you who broke his neck?'

'It was not.' Tuddenham was adamant. 'Is that how he died, then?'

Lestrade finished his drink.

'No, Mr Tuddenham, it wasn't. Can you account for your movements on the twentieth inst?' And as he said it he realised the futility of his breath and changed tack. 'Where were you last Monday?'

'At sea, with me 'ol' family, and that's gospel.'

And from a man named John, with sons called Matthew, Mark and Luke, that seemed fair enough.

Lestrade ate a hearty breakfast – of crab – while Bradstreet resolutely looked the other way and sipped his water. As Blogg had surmised, Bradstreet had come up with nothing in connection with the foreign-sounding ship moored off the lighthouse. He had of course come up with much else, but it was not material to the case. Then out into the cold grey of the first morning of May, 1893. Over the cobbles the policemen trudged, wrapping their Donegals around them. Constable Rook dragged their valises and loaded them onto the station wagon. Much to the chagrin of Bradstreet's stomach, it lurched forward to the driver's whip, and they were gone, rattling out of Cromer across the pastureland of Norfolk.

'God, it's flat,' was really the only comment Bradstreet could muster.

'I smell something,' said Lestrade, trying to doze under his tilted bowler.

'I'm sorry, sir. I thought I'd sponged my waistcoat.'

'Not you, Bradstreet. I was being metaphorical.' He hoped that was the right word. 'I smell conspiracy.'

'Anarchists?' Bradstreet had woken up.

Lestrade opened a weary eye from under the rim of his hat. The question was not worthy of comment, but Bradstreet would not leave it alone. 'So that's why we're going to Sandringham. I knew it wasn't just the coachman you were after. It's the Royal Family, isn't it? They're in danger.'

'For all I know, Bradstreet, a madman with a Maxim has killed them all and they're lying on Sandringham's lawns as we speak, but that's not my case. I'm concerned with Bill Bentley, lighthouse keeper of Cromer. Your views?'

'An old man.' Bradstreet was marshalling his powers of detection. 'Suffocated. That would be easy. He died – let me see – latish on Monday afternoon, probably. Perhaps he was taking a nap.'

'Motive?'

'Not robbery. Nothing had been taken – Blogg told us that.

Didn't he? I wasn't really concentrating on his boat.'

'Not robbery,' Lestrade agreed. 'Anarchy?'

Bradstreet took Lestrade's point. The obsession of Inspector Gregson loomed less large in a station wagon lurching through the dawn of a sleepy Norfolk.

Even so, the mysterious ship could not be ignored.

'We can't ignore the mysterious ship, sir.'

'No, we can't,' said Lestrade. 'But you Special Branch see *agents provocateurs* everywhere. A foreign-sounding name that only one witness remembers, but not well enough. I don't think it's anarchy, Bradstreet.'

'Not anarchy,' echoed Bradstreet.

'Well then. Old scores?' Lestrade offered.

'Vengeance. The Tuddenhams. But they have an alibi. They were at sea.'

'It's not watertight, if you'll excuse the pun, but every sense I've got tells me they're clean. Oh, they're up to their rowlocks in smuggling and even a bit of wrecking if the chance comes their way, but that troupe of aboriginals didn't kill Bill Bentley.'

'Family then? His daughter? His son-in-law? What was he worth?'

'I like the deviousness of your mind, Bradstreet, but he was worth pretty well what he stood up in. No stashed cash, no annuities, no private means.'

'So, where are we then, sir?'

Lestrade glanced out of the window.

'Fakenham,' said Lestrade.

No need to be offensive, thought Bradstreet, but he did not dare say so to the little ferret-faced man beside him. After all, he'd seen the size of Matthew Tuddenham, probably still spark out on a table in a back room of the Cuttlefish, and was just a little in awe of his guv'nor now.

It was Lestrade who told the constable to pull off the road and to wait with the wagon, sheltered under the trees. He and Bradstreet walked to the main gates, huge, elaborate, wrought iron, a masterpiece of royal heraldry. A liveried lackey opened them after establishing who was who. The detectives discussed tactics as they followed the widening driveway under the elms and cedars. They would not go to the main house. Protocol and all that. If the coachman who played chess with Bentley was their man, his royal master would hear of it soon enough. Bradstreet made his way direct to the stables, Lestrade by a more circuitous route to the woodworking school, where Close the coachman also had duties.

But before he could get there the inspector took a wrong turn and found himself in the confines of a sheltered garden edged with privet. A fountain played in the centre and although it was far from warm, a solitary figure sat taking tea on the matchless lawn. The figure had his back to Lestrade and was wearing a foreign-looking tunic, sky blue, laced in gold. Lestrade turned to go, but was stopped in his tracks by a gruff command, 'Halt!' Lestrade did. The figure rose from his seat, still carrying the delicate porcelain cup and saucer and approached him.

'Who are you?' The accent was clipped, foreign. Kraut, Lestrade hazarded.

'Inspector Lestrade, sir, Scotland Yard.'

'Scotland ... ach, zo.' The figure transferred his cup and saucer to his left hand rather awkwardly and saluted stiffly, his heels clicking together in what Lestrade knew was a Prussian tradition. With sudden realisation, it dawned upon him. The character before him with the fierce grey eyes, the hearty manner and the ludicrous upturned moustache was the King of Germany. Lestrade returned the bow.

'I am always impressed,' the Kaiser was saying, leading Lestrade to his table, 'by the efficiency of ze British police. Even zo I am travelling incognito, you fellows are neffer ferry far away, eh?'

'I am here on a case, sir,' pointed out Lestrade. The Kaiser looked at Lestrade's posture as he took the proffered chair, wondering perhaps whether it was an English custom for policemen to sit on suitcases. But then, he had noticed no hand luggage. Neither did Lestrade seem to be sitting uncomfortably. He decided to let the moment pass.

'You are from ze ... now, vat did Bertie call it?... ze Special Irish Trunk, yah?'

'Special Irish Branch. No, sir, I am from H division, sir. We specialise in murder.'

'Murder?' The Kaiser poured Lestrade a cup of tea. 'Tell me, hev you read ze *Handbuch für Untersuchungsrichter*? Ve Germans are, of course, ahead of the world when it comes to the science of forensics.'

No, Lestrade had not read it.

'For instance, how would you tell if someone had been strangled?'

'Discolouration of the skin, bulging eyes and tongue, perhaps broken neck, bruising certainly on the throat—'

'Yes, yes,' said the Kaiser rather patronisingly, 'but be specific.'

Lestrade failed to see how much more specific he could be, but before he had time to try again, the Kaiser had grabbed his hand and placed it on his own neck. 'Now,' he said, 'ze fingers are positioned zo. Vat marks vould zis leave?'

Lestrade felt quite decidedly uncomfortable with the Kaiser's throat and life in his hands, but before he could move or answer, the hedges were alive with uniformed men who leapt upon him. The Kaiser sprang back as the table, tea, chairs and inspector sprawled across the grass.

'Don't worry, sir, we've got him,' Lestrade heard a burly sergeant say as he felt the cuffs click on his wrists, wrenched painfully behind his back.

'Damned anarchists!' A booming voice behind the struggling company caused them all to turn. 'Lestrade!'

'Gregson.' Lestrade was peering round from the kneeling position into which the half-dozen constables had forced him. 'Would you mind calling off your monkeys before one of them gets hurt?'

'Ach, I see,' roared the Kaiser, 'zis is a test, yah? To keep your staff on zeir toes. Yes, ferry good, yah.'

It was not Lestrade's toes that worried him at that moment. At least, he would not have given them priority over his neck and wrists, aching dully under the edge of a couple of truncheons.

'What the hell are you doing here, Lestrade? Muscling in on my patch?'

'Gregson, I wouldn't willingly enter your patch if you paid me. Now get these bloody handcuffs off me!'

A constable complied and the blood began to flow back into Lestrade's fingers.

'I'm following a line of enquiry, with your Sergeant Bradstreet.'

'Line of enquiry?' Tobias Gregson was suspicious. 'You're up to something, Lestrade. Your pardon, Your Imperial Majesty,' and he bowed almost double to the Kaiser, who was obviously amused by the whole thing and then whisked Lestrade into the bushes. 'Look, Lestrade. These bloody foreigners come over here at the drop of a hat. I had a call yesterday – a telegram – to say he was staying at Sandringham as a guest of His Royal Highness. I expect His Royal Highness is as browned off with Villy as I am. But I had to be here. Frost sent me packing on the first train. And as if this isn't difficult enough – he goes where he likes, when he likes, refuses a bodyguard – you have to turn up like a bad penny, trying to strangle the man.'

'I'm pursuing a murder enquiry, Gregson,' Lestrade spat back at him (all this in vicious whispers, Gregson occasionally smiling and waving at the Kaiser while the constables righted his table and salvaged what was left of his currant buns). 'And you can play bloody nursemaid to that,' he pointed contemptuously, 'all you like. But get in my way again, and I'll get you back on the beat.'

'How is he involved in murder?' Gregson demanded to know.

'Not him, somebody else.'

'Who?'

'That's my business.'

'If you're interrogating a Head of State of a major European power, it becomes my business.'

'I'm not interrogating *him*. How many more times?'

'Lestrade, you are evading my questions. If I didn't know better, I'd say . . . God, you're not a Communist, are you?'

'If I were, Gregson, I'm sure you'd be among the first to know.'

'Well, I never was very sure about some of McNaghten's

appointments. Wait a minute, you were there on Bloody Sunday, weren't you?'

'That was six years ago, Gregson. Talk about the long memory of the law.'

'We have our uses.'

'Gregson, you can look under every bed in Sandringham for Communists, anarchists, shopping lists, whatever you like. All you'll catch is your own tail. Me, I've got a murderer to catch,' and Lestrade broke away from the bitchy conversation under the privet, and, barely acknowledging the Kaiser, who was now busy instructing the constables in truncheon drill, made for the stables and Bradstreet.

'I warn you, Lestrade,' Gregson shouted after him; 'this will go further.'

Hell Broth

Jacob sat in the attic room, cold and alone. The sun didn't seem to enter the cobwebbed windows, but the wind shivered the yellowed nets and rattled the door behind him. He took up the pen again and wrote.

Sir, I must warn you that . . . and again the muse failed him. He threw the crumpled paper to join the others littering the floor. He must have been here an hour, perhaps two, and had got no further in his letter than the first line. At least he had addressed the envelope, *To Whom It May Concern, New Scotland Yard, London.*

The whole thing was too preposterous, too outrageous — who would believe him? He must go in person. And yet. What of them? Each rattle of the latch saw him turning, paralysed for a moment with fear. Then finer emotions took him. What of him? It was a matter of honour, really. A family affair. Across the wilderness of rooftops he heard a church clock striking. Six. He could stay no longer. He would write to the Yard again later, when he could. Now, he had to go north.

They stood before Nimrod Frost in his office. Tobias Gregson, thick set, squat, fuming. Sholto Lestrade, taller, thinner, calmer. The pattern Frost was prepared for, the pattern that so angered Gregson.

'So, that's it, is it?' Frost was glowering at Lestrade, but talking to Gregson.

'I wouldn't belittle it, sir. If need be, I can go to the Home Secretary himself.'

Frost turned an odd sort of white. 'Don't you threaten me with the Home Secretary, laddie. I'm not at all sure you're necessary on this Force, Gregson. In fact, once this Home Rule nonsense is over, I'm considering scrapping Special Branch once and for all.'

Gregson was speechless. He stood there with his mouth open.

'No need for you to smirk, Lestrade. You tread with your great feet,' again the unfair jibe, 'all over Norfolk, harassing European royalty. Who the hell do you think you are?'

Lestrade opened his mouth, but in the event got no further than Gregson. Frost wallowed to his feet. 'Consider yourself under suspension, Lestrade. Half pay. Go home. Cool off.'

Now it was Lestrade's turn to be speechless. Gregson was smirking triumphantly while Frost rumbled out a tirade against inspectors who could not operate efficiently, about what the yard was coming to, blah, blah, blah.

'Now, get out, both of you.'

Gregson turned for the door, smarting under Frost's attack, but pleased and justified as well.

'Lestrade, before you go.'

Frost slumped into his chair and fixed the inspector with his sharp little eyes.

'I know what you're thinking, Lestrade. Twenty years on the Force. All for nothing. What will you do now?'

'Grow geraniums, like other retired coppers.' Lestrade shrugged.

'Do that if you like but first I've got a little assignment for you.'

Lestrade looked at his chief. That couldn't be a smile playing around Frost's blubbery lips, could it? No, a trick of the light.

'I thought I was suspended – indefinitely,' he said.

'So you are.' Frost struggled to his feet. 'Show me your hands.' Lestrade held them out. 'You'll have to take that bandage off. And toughen them up. Get yourself some rags. Don't shave from today. Eat as little as you can.'

'Sir?' Lestrade already knew Frost too well to believe the man had cracked, yet certainly he couldn't follow his train of thought.

'Can you do a Lancashire accent?'

'No.'

'Cockney up your own, then. Bow Bells stuff, yes?'

'Yes, if I must.'

'You must. How will Mrs Manchester take it?'

'Sir?'

'Don't hedge, Lestrade. You have a housekeeper named Mrs Manchester, haven't you? Sarah Manchester? Aged sixty-one?'

Lestrade smirked. 'Is that a crime?'

'On the contrary. I'm glad to see my inspectors improving their social position. It gives them the air of authority they ought to have. But you'll have to tell her you'll be away for a while – one month, two, who knows?'

'I have a feeling you do, sir.'

Frost chuckled mirthlessly. 'Quite right, I do. You spoke of a conspiracy, Lestrade. Well, Gregson might not accept that, but I think you may have something. Three old men in as many months, dead from poisoning or suffocation – all made to look like the ravages of time. It's a coincidence, Lestrade.'

Lestrade was hearing his own words bounce back at him.

'Well, I've got a fourth for you, I think.'

Lestrade was all ears – especially now the tip of his nose had gone.

'An inmate of Manchester Workhouse, Lestrade. Another old man. Nothing odd in that, you might think. Old men die in workhouses every day. Except that this one was poisoned, like the others. But this one was obvious – strychnine. Very messy.'

'One murderer for them all?' Lestrade was thinking out loud.

'That's for you to find out,' Frost answered. 'Give yourself a week to roughen up. Then go to Manchester and get yourself committed.'

'Sir?'

'Special request from Superintendent Olds. Jack and I were at school together back in. . . back in the old days. His men are too well known for undercover work. But yours is a new face, Lestrade. We must think of a new name for you, a new identity. Get into that workhouse and find out how that old man died.'

'Why undercover, sir? Why not make enquiries in the usual way?'

'As I said, Lestrade. Conspiracy. You know the worst thing about conspiracies? You never know who's involved. It could be Jack Olds. The entire Manchester Board of Guardians of the Poor. It could be me . . .' A pause. 'For all I know, Lestrade, it could even be you. But we'll have to chance that, won't we?'

'And the suspension?'

'As far as the rest of the Force knows, Lestrade, you are out, at least for a while. Only you and I will know different. You can use Charlo as a go-between. Don't come to the Yard yourself. How's he shaping up, by the way?'

'I wish I knew, sir. All I've seen of him is a red nose and he didn't exactly say a lot between sneezes. He should be in my office now.'

Frost extended a chubby, powerful hand, and as Lestrade caught it he said, 'Keep your wits about you, lad. It's a rough world north of Hampstead. Think of it as a challenge.'

Lestrade smiled.

'And Inspector . . . Don't go annoying any more Visiting European Nobs. Or your suspension might be real.'

Sergeant Hector Charlo was not in Lestrade's office. He had attempted to rise, said the note that *was* there, from his bed of pain, but his doctor had advised him to stay where he was. As he feared, the cold was bronchitis and the doctor had warned of pneumonia if he left his boudoir. There was even a doctor's note confirming it, pinned to Charlo's spidery, handwritten missive. The inspector was to rest assured, the sergeant would be back on duty just as soon as the swellings had gone down. Mind you, his back wasn't what it was . . .

Manchester. The city. Not the housekeeper. It had a tart and a school named after it. Lestrade had never been before, but Frost had told him before he left the metropolis that it would be raining. It was. Grey rain was driving across a grey city. Its buildings were uninspiring and when Lestrade walked through it he found himself jostling with labourers on the last stages of cutting the Ship Canal which was to link the cottonopolis with the Mersey. He spent the day, with the rain soaking to his skin, acquainting himself with the place. He didn't like it. After this, the workhouse would come as a relief.

It was night before he found it – a long, low building in the shape of a cross, no doubt the pride and joy of some civic do-gooder under the shadow of the great Chadwick. He was admitted through a side door by an overseer with a hacking cough, to whom Lestrade gave his chit. By the guttering light of a solitary candle, the overseer read it: *James Lister, labourer*. It was an alias Lestrade had used before. The overseer peered at him through a greasy pince-nez. He saw the usual run-of-the-workhouse vagrant, unkempt, dishevelled, not perhaps as bowed of back or world weary as they usually were, but a month or two in this place, he knew, would alter that.

'Last known address?' The overseer, at this time of night, was forced to do his own paperwork. He perched on the upright desk that Mr Dickens had probably written on about fifty years before. Or if not him, then certainly Mr Disraeli.

'Last known address?' he repeated, quill poised.

'Ratcliffe Highway,' Lestrade lied.

'Where?'

'London.' Had the man heard of it, Lestrade wondered?

He scratched something incomprehensible on the ledger.

'Right, turn out your pockets.'

Lestrade complied. One pocket knife, handle broken, a length of string, one apple. 'Stolen?' asked the overseer. No comment. Lestrade would play it dumb with the authorities. He knew a chirpy workhouse inmate was as unpopular as a chirpy prisoner. And, looking about him, this was very little different from stir. 'Tuppence ha'penny.' The overseer slipped the change into his pocket and, as if to anticipate Lestrade's protest, said, 'which will go towards your keep.'

The overseer spat copiously in a corner and slammed shut the ledger. He beckoned Lestrade to a door in a grey wall, on which he knocked. A grille slid back and a face appeared.

'Male, age unknown, former labourer. Bath, bed and oakum.'

Lestrade shuffled down endless corridors, dark and dank. Overhead in the lanterns' flicker he caught the elaborate gilt hypocrisy of the Manchester Board of Guardians, 'God is Love, God is Faith, God is Trust, God is Good,' and he was forced into the conclusion that God was probably Somewhere Else. He shambled more convincingly now, aware of his warders at his elbows, though they barely noticed him. He stooped, tilted his head to one side. Perhaps deafness might be worth a try. After all, he was physically fit enough for labouring work. His presentation at the House of Industry had to be – and to remain – legitimate.

'Strip.'

He did, standing naked in the dark of a circular room, in the centre of which he could see by the lantern's light, was a bath. Had they heard of the Poplar Reform Movement this far north? he wondered. And his question was answered as they pushed him roughly into the icy water.

'One hot bath,' said the warder and he was thrown a grubby towel to dry himself. His rags were bundled together and tied with string. 'For your release,' the warder told him and he was given a thick, drab fustian jacket and trousers. This place, he mused to himself, makes Cold Bath Fields look like the Strand Palace.

He was shunted into the East Wing, for adult males between sixteen and sixty. His bed was a trough: rough, splintered wood worn smooth by countless derelicts collapsing into it. The mattress was thin, straw-stuffed and the sheet a single layer of cotton. It was past May 1st and the blankets had been withdrawn.

'No beer. No spirits. No tobacco. No spilling your seed on the ground,' and the warders left. Lestrade let his eyes attune to the darkness. A long, dank room, stone floor, with high barred windows the length of it. The noise was of snoring, coughing, and the occasional breaking of wind – not unlike the sergeants' room at the Yard. But the smell was different. It was the smell of poverty, of despair, of death.

He didn't sleep at all, but the morning bell rang as

punctually as ever. Five o'clock. Cold water, what passed for
a meal of bread and black pudding, which Lestrade had never
seen before and didn't really want to see again and then out to
the labour yards to pick oakum. He studied the faces around
him, grey, lifeless, identical. It wasn't easy to tell a man's age
in here, much less his former calling. A pile of evil-smelling
hemp was thrown at him. Like the others, he adopted the
position of back against the wall of his stall, cross-legged, and
proceeded to do as they did, hammering the rope with a
broken mallet, teasing out the greasy, sharp threads until his
hands were a mass of blood. At the end of the first day, he had
spoken to no one, no one had spoken to him. He had failed to
reach his quota of three and one half pounds of oakum. He
was given a day to rectify that or it would be loss of privileges
– no meals for two days.

He endured the night of hacking coughs, the tuberculous
hours, yet again, wondering why exactly Nimrod Frost had
chosen him for this, and the morning bell clanged the
Unfaithful to work again. After hell broth on the fifth day,
his hands red raw but his quota achieved, Lestrade made his
first contact – a knot of men of varying ages, their skins the
colour of the workhouse walls. Yes, they had known Richard
Brown. How old was he? God knew, they didn't. Everybody
looked the same age in here. All they knew was that he had
worked on the canal side and when his rheumatics got too
much, he came in here. Nice enough bloke. Honest. Mind
you, he died funny.

'Oh?' Lestrade was all ears.

'Where did the say tha knew 'im from?'

'In the docks.' Lestrade hedged.

'Liverpool?'

'Yes. How do you mean, he died funny?'

'Well,' another inmate chimed in, ''e were all reet one
mornin', then be night time, 'e were gone.'

'And 'is face,' whispered another.

'What about it?' asked Lestrade.

'Grinnin' 'e were, like the devil 'isself.'

Lestrade felt the hairs rise on the back of his neck, where
the short crop given by the warder three days ago was still

smarting from the nicks of the razor.

'I seen plenty of dead men. They die every day in 'ere – and t'womenfolk, and t'kids,' another went on, 'but nothing like 'im. He was smiling with 'is eyes bright and 'is teeth bared. Like a rabid dog, 'e were.'

'I saw 'im die. I were wi'im.' All eyes turned to the Little Fly in the corner.

'Tha never said,' another chided him. 'I thought 'e were alone in bed.'

'Nay, I were going to ask 'im for some snout when 'e went rigid. He screamed out – you all must've 'eard it.' They hadn't. ''E arched 'is back a couple of times, like 'avin' a fit, like, and 'e died. It were all over very quick.'

So was the conversation. A warder rang a bell deep in the bowels of the workhouse and the inmates scattered, like the zombies of a Gothic novel – the undead going about their business. Silence, but for the coughs, reigned.

It had been confirmed. Lestrade's ravaged fingers curled painfully round the mallet again. The classic symptoms of strychnine poisoning. But this time Lestrade had to go further. He had to see the doctor who pronounced Richard Brown dead – and there was only one way to do that. He waited until the moment was right, heart pounding with the concentration, sweat breaking out on his forehead, then crushed his thumb with a mallet. He rolled sideways, crying out in agony. A warder was at his side, prodding him with his truncheon, 'You there, Lister. What's t'matter wi' ye?'

Lestrade held up the blackening digit.

'Malingering bastard,' was the warder's only comment, and he went away. Lestrade knelt there in pain and surprise until he passed out. The rest was easy.

When he awoke he was in a different room. Not the dormitory of the East Wing, but in a hospital room.

'Oh, so you're awake are you?' A burly woman with a starched but grubby apron stood before him, sleeves rolled to reveal muscles not out of place on a circus strongman, hair strained back in a silver bun. 'Malingering bastard,' she grumbled, tucked Lestrade in bed even harder and stalked off,

bellowing orders to other unfortunate inmates, whose terminal tuberculosis or tertiary syphilis had brought them to their
last days in the infirmary of the Manchester House of
Industry, Openshaw district.

It was the best part of a day before his quarry arrived, a
sallow-faced man in his mid-forties, shabby frock coat and
faded silk vest. He handled Lestrade's thumb with something
less than a charming bedside manner, but was alarmed when
the inspector yanked him down to pillow level with his good
hand. 'I am Inspector Lestrade of Scotland Yard. I must speak
with you on an urgent matter of the gravest importance.'

The doctor pulled away, shaken. He recovered himself.
'See him over there.' He pointed to an old man staring at the
ceiling, his fingers endlessly fiddling with his sheets. 'He
thinks he's Nero. And I of course am Florence Nightingale.
This one can chop wood with his right hand. There's
obviously nothing wrong with that. Only his mind and his
thumb need attention. Wood chopping tomorrow!' he barked
at an accompanying warder. 'Let him sleep here tonight,' and
he swept away. Lestrade's silent protestations as he craned out
of bed were met with a swift tap from the burly woman, who
had miraculously reappeared at his bedside. 'No broth for
you tonight, me lad. Grabbin' the doctor like that, indeed!
Who do you think you are?'

'Napoleon Buonaparte,' said Lestrade and sank down in
discomfort and despair into his bed.

Most of the night was spent fighting off the advances of an
old cottage loaf who would not take no for an answer. In the
end, Lestrade brought his knee up rather sharply into the old
man's groin, which cooled his ardour more than somewhat –
and probably made him sing in a rather higher key. Nero in
the meantime was composing odes of indescribable nonsense
and the night would have been funny had it not been so
unutterably sad. An inspector of Scotland Yard, Lestrade kept
telling himself, had seen it all before. Remember that, keep
your identity and this madhouse won't get you. An inspector
of Scotland Yard. Remember. ... Or was it Napoleon
Buonaparte?

The dawn saw Lestrade standing with the others, huddled

against the driving rain. God, did it never stop raining in
Manchester? Beyond the limits of the city, mused Lestrade, in
the airy uplands of Failsworth and Stalybridge (he had studied
the whole area on a map) the sun shone out in splendour, but
the smoke of the cottonopolis and the gleam of the cotton
masters' brass conspired to reflect it back and keep it out of
inner Manchester. Or perhaps even the yards of the House of
Industry. Perhaps even beyond those high, grey walls, the
world was turning still.

A whistle signalled a break in work. The woodcutters
stopped. But this was no rest period. Even without his
half-hunter, Lestrade kept his sense of time. The bells never
missed. It was not rest period for an hour or more. The gates
of the yard opened to admit a Visiting Pair of Dignitaries. A
good-looking lady, perhaps thirty or so, swept in in a flourish
of velvets and silks. The sweetness of her perfume flooded the
air of sweat and sawdust. From nowhere, little workhouse
children, the friendless boys and girls, scampered to her. She
bent to them, kissing them, distributing sweets and liquorice.

'That's Mrs Lawrenson,' came the whispered answer to
Lestrade's query. 'She comes twice a year to give us baccy and
the kids sweets. She brings pins and combs for the womenfolk.'

'That's charitable of her,' Lestrade commented.

'You don't often get that. I was in the workhouse at
Kensington a year or two back.' Lestrade thought he
recognised the south-London drawl. 'Bloody Miss Louisa
Twining stoppin' our porter. Bloody do-gooder. This un's all
right, though. Knows how to treat a man proper, she does.'

'Aye,' whispered another. 'I wouldn't mind changing my
place with that Dandy Jack of hers. I bet she's a real hot'un
between the sheets.'

'Just remember,' the Londoner broke into verse:

> 'The paupers is meek and lowly,
> With their "Thankee kindly, mum"'s;
> So long as they fill their stomachs,
> What matter it whence it comes?'

'Is that Mr Lawrenson?' Lestrade asked, though he couldn't
see the gentleman with her very clearly.

'Dunno,' said the Londoner. 'Fancy done up though, ain't 'e?'

'Nay,' the Mancunian spat a gob into the sawdust. 'I seen 'im when they came last Christmas. Introduced to us, 'e was. 'E's 'er intended. Name of Bandicoot.'

Lestrade dropped his axe, clanging loudly on the cobbles of the yard.

'Watch out, you clumsy ba . . .' and the Mancunian broke off as Mrs Lawrenson made her way towards the clump of woodchoppers.

'Good morning, gentlemen,' she beamed. 'Not a fine one, I fear.'

'Your radiance is sun enough for us, ma'am,' the poetic Londoner replied.

Mrs Lawrenson curtsied graciously and began to distribute largesse in the form of tobacco. 'Harry, help me here.'

'Of course, dearest,' and the tall, good-looking fiancé lent a hand. As he came to Lestrade, he stared in astonishment, his jaw hanging open. 'Good God,' was all he could say. All eyes turned to Lestrade.

'What is it, Heart?' Mrs Lawrenson asked.

Lestrade burned his eyes fiercely into the fiancé's. He could tell that it wasn't doing the trick. 'James Lister, sir, from the Ratcliffe Highway, labourer.'

'Has it come to this?' Bandicoot persisted. What an idiot, Lestrade fumed inwardly. Still the same copper of very little brain he used to be two years ago. What though he owed his life to the man, this was no way to treat him now, breaking his cover on an assignment.

'Do you know this man?' Mrs Lawrenson asked.

'No, ma'am,' Lestrade broke in. 'Begging your pardon, sir,' and then with vehemence, 'You must be confusing me with someone else.' He felt his stage Cockney fooling no one, but Mrs Lawrenson, accepting the statement at face value, gently pulled the uncomprehending Bandicoot away.

The others still looked a little oddly at Lestrade, not least the warders, whose truncheons were not in evidence this morning. Mrs Lawrenson swept away, with soothing words of comfort, surrounded by workhouse children, gobbling and sucking gratefully on their sweets. As the whistle signalled the men back to work, two warders strolled past Lestrade's group. 'She's 'ere a lot these days. Only, what were it, two weeks back? Three?'

'Nay, it weren't that recent,' said his mate.

'Aye, it were. Don't you remember? She visited Brown on t' day 'e died. No wonder t' old bastard died wi' a smile on his lips.'

Lestrade's ears pricked up. Was that it? Was that how strychnine was administered in this hell-hole? By the unsuspected hand of a social worker? A sister of mercy? Of course. It must be. Why else had Mrs Lawrenson visited Richard Brown? Had she visited him alone? Had she visited others? Had those other visits merely been to disguise her real purpose? Had she given anything to Richard Brown? What about a plug of snout? Strychnine on the tobacco. Yes, it was too easy. But she was Bandicoot's lady. His intended. Had that muddle-headed ex-constable from the right side of the tracks, old Etonian and friend of kings, taken a viper to his bosom? And while the inmates nearest the gates were secretly admiring Mrs Lawrenson's bosom, Lestrade hatched a plan.

He had to wait more than a month before he could make any move. Then, armed with a chit signed by a Guardian of the poor, he trudged out of the Openshaw Workhouse in search of work. Three others with him went straight to the nearest tap room, in the hopes of cadging or stealing the price of a pint. One, perhaps with greater resolve than they, set out for the diggings at the canal. But then it was easier for him; he *was* teetotal. Lestrade was choosier in his search for employment. He passed the rows of bleak, mean streets, silhouetted against the glower of the Manchester sky. Why were so many of them called Coronation Street, he wondered? He passed the gaunt, monolithic cotton mills, rows and rows of windows, repaired and buttressed against the escape of valuable steam. He passed the queues of women waiting their turn, with the resignation of the poor, at the standpipes. He avoided signs saying 'Cotton operatives wanted' and the pairs of uniformed policemen of the Manchester Constabulary. He was looking for one place of employment only – at the home of Mrs Lawrenson.

He had covered many miles in his workhouse hobnails before he found it, a large town house surrounded by acacias and planes. Dogs barked at his entry and the door was opened by a pompous butler of the old school, Scots and sandy-haired.

'Who is it, Dudson?' a voice called from the hall.

'A vagrant, ma'am. A person of no consequence. Shall I give a shilling, ma'am?' 'And may I keep the change?' he muttered under his breath.

Mrs Lawrenson appeared, gorgeous in a swirl of crimson satin – the afternoon dress of the rich. 'No, poor fellow. Come in, come in,' and she extended a hand and helped Lestrade over the threshold. Dudson, though used to this sight a hundredfold, showed with every movement of his body that he had never approved. What, he wondered for the umpteenth time, was a good Lowland Liberal like himself doing in the employ of a Socialist? And he was careful to keep upwind of Lestrade.

'Tea, Dudson. In the drawing room.'

The butler bowed to the inevitable and vanished, clapping hands to attract unseen maids.

'Pray, be seated.' Mrs Lawrenson extended a hand to the sofa.

'I'm dirty, ma'am.' For the moment Lestrade kept up his Cockney idiot.

'Nothing that can't be cleaned. Dirt, like poverty, is only skin deep. Are you in search of work?'

Lestrade decided to drop the guise and go for the kill.

'If I don't complete this case, I may be.'

Mrs Lawrenson looked a little taken aback at the brightness of the answer, the loss of accent. She peered for the first time under the grime, the blackened hands and the blue shaven head and caught the flash of eyes, purposeful, sure, even haunting.

'Who are you?' she found herself saying.

'Inspector Sholto Lestrade, ma'am, Scotland Yard.' He rose and bowed stiffly but watched her every reaction. She broke into a merry, musical laugh. 'Lestrade. Why, Harry has spoken of you so often. But why . . .?' Then it dawned. 'Wait, you were in Openshaw Workhouse, last month. *That* was why Harry was so odd. He recognised you.'

'He did indeed. It was all I could do to shut him up.'

'Oh, he is a silly boy, isn't he? Hasn't the brains he was born with.' A sudden seriousness. 'So, you are on a case, incognito?'

Lestrade was about to say 'No. In the workhouse,' when the timely entry of Dudson with the tea saved him unawares from social embarrassment.

'I thought I'd better bring the tea myself, ma'am,' explained Dudson in his impeccable Lowland-Liberal delivery, 'bearing in mind the present company.' Had there been a clothes peg handy, Lestrade felt sure it would have been clamped firmly on the butler's nose.

'Vagrant be damned!' cried Harry Bandicoot as he rushed into the room seconds behind Dudson. 'This is Inspector Lestrade of Scotland Yard. You mind your p's and q's, Dudson, or he'll feel your collar.'

The very thought of Lestrade's grimy hand coming anywhere near Dudson's collar made the butler pale. He had read that the police were badly paid, but could it be as bad as this?

'What do I call you?' Bandicoot extended his hand. '"Sir", it always was. And yet now . . .'

'The least I can do for a man who saved my life is to let him call me Sholto, Harry,' and the two men shook hands warmly.

'You've met Letitia?' said Bandicoot, indicating Mrs Lawrenson.

'Bless you,' said Lestrade. 'Oh, I see. Yes, indeed.'

'Sit down, sir . . . er . . . Sholto. Please. Tell us why the disguise.'

'Undercover,' said Lestrade, and flashed a glance at the butler eavesdropping splendidly near the door.

'That will be all, Dudson.' Bandicoot flicked him away like a fly in summer.

Letitia poured the tea, and handed round the Madeira cake.

'It's rather difficult,' Lestrade began. 'You're a member of the public now, Harry. And it's I who should be calling you "sir".'

'We only worked on one case, Sholto, but I would hope we may be friends. I will never forget Hengler's Circus that night.'

'No more will I. It was nearly my last.'

'Well, then.' Bandicoot's mood lifted. 'You must have come here for a purpose. You're not a man who makes social calls. I remember that much.'

'May I speak to you alone?'

'Sholto,' began Bandicoot, a trifle outraged.

'No, no, dearest heart, the inspector has his reasons. Besides, I have letters to write. Mr Morris will be in Manchester next month and I have not arranged the details with him. I shall be in the study . . . should you need me,' and she looked meaningfully at Lestrade. The men rose as she left the room.

'Look, Sholto,' Harry Bandicoot's new-found independence had increased his self-confidence; 'you may have been my guv'nor once, but that doesn't give you the right to pull rank now. Letitia and I are to be married in four months. In fact,' and he paced the room, 'in fact, she wrote you an invitation only last week. It's probably sitting on your desk at the Yard.'

Lestrade walked to the window, then turned back to the ex-constable.

'What do you know of Letitia?' he was bound to ask.

'Know? That I love her, of course. And that she loves me. And that's all I need to know.' Indignation was followed by a realisation. 'Why are you asking all these questions?'

'I've only asked you one.'

'All right.' Bandicoot was more reasonable, remembering his police training. 'Let me ask you one. What has Letitia to do with the case you're working on?'

Lestrade answered with another question. 'Who is Mr Morris?'

'William Morris, of the Kelmscott Press.'

'The Socialist?' He sounded like Gregson.

'Yes, he's a Socialist. He's also an artist, a writer, a thinker and a Great Man.'

'Like Sherlock Holmes was a Great Detective?'

'No, not like Holmes!' Bandicoot was thundering in a way Lestrade had not seen before. Then calmer, 'Sholto, as a vagrant you were welcome here. As a policeman, I'm not so sure. Unless you tell me what this is all about, I must ask you to leave.'

Lestrade looked at Bandicoot. He was half a head taller, considerably broader, and eleven years his junior. Furthermore, he had not lived on hell broth and beef tea for the past five weeks and his hair, unlike Lestrade's, was not falling out. Anyway, physical attributes apart, this man was Harry Bandicoot, the curly-headed, good-natured young constable who had shot and killed one of the most accomplished murderers of the century to save Lestrade's life. He couldn't let it come to blows. Besides, he hadn't got his knuckle-duster.

'All right, but you must promise to answer some questions first – for old times' sake.' He didn't want to say for auld lang syne in case Dudson was listening at the door. Bandicoot sat down, rational, reasonable again.

'How often does Letitia visit Openshaw Workhouse?'

'A few times a year, I believe. Christmas and the spring, certainly. Other times if she has the opportunity.'

'Why?'

'Why?' Bandicoot appeared genuinely taken aback. 'She believes in her fellow man, Sholto. You and I may have seen the dregs of humanity on whom any amount of sympathy would be wasted. But Letitia believes man can change his base nature.'

'What about Richard Brown's base nature?'

'Who?'

'The name means nothing to you?'

'No.'

'What about Bill Bentley?'

Nothing.

'Joe Towers?'

Still nothing. Bandicoot was as blank as ever he was.

'Richard Brown was visited by your lady love some seven weeks ago,' Lestrade offered by way of explanation. 'Is she in the habit of visiting individuals in the workhouse?'

'Not usually, no, but it has been known. Sholto, what exactly are you accusing her of?'

Lestrade let out a long sigh. 'Probably nothing,' he said; 'possibly murder. Would you ask her to join us?'

Lestrade knew he was breaking all the rules in the book, letting Bandicoot fetch a suspect himself, with all the emotional ties he had with her. But Lestrade was having a private bet with himself that Bandicoot was still too much of a policeman to permit anything untoward. A bolt for the backdoor? A rush to the stable? A concocted story at the very least? But no, a few seconds and Letitia Lawrenson stood before him, her intended bridegroom at her side.

'Did you know Richard Brown?' Lestrade was standing facing her, eyes and voice as cold as the workhouse hot bath.

Mrs Lawrenson visibly sank. 'So you know?' She waved aside Bandicoot's outstretched arm. 'No, Harry. It's time I . . . what is it you policemen say? . . . came clean?'

'Letitia, don't—'

'Letitia Lawrenson,' Lestrade broke in, 'you are not obliged to say anything, but I must caution you—'

'No, Inspector,' Letitia cut him short, 'this is not a confession to you. It is a confession to Harry.'

And all three of them sat down to hear it.

'George, my husband, died six years ago; he was killed in a mountaineering expedition, Inspector – the Matterhorn. When he died I was twenty-two, scarcely a woman at all. Some women might have broken down, withdrawn behind the weeds of widowhood as the Queen did, I have read. I found a cause, Inspector. The people. Good, honest people, like your friends in Openshaw. I buried my love for my husband in them.' Bandicoot held her hand, tenderly, for a fist so large.

'But, my dearest, I know all this,' he said.

'What you don't know,' and she pulled herself away from him to the window, 'is that I had an admirer. I never told you about him because . . . because, well, it was all over nearly a year ago.'

'Well then . . .' Bandicoot offered acceptance, but Letitia spun round; 'he was sixty-three years old, Harry. Old enough to be my father.'

The policemen, past and present, looked at each other.

'Richard Brown?' asked Lestrade.

Letitia took her eyes with difficulty away from Harry Bandicoot. 'No, Inspector. Richard Brown knew this man in the Army. He worked on his estate for a while, but drifted away in later years. I came to know him for a time before he left. His rheumatism had got worse very quickly. When I first saw him in Openshaw I could scarcely believe it was the same man. I visited him when I could. I learned later he died on the day of my last visit.'

So now we are getting somewhere, Lestrade hoped.

'Did you give him anything?' he asked.

'Some tobacco. And some words of comfort.'

'Tobacco,' repeated Lestrade, almost hoping now he was wrong.

'Yes, as I gave you and the rest some on my most recent visit. As a matter of fact, I had neglected to bring any on the day I visited old Richard. The surgeon gave me some.'

'The surgeon?' repeated Lestrade. 'Do you know how Richard Brown died?' he asked.

'A convulsion, the surgeon told me,' Letitia answered. 'He would say no more.'

'The surgeon?' Lestrade was beginning to sound like a wax cylinder.

'Yes, Dr Foster.'

He couldn't be from Gloucester, could he? thought Lestrade. But this was hardly the time to be flippant. 'This Foster. Was he the man who gave you the tobacco?'

'No. Dr Foster joined the infirmary a day or so after Richard Brown's death, I believe.'

'So who gave you the tobacco, Mrs Lawrenson?' Lestrade was persistent.

'Well, presumably Dr Foster's predecessor. I didn't have much to do with the medical team. I believe his name was Corfield.'

'Corfield. Corfield.' Lestrade had heard that name some-where, but he couldn't remember where.

'And you didn't poison Richard Brown?' Lestrade was to the point.

Bandicoot and Letitia looked at him speechless. It was she who found her tongue first.

'Inspector, I told you my confession was for Harry. I was ... close ... to a man nearly forty years my senior, and that within the last year. I could not believe ... cannot believe Harry could still love me once he knew that. But dear God, can either of you think me guilty of murdering that dear, sweet old man?'

Lestrade collected together his rags. 'No, Mrs Lawrenson. We can't. I am very sorry to have bothered you. I will take my leave. But first, I must know the name of this man, on whose estate Richard Brown worked.'

'Inspector, I cannot tell you that.'

'Old ghosts,' said Bandicoot. 'Better let them lie.' And he took Letitia's hand firmly in his.

'I hope you will both be very happy,' said Lestrade and made for the door. As he turned, they were locked in each other's arms, oblivious to his going.

In the hall the pompous Mr Dudson approached him. 'Er ... Inspector ... I could not help overhearing. The man you seek is Major General Edward Harnett. I ... er ... hope I have been ... helpful to you.' The Scotsman was actually rubbing his hands together in anticipation. 'Is there a reward?'

'Oh, yes,' smiled Lestrade. 'There's always a reward for people who listen at keyholes,' and he jabbed two grimy fingers into the butler's eyeballs. Dudson fell back, screaming in pain and Lestrade was on the steps before Bandicoot caught up with him.

'Sholto. Don't go. You see, I knew Letitia wasn't your man. Please, stay to dinner. A bath? A soft bed? Letitia insists.'

'Tempting indeed, Harry. But I'd better not. How will I face the hell broth tomorrow after a fine meal tonight? Besides,' he began scratching, 'there are too many of us.'

'Will we see you at the wedding?'

'You might, Banders old thing, you might. Oh, and by the way,' he pointed to the doubled-up sobbing form of Dudson, 'I recommend you get yourself some new staff,' and he turned into the rain.

Daisy, Daisy

It was appreciably easier getting in than getting out; Lestrade's overhasty grasping of the workhouse doctor's lapels had earned him something of a reputation. God knows to how many people the good doctor had repeated Lestrade's bizarre claim to be an inspector from Scotland Yard. Perhaps for that reason, perhaps for others, Lestrade found himself watched more closely than before. He had returned to Openshaw that evening without employ – not unusual in the Manchester of the nineties. Times were hard and despite the 'Hands Wanted' signs, workhouse Hands were not required. At least Lestrade had eliminated Mrs Lawrenson from his enquiries, but before he could follow up Dudson's tip, he had to see the good doctor again.

Days followed days slower than Lestrade had known. And in the course of them he noticed a shadow; a slim young fellow who watched him more closely than the warders. In a rest period late on the Wednesday, he engaged Lestrade in conversation, though the inspector's mind was elsewhere. He was what Madge of *Truth* referred to as a contemptible cur. Educated at Charterhouse, he had fallen on hard times and his family, of nouveau riche stock from Altrincham, had deserted him. A few indiscreet card games, a torrid affair with the daughter of a Stalybridge banker and he found himself in here, in coat crawling with company and his once immaculate hands ragged with oakum. He could leave tomorrow. They all could. Couldn't they? Lestrade looked at him. He wasn't at all sure *he* could.

'A bounder. That's what her father called me,' said the young man, looking up from his knees drawn tight under his chin. 'Just before he had me horse-whipped. Want to see?'

Lestrade declined the offer. He had decided the Bounder was harmless enough. He wasn't a threat, a plant by the authorities. The very improbability of his story ruled that out. He was just lonely, feeling sorry for himself. Lestrade nodded, shook his head, said 'Yes' and 'No' a few times, more or less, he hoped, in the right places. He was waiting for night, for the sound barrage of hawking and spitting. The lights flickered out at ten as they always did. He did not have long.

Time was of the essence. Noiselessly he slipped out of his trough and between the rows of snoring men. A faint light shone from the bull's-eye, swinging in the wind of the labour yards. Beneath the oakum, when he wasn't being watched, Lestrade had been hammering into shape the iron wedge he had wrenched from the rotten wood of his bed. It had taken him a week, but it was ready. He slipped it between the door and the jamb. Damn. Too tight. He bent it against the door and it clicked into position. No danger in the cacophony of coughs behind him of the door being heard. He swung it open and was about to close it when he felt fingers grip his arm. He swung round, ready to slam the door on whoever it was and in the dim light recognised the Bounder.

'Take me with you,' he rasped.

'What do you mean?'

'You're going over the wall.'

There was really nowhere else Lestrade could have been going. The latrine was at the far end of the room. Midnight raids on the pantry belonged to the days of Charterhouse and if this was sleepwalking, Lestrade was a very determined example of it.

'And you can go through the door tomorrow. Go back to bed, man.'

'I can't stand another night in . . . there.' The Bounder was quaking.

'They'll be after you by morning.'

'What for – breaking and exiting?'

Lestrade did not appreciate the light relief.

'All right, but keep low, keep quiet and do everything I tell you.'

They ran across the yard, the inspector and his shadow, scattering rats to left and right. Lestrade flattened himself against the wall, ramming the Bounder into a corner. A whistling warder lurched across the steps on the way to the outer gate. He paused, looked briefly around and then fumbled with his trouser buttons. The Bounder raised his nose helplessly in anticipation of a sneeze and Lestrade clapped his good hand over his face. The sensation in the Bounder's nose went away as the warder adjusted his clothing and growled, 'Who's there?'

Lestrade pressed his conveniently flat-tipped nose further into the stone.

'Oh, it's you, Doctor. Just off home?'

'That's right. I've got my keys. You needn't bother,' pre-empting the warder's attempt in the darkness to find the relevant key.

'Good night to you, then, sir,' and he went on his way.

Couldn't be better, mused Lestrade and springing back from the wall rolled under the doctor's feet, bringing him down in the straw with a crunch. Before he could cry out, Lestrade had straddled him, a hand over his mouth and a forearm at his throat.

'One sound and you're a dead man,' he hissed in his ear.

The Bounder sat in the shadows, amazed.

Something in the glint of Lestrade's eyes told the doctor he meant business. And something in the doctor's eyes told Lestrade he could relax his grip. He hauled the man upright.

'To resume our conversation of a couple of weeks ago. I am Inspector Lestrade of Scotland Yard. Were I not attired in the sartorial elegance of Openshaw District Workhouse, I would be able to prove it. As it stands, you must take my word for it, Doctor Foster, and I am not a patient man.'

If this man is insane, thought Foster, he's extraordinarily single-minded. But then, wasn't that a symptom of one kind of clinical madness? He wished he'd been to that lecture.

'You signed the death papers on Richard Brown?'

'I did.' The lunatic was well informed.

'Cause of death?'

Silence.

'Doctor, you are familiar with all sorts of deaths in establishments like these. What was the cause of his?'

Foster relaxed with a shrug. 'Actually, I'm not very experienced in establishments like these, as you put it. My practice was not ... well, let's just say things were not working out. I became a Poor Law doctor. Openshaw is my first workhouse.'

'How long have you been here?' The soggy, rat-soiled floor of a workhouse labour yard was not the ideal place for a prolonged interview. Lestrade was trying to hurry things up.

'A few weeks. Look,' the doctor's tone changed, 'are you who you say you are?'

'On my word as an English gentleman,' was the least fatuous thing Lestrade could think of.

'All right. I'll trust you. I'll have to. It was I who contacted the Manchester Police. I managed to obtain an interview with Chief Superintendent Olds. I couldn't make much of it. After all, I didn't know – don't know – if the authorities are involved.'

'Authorities?'

'Richard Brown died of strychnine poisoning, Inspector. Risus sardonicus. Heard of it?'

'Strychnine, yes.' Lestrade rested back on his heels. 'What's the other? A monkey?'

'The smile of death, Inspector. The poison causes the muscles of the face to contract, baring the teeth in a maniacal grin. It's not something I'll forget. Ever.'

'What's your point about the authorities?' Lestrade persisted.

'You've been in here, Lestrade. How many inmates do you know who have access to strychnine?'

'It wasn't Mrs Lawrenson, who visited him on the day he died. Although unwittingly she may have given him tainted tobacco.'

'Tobacco,' Foster shouted, until Lestrade's hand silenced him. 'Of course,' he went on in a whisper, 'that's it.'

'No, it's not. We want the man who gave the tobacco to the lady.'

'So our murderer is a tobacconist?'

'Not necessarily, Doctor.'

'Have you asked her?'

'Of course. She obtained the tobacco from your pre-decessor.'

'Prior?'

'Prior to what?'

'No, no. Dr Prior. That was the name of my predecessor.'
Lestrade didn't follow. 'Not Corfield?' he said.

'Corfield? No. Wait a minute. I believe the name does appear in the day book.'

'What's that?'

'As surgeon and practitioner to Openshaw, I have to sign daily in the day book, as evidence of my attendance on duty; otherwise they don't pay me.'

'And you say Corfield's name is in it?'

'Yes. He was probably a *locum tenens* for Prior.'

'A what?' This man was speaking a different language.

'That means he filled in for Dr Prior if the man was off sick or otherwise unable to attend the infirmary.'

'Do you remember when Corfield's name appears last? Think, man. This could be vital.'

'Er . . .' Foster's face screwed up with the effort. 'I think it was May the tenth. Good God!'

'What?'

'That was the day that Richard Brown died.'

'This Corfield,' Lestrade went on, 'have you ever seen him?'

'Never. But I don't understand. Why wasn't I told you were here, incognito?'

Lestrade knew the meaning of that one now. He wouldn't show ignorance again.

'You wouldn't have been the first murderer to report his suspicions of the crime to the police.'

'You mean . . . you mean I was a suspect?' Foster was outraged.

Lestrade straightened. 'When exactly did you take up your present post?'

'May the seventeenth. A week to the day after Brown died.'

Lestrade turned to the Bounder. 'Laddie, you've heard a

few things tonight it would be better you forgot.'

'Inspector . . .' and he started to say something, then fell back into the shadows. 'What things are they?' He grinned uneasily.

Lestrade patted him condescendingly on the cheek. Foster unlocked the outer gate and the three of them slipped into the night.

'One last question,' whispered Lestrade. 'Do you in fact come from Gloucester?'

'No, actually I . . .' and the doctor's face hardened into the resolution of ages as he caught Lestrade's smirk.

With one Bounder, Lestrade was free.

Letitia Lawrenson was of little more use to Lestrade than Foster had been as to the physical description of Doctor Corfield. Greying, she thought, quite distinguished. But other than that, she could not help. And she begged Lestrade to believe, in Bandicoot's absence, that she did not habitually find older men attractive. That was one reason why she had not particularly noticed Corfield. It was one reason indeed, though not paramount, why she was marrying Harry . . . .

They sat beneath the sheltering arms of a Cedar of Lebanon. The Prince and his lady. Below them, in rolling ground falling away from the great house, stretched Derwentwater in Derwent Dale and away to their left the hills of Stanage Edge and High Neb. The incredible summer of 1893 really began then, in the shimmering heat of July's end, and for them it began at Ladybower, overlooking the Derwent.

It was into this idyllic scene, the *fin de siècle* sun throwing long, deep shadows across the lawns, there walked a man in a shabby duster coat, worn among the *nouveaux* and *anciens riches* for driving their horseless carriages. His hair was cropped short, in the manner of the working classes, and he didn't appear to have eaten well for some time. His skin had the jaundiced look of old parchment and he seemed unused to the fresh air. But his step was jaunty enough and he threw the Gladstone bag to the ground as the station wagon lurched to a halt beside him.

'You take a devil of a lot of finding, Inspector.' The

asthmatic wheeze behind the muffler was vaguely familiar.

'Charlo?' Lestrade peered into the gloom of the cab.

'The same, Inspector. As you see, much recovered,' and he fell into a paroxysm of coughing.

'How did you find me?'

'It wasn't easy, sir. But duty called. May I ask, sir, what we are working on?'

Isn't 'we' a little presumptuous? thought Lestrade, but the man had obviously been suffering.

'Get rid of this wagon and walk with me,' he said. 'I'll explain as we go.'

The constable snapped the whip and rattled away down the drive. In the dust and gnats of the summer evening, the policemen strolled down the drive.

'How can you bear that scarf in all this?' Lestrade gestured to the heat of the day.

'Oh, I have to be careful, sir. I've never been strong, you see. Even as a child—'

'Yes, let's leave that stone unturned, shall we, Charlo? I'm going to use you as a brick wall to bounce a few ideas off. Ready?' And Lestrade told Charlo all he knew.

'Which leaves me,' said Lestrade as they crossed the Palladian bridge, 'two niggling questions. If I can answer them, I'm close to my man.'

'Sir?'

'How is your grasp of languages? What do you make of Blogg's "Ora Rosa"?'

'That being . . .?'

'Come on, Charlo, concentrate. That's the name Blogg thinks he remembers on the boat – er, ship – moored at Cromer Lighthouse.'

'It's all a bit vague really, isn't it?' Charlo was adjusting his eye shade to avoid the glare of the setting sun. 'I'm not sure Blogg knows anything.'

'I should have thought an up-and-coming pillar of the Yard like you would have had a command of languages, Charlo,' Lestrade persisted. 'I thought it was Spanish. Bradstreet thought Italian. What's your reading of it?'

'Perhaps it was neither, sir. What if Blogg's "Rosa" was

really someone's name? How far away was he when he saw it?'

Lestrade hadn't checked that.

'It's true, I do have a certain natural linguistic talent.' Lestrade had obviously touched his sergeant's vanity. 'If I'm right, it means "scent of roses". But that doesn't make much sense, does it?'

'About as much as this case does at the moment. What about the name Corfield? The *locum tenant* doctor at Openshaw? Does that sound familiar to you?'

Charlo searched his memory. He'd known lots of doctors in his time, but he couldn't help his governor on this one.

'Excuse me,' Lestrade called to the couple sitting under the tree. 'It's a devil of a way from the gate. Am I right for the house?'

'Over the rise,' the Prince called back. 'You can't miss it. Thirty-two bedrooms, Palladian style, copper cupola. Usual thing.'

'Are you house guests?' the lady asked, gliding over the lawn towards them.

By now, recognition had dawned on the dusty traveller. 'Not exactly, ma'am. Your Royal Highness,' and he nodded in a stiff bow.

'Good God,' the Prince chuckled, waddling behind the lady to the drive. 'You've been taking lessons from my nephew. That reminds me, Daisy, the damned whippersnapper is bringing the *Meteor* to Cowes this year. He's bound to win the Cup, damn his eyes.'

'Ssshh, Bertie.' Daisy motioned towards the traveller. 'I'm not sure these gentlemen are Edward's guests. . . .'

'Allow me to introduce myself, sir. Inspector Sholto Lestrade, Scotland Yard. This is Sergeant Charlo.'

'Good God,' said the Prince again. 'Your husband?' He turned to Daisy, nudging her with a well-padded elbow.

'Bertie!' She rapped his chest with her fan.

'Wait a minute . . . that name is familiar,' said the Prince. 'Haven't we met?'

'I am flattered Your Highness remembers me. It was the Commissioner's Ball, eighteen ninety-one. You and the late

Duke were guests of honour.'

'Aha!' the Prince roared again. 'Harlequin!'

'Correct, sire.'

'Would you believe it, Daisy, this man was got up as Harlequin. One of old McNaghten's best men.' Then, more confidential, 'I seem to remember you made a fool of my son.'

'My apologies, sir.'

'Don't wish to speak ill of the dead, eh? No, Lestrade, don't let it bother you. Eddie had his fling. We none of us are masters of our fates, eh? Anyway, if my memory serves me correctly, he was being his usual boorish self, annoying a lady; cracking creature, dark eyes, dark hair ...' and he cleared his throat forcefully, having caught Daisy's eye catching his. A new tack, 'So who's this new chappie ... er ... Orion Snow?'

'Nimrod Frost, sir.'

'Yes, of course. Sorting out the sheep from the goats, eh? Well, new shepherds will. And your case, Lestrade? What brings you to Ladybower?'

'As ever, sir, I fear I cannot divulge ...'

'Oh, quite, quite. But come, Lestrade, your professional advice at least. I've heard that some chappie has written some nonsense about tracing cracksmen and the like by the pattern on the end of a man's fingers. That can't be true, surely?'

'There are those who say it is, sir.'

'What about you, man? Commit yourself.'

To a workhouse, thought Lestrade, no, never again. 'Let's just say I shall keep an open mind, sir.'

The Prince roared again. 'Well, let's see what old Harnett's been up to, the dog. I assume you have come to see the master of the house?'

'We have, sir.'

'Right, we'll walk with you. Oh, Lestrade, now that Mr Gladstone has at last persuaded Mama – that's the Queen, by the way, I think I mentioned her when we last met – to let me see Cabinet papers, I'm a pretty busy chappie. I must be away before dinner on pressing affairs of State. I take it I *can* leave? I mean, I'm not part of your enquiries?'

'No, sir.'

'Good, then you must squire Lady Warwick here this evening.'

Lestrade was a little non-plussed. 'Your Highness, I . . .'

Daisy Warwick took the detective's arm. 'You're not refusing a royal command?' she mocked, wide-eyed.

'Ma'am, I'm hardly dressed for . . .'

'Oh, Eddie Harnett will have something for you and your chappie here. The truth is, Lestrade, I don't trust the other old lechers here this weekend. I know Daisy's safe in the arms of the law. Metaphorically speaking, of course.'

And they walked, Lady Warwick arm in arm with the Prince and the inspector, towards the house. Charlo tagged behind.

Major-General Edward Harnett, Master of Ladybower, sat on the edge of a leather sofa with outstretched arm. He was dressed in his scarlet uniform, dripping with gold, a plumed cocked hat on his head. The only incongruity, apart from the fact that his charger was mere horse-hair, was the glass of Cognac in his rein hand. In front of him, agonising over every stroke and flourish, crouched an artist of the Bohemian set, swathed in smock and beret.

'I don't think I can help you, Lestrade,' the general was saying. 'I'm sorry old Brown has gone, but I can't see why this is a police matter – and Scotland Yard at that. Oh, do hurry, Mr Sickert, my arm is killing me. This damned Mameluke is heavy,' and he twirled the sword wearily.

'Richard Brown was murdered, sir.'

Sickert's brush slid inexorably over the canvas, driving scarlet across the general's moustaches. 'Is something amiss, Mr Sickert?'

'Er . . . no, no.' The artist fumbled with his turpentine substitute, 'Murders. Violence. Such things bother me.' He visibly paled.

'You know where the latrine is, man,' the general motioned and the artist sped for the door. 'Sickert by name and Sickert by nature.' He yawned. 'Still, it gives me a chance to "dismount", what? Drink, Lestrade? Charlo?'

'Not when we're on duty, sir – but that's not for an hour or two. Brandy, please.'

'A glass of water, please,' said Charlo, and as if to avoid the glances, 'It's my stomach, you see.'

'Brown was murdered?' Harnett took the weight off his boots. 'How?'

'Strychnine.'

'Poisoning. Good God,' and Harnett swigged his glass. 'Why?'

'I hoped you might tell me, sir. When did you see him last?'

'God knows. He left me . . . ooh . . . nearly three years ago now. I never really knew why. He seemed happy enough. Perhaps the call of the city. Manchester claimed him.'

'Did he have any enemies here?'

'Here? No, I don't think so. In fact, he was a popular man. Scrupulously honest. He always was, right from way back, in the Crimea.'

'The Crimea?'

'Yes, he was my orderly for a time. But then, he was Lord Cardigan's orderly too – and Colonel Douglas'. A very orderly man, you might say.'

'His regiment then, sir?' Lestrade pursued.

'The Eleventh Hussars, Prince Albert's Own,' and Harnett raised his glass in a toast. 'God love 'em. Tell me, Lestrade, why the death, albeit murder, of a lonely old labourer commands the attention of Scotland Yard? I thought you chaps guarded the Crown Jewels, that sort of thing.'

'It's a long story, sir. And I fear I am not at liberty to tell you.'

'Ah, quite, quite. Anyway, it's almost dinner time and I must see His Royal Highness to the station. See my man, Burroughs, he'll kit you both out. I insist you stay for breakfast too; Mrs Carpenter's kedgeree is legendary.'

One couldn't say fairer than that.

Dinner was superb. After weeks on hell broth and only a day of London fare before catching a train north again, Lestrade wasn't sure he was up to it – twelve courses, eyes dazzled by the crested silver, brain seething with the champagne. Charlo declined most of it, devouring what seemed to be large

quantities of Carter's Little Liver Pills. Half the county
seemed to be there; ladies in their pearls and diamonds,
gentlemen of the Hunt in their elegant black and white. But
Sholto Lestrade found himself looking increasingly at his
beautiful escort, Daisy, Countess of Warwick. A hostile
observer would have found the mouth too hard, the
eyebrows too dark, but Lestrade, mellowed by wine and the
sparkling conversation, was far from hostile. He forgot, in
the course of things, that the tails lent to him by the general
were rather too roomy, that his neck swam in the collar like
Gladstone's, an old tortoise reaching for a cabbage leaf, and
that the jacket shoulders drooped off his own. It had been a
long time since he had found himself in such company.

He tolerated the exclusion of the ladies after the coffee with
a marked reluctance, but Daisy Warwick's hand lingered
longer than was strictly necessary in his. She blew him a kiss
with her eyes.

He lit his cigar from the candelabra and made himself as
much a part of the conversation as he could. Harnett was
reliving the Ashanti War in one corner, surrounded by
crimson-faced cronies of the old school. Elsewhere, the old
chestnut of Home Rule was being trotted out, if one did trot
out chestnuts. Charlo rotated around the room in the
opposite direction from Lestrade, avoiding the smoke and
keeping, as his guv'nor had suggested, his ear to the ground.
And horses dominated the field in other corners. Those
buffoons in the Quorn. Who was tipped at Epsom this year?
And Goodwood? And in the Prince's absence, Persimmon
was a Shetland pony fit only for the knacker's yard. Or
perhaps a police horse. Lestrade, incognito again, refused to
bridle at that.

'Now Bertie's gone, we could play baccarat,' suggested a
guest.

'Damned bad form,' growled another and flopped back
into the champagne fug of his corner.

'Let's look at the garden,' a soft voice whispered in
Lestrade's ear and Daisy, as bored with female company in
the next room as he was by male, swept him out on to the
balcony.

It was a glorious evening, that one in late-July, over the

Derwent at Ladybower. And they walked hand in hand over the sun-gilded lawns, the Detective and the lady.

'Do I shock you, Sholto?'

'Ma'am?'

'Oh, come.' She shook his hand teasingly. 'You can call me Daisy.'

'If I may say so, ma'am, we are from different stations, you and I.'

'Bow Street and Clerkenwell?' she quipped.

Lestrade stifled his smile.

'Ah, I saw it, Sholto. You almost cracked, then. Seriously, Inspector Lestrade of Scotland Yard, you won't compromise your position – or derelict your duty – by calling me Daisy. Just this once.'

She turned and took both his hands in hers, gazing into his eyes. What's behind them? she wondered. What makes this man? What kind of man becomes an inspector of detectives? What sights have those eyes looked on?

'Very well. Just this once,' he said, 'Daisy.'

She laughed, a bright, tinkling sound that danced with the rose trees down the lawns. 'You know, dear Bertie thinks the world of you, Sholto. He likes you.' And then suddenly serious, 'Isn't it nice to be liked, Sholto?'

He nodded, unsure of himself, missing the familiarity of danger, the boredom of routine. Walter Dew with his inane grin, his cup of tea at the ready. Sergeant Dixon with his 'Mind how you go.' Nimrod Frost with his ferret eyes and his wobbling girth. It all seemed an eternity ago. And here he was, a suspended policeman, gazing into the dark, hypnotic eyes of a countess of the realm, on the lawns of Ladybower, eighteen hundred and ninety-three.

'You knew Eddie?' she went on.

'Let's just say we met.' He remained cryptic.

'Tell me, this lady Eddie was annoying at the commissioner's ball. How did Bertie describe her? Dark hair? Dark eyes? Mrs Lestrade?'

'No.' Lestrade straightened. 'No, there is no Mrs Lestrade.'

Daisy smiled to herself in the dusk.

'Who was she, Sholto?'

'Someone,' he said, fighting down the memory.

'Someone?' Her voice was a whisper, her mouth closing towards his chest.

'Her name was Constance. Constance Mauleverer.'

Daisy stepped back. 'And you loved her?'

Lestrade nodded.

'You love her still?'

He did not nod this time, but walked on. 'I met an old friend of mine recently, Daisy – a young constable I knew when I knew Constance. He said something I shan't forget. He said "Old ghosts. Better let them lie."'

'I wonder if Constance feels that way.'

There was something in the way Daisy said that that made Lestrade catch his breath. He stopped and looked at her. 'Yes, Sholto. I know Constance Mauleverer. Have you forgotten that my husband is now Earl of Warwick? The Mauleverers lived at Guy's Cliffe, didn't they? I remember when Albert Mauleverer was killed. Were you on that case?' Realisation dawned.

Lestrade nodded. 'For a time, I thought I'd go back to Guy's Cliffe.' he said. 'Find her. When we parted, it was like losing a part of myself.'

Daisy sat on the cool grass under the Cedar of Lebanon and spread her gown.

'She's gone, Sholto. Gone for ever.'

'Do you know where?' Lestrade sat beside her.

She looked at him hard. 'Yes,' she said slowly, and placed her fingers on his lips to stop the next question. 'And I'm not going to tell you. Your friend was right, Sholto. Let old ghosts lie.' And she curled her hand round his neck, drawing him to her.

Their lips met under the boughs of the cedar. From somewhere in the woods a peacock called, echoing across the lawns. Daisy Warwick was an expert at seduction of this type. Her mouth was warm and yielding, her fingers running tantalisingly through the fuzzy crop of hair.

'For one night, Sholto,' she whispered, gazing into his eyes, 'forget Constance.'

'As you will forget Bertie?' he asked.

She smiled. 'I have always thought,' she said, 'there are degrees of love. My husband and I are ... comfortable together,' and she kissed him again. 'Conventionally so. Bertie is like ... a rich old uncle. We don't ... well, I'll leave that to your imagination. He's a darling, he feels like an old glove, warm, moulded to your hand.' Her tongue found his in the French manner, to which Lestrade was unused. 'And there is the degree of a summer night, Sholto, when a man and a woman are thrown together by chance, to enjoy the moment, to enjoy each other. No regrets, no second thoughts, just the moment ...' and she sprawled beneath him on the grass, wild with the cool scent of clover and honeysuckle, opening her bodice to his searching fingers.

Mrs Carpenter's kedgeree was as magnificent as Harnett had predicted. Lestrade tucked in with a will and maidservants came and went with clashing tureens. If anyone had seen the figures writhing under the cedars the previous night, they were not letting on. Such servants were used to such sights. Harnett chose them for their discretion. Charlo toyed with a water biscuit.

'What did you get last night?' Lestrade asked him.

'Rather less than you, sir, I should imagine.'

Two gentlemen joined them whom they had not noticed at dinner. They were both middle-aged, heavily built, one with a centre parting and a walrus moustache which put Lestrade's in the shade. They grunted good morning to the policemen, simultaneously stuffed napkins into their cravats and waited in silence while coffee was poured.

'What's this?' one of them grunted to the other, fingering his breakfast.

'It's a croissant, you peasant. The circular thing it is resting on is called a plate.'

'Bumroll,' and the two men looked up and around in case someone should take umbrage at their conversation.

'Croissant? That's French isn't it? What the hell is it doing at an Englishman's table?'

'The word "chauvinist" is French as well, Sullivan, but it fits you like a glove. How can you be such a philistine?'

Lestrade listened with half an ear, but his thoughts still whirled with the events of the night before and his back ached. Sullivan glanced around again, then rapped his spoon savagely on the back of his companion's hand. Lestrade looked up as the companion jack-knifed in pain, banging his head sharply on the table.

'Oh, careless, William, careless. You'll do yourself an injury, dear friend.'

William stared maniacally at his companion, then caught Lestrade looking bemusedly at him, and attempted a chuckle. 'Yes, silly of me. I . . . er . . . tripped. Allow me to introduce myself, William Gilbert.'

'The playwright?' asked Lestrade.

Gilbert bowed.

'William *Schwenck* Gilbert,' bubbled his companion, and collapsed in fits of mocking laughter.

'And you, sir?' asked Lestrade.

'*Sir* Arthur Sullivan, at your service.'

'You sycophantic crawler,' hissed Gilbert. 'Why Her Majesty did you the honour of . . .'

'I am honoured, gentlemen.' Lestrade finished his coffee.

'And who might you be, sir?' Sullivan asked.

'Sholto Lestrade, of Scotland Yard.' He saw no reason to hide the fact. 'This is Sergeant Charlo.'

The playwright and the musician advanced on them, napkins still dangling and sat on either side. '*The* Scotland Yard?' Gilbert asked him.

'Well,' said Lestrade, unsure whether their interest was criminal or architectural, '*New* Scotland Yard.'

'Have you seen, dear Lestrade, our *Pirates of Penzance*?' Sullivan asked him.

'Don't you mean "my" *Pirates*?' Gilbert corrected him.

'Bitch,' hissed Sullivan.

'I believe I have,' Lestrade answered, becoming increasingly edgy in the presence of these two maniacs.

'Good,' said Gilbert. 'Now then. The portrayal of the policemen. Was it fair? Is a policeman's lot not a happy one? Eh, Charlo? Eh?'

'Tarantara,' broke in Sullivan and launched into a stanza,

fingers pounding dramatically on the tablecloth. Gilbert looked coldly at him.

'I believe your sub-title for the piece was "The Slave of Duty",' said Charlo.

'Ah, a fan,' beamed Gilbert, clasping his hands together poetically.

'Now that fits a policeman very well,' said Lestrade.

'Have you heard my *Haddon Hall*?' Sullivan asked.

'Nobody has,' snapped Gilbert. 'Let's face it, Arthur dear, without me you're a flop.'

Sullivan leapt to his feet. 'Flop, am I? You conceited imbecile. You have the talent of that scrambled egg.'

'Kedgeree,' said Lestrade and mentally withered as he realised he had entered the colleagues' quarrel. He had no place there and was about to rise and make his excuses when Edward Harnett entered the room, pale and stern faced. The bickering ceased as Gilbert and Sullivan noticed the deathly appearance of their host.

'Lestrade,' said Harnett. 'You'd better come with me.'

The inspector whipped the napkin from his collar and he and Charlo followed the general through the marbled hall. Lady Warwick reached the bottom of the stairs as they passed. She took Lestrade's arm.

'Not now, Daisy,' barked Harnett. 'A man is dead,' and her hand fell away as the inspector walked into the sunlight.

He lay on a handcart, head lolling back, grey hair sweeping the ground. He wore the leather gaiters of a labourer, a shabby waistcoat and rolled sleeves.

'The others found him this morning.' Harnett motioned to a knot of grim-faced labourers nearby.

'Where?' Lestrade asked.

'Out by the Lower Meadow, sir,' one of them answered. 'Hedging we were.'

'Is there somewhere I can examine the body?' Lestrade asked Harnett.

'Yes, of course. You men, take old Jim to the outhouse.' Charlo wrapped his muffler around his face, presumably against the raw cold of the July morning and followed the bier and the pall bearers. 'Lestrade.' Harnett took the inspector aside. 'It's his heart, surely? Nothing suspicious, is there?'

'Then why did you call me?'

'All right, I must admit, it's damned odd. If you'd have asked me last night to pick out the fittest man on my estate, I'd have said Jim Hodges, without a doubt. And yet this morning . . . It's damned odd.'

'How old was he?'

'I don't know. Sixty or so. Best damned hedger I had. The men used to joke about it – Hodges the Hedger, they called him. What will I do for a decent hedger now?'

'I shall need your help, General.'

'Of course, dear chap. Anything.'

'I shall need to speak to your guests and to your staff. All of them. Can you arrange that?'

'Er . . . I suppose so. But look, you can't hold up my guests for long. Most of them will be going today. Some already have.'

'Ask them to assemble in the drawing room, would you? And inform the local police force. I shall need constables.'

Lestrade's difficulty, apart from the scale of the investigation, was that technically, as far as anyone other than Nimrod Frost knew, he was under suspension. As such, he had no actual right to be making enquiries at all. If this was a routine sudden death, he decided, he would turn the whole thing over to a local sergeant and make a discreet exit. Charlo was chancing his arm too to be working with a suspended man. It was high time Nimrod Frost made up his mind about that. But Lestrade feared that this death would be far from routine. It fitted all too well the familiar pattern of those with which he had been involved over the past weeks.

He locked the outhouse door and examined the body. When forced to, Lestrade relied on coroners' verdicts for this work, but they operated too late in many cases, when valuable clues had gone. Besides, they didn't know a great deal more than he did. Some of them a damned sight less. His attention was drawn to the cuts on Hodges' left forearm, over a much older scar. There was a small amount of fresh blood on the arm, trickling down towards the wrist. On an impulse and checking first to see no one was around, he first sniffed the arm, then licked the scratches. He spat viciously, the taste bitter and acrid. No blood of his own ever tasted like that and, he suspected, neither did anyone else's. He must get to a chemist's as soon as possible. It was poison, he was sure. But what?

As to its administration, that was easy, but ingenious. Lestrade went with the hedgers to the spot where they had found the body. The inspector checked the hedge – brambles, sharp ones with thick, purplish stems. He ran his fingers over their points and sniffed and licked while the labourers looked on in amazement. He spat again – the same bitter taste. He quizzed the labourers on the make-up of the hedge. They confirmed his townie's verdict – bramble, with a threat of blackthorn. He had them hack off a few pieces for testing, although he knew he couldn't take it back to the Yard. He would have to find a competent chemist in Manchester.

Lestrade had not spoken to Charlo throughout. He had noticed him swaying a little as he watched his guv'nor examine the body. Now, in the sun, as the labourers returned to their work and their gossiping he took him by the arm.

'Are you alright, Charlo?'

'I'm not quite myself, sir. I've never really been one for the sights. It's blood, you know. Brings me out in a rash.'

'Yes, quite.' Lestrade found himself wondering what Frost's idea of a good boy was. Still, he'd tracked the inspector down to this neck of the woods; he must have some merit in him. 'I shall need help in interrogation. Are you up to that?'

'Oh, yes, sir. Yes,' and he gulped in the country air. 'Now I'm away from . . . the deceased . . . I feel much stronger.'

Lestrade and Charlo stayed at Ladybower for four days. On the first they and two local sergeants interviewed the thirteen guests that remained. Gilbert and Sullivan were as bitchy to each other and about each other as ever, each of them sure that the other was Lestrade's man. Gilbert in particular said he felt sure the cause of death was listening to Sullivan's music. Lestrade ruled them out as serious suspects. Bearing in mind that the guests were now prisoners at Ladybower, they held up remarkably well under questioning.

Lestrade deliberately left Daisy Warwick until last.

'I have kept you waiting, Lady Warwick. I am sorry.'

Daisy noticed the new frostiness in Lestrade, but chose to ignore it.

'That's all right, Sholto. If I can help in any way in this dreadful business. That poor man. . . .'

'Do you feel for the labouring poor, ma'am?'

'As a matter of fact, I do.' Daisy was as arch as the inspector. 'Although I'm not really sure I understand the question.'

'Did you know the deceased?'

'No. I didn't.'

'Are you familiar with poisons and their administration?'

'Good Lord, no.'

'The Prince of Wales left in a great hurry the other night, didn't he?'

'Sholto, you can't possibly think that Bertie or I had anything to do with that poor man's death?'

Lestrade relented. 'No,' he said, 'but you must appreciate I must have my suspicions, even about the heir to the throne. About the other night . . .'

Daisy rose and held her fingers to her lips. 'Old ghosts,' she said and swept, as gorgeous as ever, from the room.

The subsequent days saw Lestrade and Charlo doggedly questioning every tenant on Harnett's estate. Jim Hodges had been popular, a practical joker, yes; but no one bore him a grudge. It was good, honest fun – like the time he had plugged the general's hunting horn with tobacco and the time he'd tied the bootlaces of the visiting Bishop of Durham together as he dozed after tea. Well, yes, the old boy had lost three teeth when he stood up, but unless Lestrade was suggesting His Grace had vengeful, murderous tendencies, it was best left alone. Lestrade decided it was. Hodges had worked on the estate the best part of thirty years. His wife had died years ago. The marriage was without issue. Charlo coughed his way through dozens of cottages, declining tea and lemonade, staying in the shade whenever he could. The result of his meticulous and painful enquiries? Nothing.

But what was of greatest interest to Lestrade, and he

learned this when he checked the old man's personal effects in his cottage, was that the link was established, at least between two of them. Wrapped in crimson cloth in a corner of a cupboard in Hodges' cottage was a medal. It had a faded blue and yellow ribbon and a single clasp, ornate, like the label on a sherry bottle, which read 'Balaclava'.

The old ghosts had come home to roost.

Soldier Old, Soldier New

It had been a long time since Nimrod Frost had ridden on an omnibus. He regarded the stairs to the upper deck as a challenge and in the shimmering sun of the last day of July he slumped heavily into the seat. Summer in the city was no joke to someone of his girth. His shirt and necessaries clung to him as if he had been wading through an Amazonian swamp. The buildings wobbled in the heat-haze as the horses, lathered and fidgety, swung left beyond the Old Lady of Threadneedle Street and on to the wider concourse of Cornhill.

The scruffy man in the tropical-weight duster sat behind him, tilted the bowler back on his head and lit a cigar.

'No shortage of cash then, Lestrade,' murmured Frost out of the corner of his mouth. The men sat back to back, like bookends of Jack Spratt and his wife.

'I could get used to suspension on half pay, sir,' the inspector answered.

'I was about to square it with Gregson,' said Frost, 'and reinstate you.'

'I'm flattered, sir, of course, but frankly on this particular case, I can probably do more as a free agent.'

'Less clutter from the Yard, eh?'

'Well, sir, triplicate does have its disadvantages.'

'Quite. Charlo's been filling me in. He's not a well man, you know. I wanted to assign him to other duties, a desk job. But he wouldn't hear of it. That's devotion, Lestrade. I like a man like that.'

And despite the fact that Lestrade had only spent a few days in Charlo's company, so did he. It was Frost's turn to light up. 'Damnably hot, isn't it?' For a while Lestrade thought he must mean the cigar and found the remark rather odd, but then the oppression of the city heat bore in on him too and he understood.

The two men spoke in stifled monosyllables, blowing rings of smoke into the air at the approach of a fellow traveller. The bookends gave nothing away. At Knightsbridge, Lestrade deftly palmed the roll of notes passed to him by Frost and got off the 'bus. The huge placard bearing the legend 'Nestlés' lurched away, topped by the lugubrious features of the Head of the Criminal Investigation Department.

Once again, Lestrade had had only time to meet his chief, collect a change or two of clothes (his salary would permit no more), leave a garbled note for Mrs Manchester and board yet another train. Why was it, he wondered as he sped north, that country air always made him sneeze? For all the heat, he loved the firmness of those city pavements, the sharp shadows of the Tower, the stench from Billingsgate, the endless suburbia of Norwood and Camberwell. It really was inconsiderate of the murderer to kill in the provinces. What were the criminal classes coming to?

He passed the high, wild hedges of Deene and the little church, lost in the wilderness of spurge and rough cocksfoot. Not that Lestrade knew these terms. A blade of grass was a blade of grass to him. So, Jim Hodges had died of aconite poisoning. He chewed again on the information he had, teasing it, worrying it until it made some sense. The aconite, mixed, the chemist in Manchester had told him, from a compound of wolfsbane, must have been smeared on the section of hedge where Hodges had been working. Who then knew where he was working? Any one of a dozen or more of his fellow workers. But Lestrade had interviewed them. And he prided himself on knowing a dishonest man when he saw one. None of these salts of the earth was a murderer. How many labourers had access to wolfsbane? And how many of them had the knowledge to prepare it? There again, there were strange things in country lore. Stranger than he knew. He longed for the pavements again, and sneezed uncontrollably.

Aconite. Aconite. Wolfsbane. The words ricochetted around Lestrade's brain. Was the chemist right? It was a rare poison, he had said. It could be absorbed through the skin. Death could result in as little as eight minutes. But anybody could have been scratched by those brambles. It was a chancy killing – dicey, uncertain. And the chemist was more interested by the printing errors in the *Guardian* that morning than he was in Lestrade's withered brambles. Still, this was 1893. The march of science in all its magnificence was at Lestrade's disposal. The trap halted suddenly and the lathered horse broke wind, depositing its load with symbolic grandeur before the front door.

Deene Park was a superb Jacobean building, a mellow grey in the heat of this first day of August. Her Ladyship, Lestrade was informed, was taking tea on the terrace. Would the gentleman care to join her? Lestrade had met Adeline Brudenell before – two years ago under rather odder circumstances. And so he was prepared for the sight that met him. A mature lady, still slim, still agile, wearing too much make-up, and a waistcoat of crimson laced with gold. On her head, at a rakish angle, a forage cap of the pill-box type. She offered tea to Lestrade.

'Young man, we've met before,' she began once the servant had bustled off about his duties. 'I never forget a face. And I believe I was there when you lost the tip of your nose.'

'Indeed you were, ma'am.' Lestrade took the proffered chair.

'Glorious weather, is it not? You know I sold my house in Highgate last year and I find Portman Square so depressing.'

'Are you not in town for the Season, ma'am?'

'Tsk, you naughty boy. I am heart-broken, of course, that you don't remember, but I am disappointed that my notoriety does not seem to have filtered through to Scotland Yard. Who am I?'

'You are Lady Cardigan,' Lestrade replied. 'A gracious lady indeed.'

'Twaddle!' Adeline rang her handbell. 'Yes, yes, I know, the relict of the Seventh Earl, the hero of Balaclava and I keep his memory alive by wearing his old uniforms. But in my day. Ah, Inspector, when Cardigan brought Adeline Horsey de Horsey to town, everyone knew it. God, how the heads turned.' She alarmed Lestrade a little by lighting up a Havana and puffing viciously at it. 'I remember the carriages, the glitter, the rides in Rotten Row and the Steyne.' Then she laughed. 'The Queen, God rot her, didn't like me. Actually, it was Albert, the sanctimonious old Prussian. I was not considered – am not considered – polite society, Inspector. Time-honoured phrases like "No better than she should be" et cetera, et cetera. Do you know, he actually resigned the colonelcy of my husband's regiment rather than be a party to me? And Her Majesty, she of the poppy eyes and elephantine girth, had herself painted out of a portrait of James explaining Balaclava to His Royal Highness! Small wonder I didn't get an invitation to the wedding.'

'Wedding ma'am?'

'Come, Inspector. Where have you been?'

'Manchester, ma'am.'

'Ah, I see, that explains it. George and May – a charming couple. I wasn't sorry to see Clarence go. I never liked him. Fancy not fighting his own duels! I never forgave him for that. Still, George will never be king. Victoria will outlive us all. I doubt if Bertie will get a chance.' She sighed. 'It's a terrible thing, longevity.'

A servant arrived, wheeling a bicycle.

'We have a guest, Meldrum,' she pointed out and the servant scurried off in search of another machine. 'You do ride?' she asked.

'Let us say I am safer in the saddle of one of these than a horse, ma'am.'

'Good. A pity though one can't ride to hounds on a Waverley. It's the five-barred gates that are the problem, you see. I never miss my morning ride, so you'll have to come with me.'

Meldrum brought a sturdy, black-painted Raleigh and Lestrade, stripping to his waistcoat at Her Ladyship's insistence, straddled it manfully and away they sped. He hadn't expected Adeline to take the steps down the terrace, but down she went, like a church. It was a physical fact, however, which Lady Cardigan may have forgotten, that for a gentleman to ride a bicycle down steps requires a great deal more courage and agility than Lestrade could, at that short notice, muster. There were twelve steps. Lestrade counted every one of them, inwardly and with feeling. Had Adeline cared to glance behind her she would have seen an altogether older and paler man.

She pedalled furiously along the lawn, dust flying out behind her, skirts billowing in the breeze and the sun flashing on the lace of her forage cap. From the hedgerows, here and there, as they crossed into the fields around Deene, labourers popped up, saluting briskly at the sound of Her Ladyship's bell. Was it the country air, Lestrade wondered? His cramped journey in the trap? His recent near-emasculation on the steps? Whatever it was, he found it very difficult to keep up with Adeline and she seemed to be increasing her pace the whole time.

It was to his intense relief then that having crossed the lake (he was pleased to see she did it via the bridge rather than by skimming the lilies) Adeline screeched to a badly oiled halt by the summer house. She waited for Lestrade to catch up.

'It was here he used to bring his maidservants,' she said. 'He used to take an evening constitutional on the terrace and wander in this direction. Minutes later you would see a woman in white, his chosen companion for the evening, scurrying across the lawn.' She became distant, with a smile on the faded lips, etched in deepest crimson. 'But,' she regained the present, 'you did not come here to reminisce.'

'As a matter of fact, Lady Cardigan, I did.'

And the inspector and the dowager sat in the shaded bower of the summer house, while Lestrade attempted to jog old memories.

'I understand that one of your late husband's orderlies in the Crimea was one James Hodges of the Eleventh Hussars. Did your husband ever speak of him?'

'My husband spoke of many people, Inspector. Most of it was malicious and disparaging. But that, I fear, was the sort of man he was. Oh, brave as a lion – and vain – but not gracious. He did not suffer fools gladly. Hodges. Hodges. Yes, of course. I remember now. Hodges was his favourite orderly. Something of a practical joker I was given to understand. But James hadn't seen him since the Crimea. That would have been eighteen fifty-four, shortly after Balaclava. His Lordship was bronchitic, you see. He had to

come home. But why these questions, Inspector? I would
have thought Hodges would have been dead by now.'

'Indeed he is, ma'am. And by the hand of another.'

'Murder?' Lady Cardigan was incredulous.

Lestrade nodded.

'Inspector, my husband has been dead for twenty-five
years. Do you assume he has reached out from his grave to
kill this Hodges? Or do you think I had a hand in it?'

'Neither, ma'am. But we of the Yard leave no stone
unturned.'

Lady Cardigan was already on another tack. 'If my
memory serves me correctly, Hodges was also orderly for a
time to John Douglas. He was colonel of the Eleventh at the
time of Balaclava.'

'Do you know where I might find him?' Lestrade asked.

'Aldershot,' Lady Cardigan answered and again her light-
ning mind was up and away. She took Lestrade's hand in hers
and gazed into his steady eyes. 'My family are afraid I will
re-marry,' she said. 'That would scotch their inheritance
plans. It would also solve my present insolvency. These old
houses cost a small fortune to run, Inspector.'

'Is that a proposal, ma'am?' Lestrade asked.

'Why not? It may not be a leap year, but I *am* the notorious
Adeline Cardigan. People expect it of me.'

Lestrade patted her hand gently and rose.

'I couldn't afford you, ma-am,' he smiled and turned to the
Raleigh. The sight of the saddle unnerved him and he kissed
Her Ladyship's hand, bade her goodbye and walked, a little
shakily, to the waiting trap.

Lady Cardigan was not being quite level with Lestrade. Yes,
John Douglas, colonel of the 11th Hussars was to be found in
the vast complex of camps at Aldershot, but he was
mouldering in a stone vault, having passed away in 1871.
Literally a dead end, thought Lestrade. Even so, for the
record, he would dig a little deeper, in the metaphorical sense,
to see what those at Aldershot could tell him about John
Douglas or his orderly, Jim Hodges.

'You're talking about forty years ago,' he heard as though
on a phonograph countless times during the day. By nightfall

he was about to retire to the cell-like visitor's room in the sergeants' quarters (the AQMG obviously didn't feel that an inspector of police merited the more salubrious apartments in the officers' block) when he bumped quite literally into an elderly gent who teetered gingerly along the curb, trying valiantly to walk in a straight line and treading through the horse manure in the gutter.

'Ah, thank you, dear boy.' The elderly officer tipped his cap and regained the pavement. 'I wunna if you'd be sho kind ..., and he aimed his swagger-stick vaguely at the door in the nearest wall. He stumbled violently and only Lestrade's presence saved him from smashing his head against the door frame. He spun round, on one leg, the other pirouetting like a skater in mid-turn, glaring accusingly at the ground. He bent nearly double, pointing threateningly at the grass.

'I've been crossing thish threshold for nigh on fifty yearsh,' he mumbled. 'I've never notished that there before.' He started upright, remembering that Lestrade was with him. 'Ah, dear boy, you're back. You have been sho kind. Would you like to join me for some liquid refes ... liquid ref ... a drink?'

'Tell me, sir,' said Lestrade, 'did you know Colonel Douglas, late of the Eleventh Hussars?'

The old man swung up a leg extraordinarily high to reveal the crimson trousers of the 11th, before his balance got the better of him and he toppled gracefully back into the shrubbery. Lestrade lifted him out and helped him into his quarters. He fumbled for a lucifer and lit the lamp. The room was a little austere, but cluttered here and there with papers.

'In the umbrella shtand,' the gent called out as he gracefully collapsed across the bed. Lestrade found the bottle of Dewar's and poured them both a glass.

'Your very good health,' slurred the old man, still prone, but his hand rock steady around the glass and his arm erect and firm, 'Mr ... er ... Mr ...?'

'Lestrade, Sholto Lestrade.'

'Solto?' the old man asked.

'Sholto,' Lestrade repeated, moving a mountain of screwed-up papers in order to find a seat. 'And you are?'

'Drunk as a lord,' the gent answered and by a feat of

astonishing agility, poured the contents of the glass from
where it was into his mouth.

He sat up.

'Allow me to introduce myself. The Reverend Wilber-
forshe Battye, late chaplain to the Eleventh, Prinsh Albert'sh
Own Hussarsh. At leasht,' he rose uncertainly to his feet,
'that'sh what it saysh on this dinner invitation,' and he waved
his glass vaguely at a card pinned to the wall, 'doeshn't it?'

'So you knew Colonel Douglas?' Lestrade asked.

'Who? Oh, yesh. I knew John. Funny thing,' he poured
himself another Scotch, 'he had the shame name as you,
y'know. Solto. Not related, are you?'

'I don't think so,' said Lestrade.

'Matter of fact,' he peered under the rim of Lestrade's
bowler, 'you don't look unlike him, y'know. He was taller.
I'd shay. And of courshe, he had a noshe.'

'A noshe?'

'Yesh,' and the chaplain waved an inebriated finger
somewhere between his eyes.

'Did you also know his orderly, James Hodges?'

'Never heard of him.'

Lestrade drew another Scotch, to drown his sorrows. It had
been a long shot, of course. He had no right to be
disappointed, really. The chances of this old wreck having
anything to help his case were pretty remote. The old man fell
back on to his bed again. Lestrade took off Battye's peaked
forage cap, folded his arms across his chest and crept towards
the door.

'Mind you,' the chaplain suddenly came to life, 'I've always
sushpected him of killing Alex Dunn, you know.' His arms
flopped down again and he began snoring, loudly, erratically.

Lestrade closed the door and silently began knocking his
head against the wall. Who was Alex Dunn? John Douglas a
murderer? Why should he bring up murder? Lestrade had not
told Chaplain Battye that he was a policeman. He ransacked
the rooms to find tea, coffee, anything to sober the old fool
up. His hand found a bottle of Vino Sacro, and a voice behind
him said, 'That'll do nishely,' and the chaplain, eyes still
closed, held out his glass for a drop. He drank it down, then
sat up, demanding another. It followed the first.

'It'sh a funny thing,' he said. 'The only thing that bringsh me round ish Vino Shacro. The waysh of the Lord are shtrange. Cheers. God Bless,' and he downed a third, shaking his head, blinking to clear his vision. 'Now, what did you want to know?'

'You mentioned something about John Douglas having murdered Alex Dunn.'

'Did I?' The chaplain was trying hard to recollect. The Communion wine had obviously sharpened him more than somewhat, because he suddenly said, 'Now, why should that be of interest to you?'

'Because I am from Shcot ... Scotland Yard,' said Lestrade, 'and murder is my business.'

'Ah, well,' the chaplain cleared his throat, 'it'sh a long shtory.'

'I have all night,' said Lestrade and settled himself down.

'Alex Dunn was the mosht brilliant officer in the Eleventh in thoshe daysh.' He downed a fourth which clarified his sibilance instantaneously. 'Tall, handsome, debonair. I had only been with the regiment a few months. My first commission. Dunn took me under his wing, as he did with all new boys. I can see him now, laughing at the head of his troop, six foot two, he stood. Shoulders like lecterns. One helluva ... oh, pardon me ... one devil of a swordsman. Born to horses of course, they all were in those days. Not like these whippersnappers of today. Public school johnnies. Wet behind the ears, most of them. They don't know one end of a horse from another.'

'Dunn?' Lestrade reminded him.

'Well, yes, some of them are. But the Eleventh ride chestnuts mostly. Anyway, to get back to Alex Dunn. I'm not one for gossip, you understand, but that's why Douglas didn't like him. He always fancied himself as a bit of a *beau sabreur*, but he wasn't in Dunn's class. And then, when he took up with Rosa ...'

'Rosa?' Lestrade repeated. That was the name of the ship moored at Cromer Lighthouse at the time of Bentley's death.

The chaplain reached across for a fifth Vino Sacro, but Lestrade clamped his hand firmly over the glass. Battye continued to pour it over his fingers and was surprised to find nothing trickling down his throat as he knocked the glass back.

'Douglas' wife. She fell for Alex Dunn hook line and sinker. Talk of the regiment, it was. She left Douglas eventually and went to live in Canada with Dunn.'

'When did Dunn die, and how?'

'Eighteen sixty-eight, I think it was.' The same year as Cardigan, thought Lestrade, if Lady Cardigan's mental calculation had been correct. Coincidence? Perhaps. 'A hunting accident, apparently. Shotgun. Very nasty. Of course, he was with the Thirty-third by then. God knows where they are stationed now.'

'The Thirty-third?' asked Lestrade.

'Oh, what's this new-fangled name for it? The Duke of Wellington's Regiment, is it? I don't know.'

'And you think Douglas pulled the trigger?'

'That was the rumour at the time. But I'm a charitable man, Solto. I prefer to think it was an accident. Of course, Rosa could tell you.'

'Rosa Douglas is still alive?'

'Yes, I think so. The last I heard she lived Warwickshire way. A village called Tysoe. But tell me, Solto, why are you chaps looking into all this now? It's been years.'

'The machinery of justice grinds slow,' said Lestrade, proud of that piece of philosophy. 'And you're sure you didn't know the name James Hodges?'

'Solto.' Chaplain Battye staggered to his feet. 'There are times when I'm not quite sure of my own,' and he fell back, snoring rapturously, on the bed.

It was a noise Lestrade had not often heard before. And never at five o'clock. It fitted in well with his dreams. A voluptuous woman was kneeling naked at the foot of his bed, breasts full and rising with desire, legs opening as he watched. When suddenly, for no reason that he could fathom, she brought two brass cymbals clanging on both sides of his head. He was standing upright, his forehead having collided with the ceiling, and his erection having crunched against the wall, when he woke up fully. Cymbals and siren were gone and in their stead the realisation that it was a bugle he was hearing.

He ripped aside the curtain to see a soldier, sickeningly smart in scarlet, blasting the reveille for all he was worth across the expanses of Laffan's Plain.

Why? mused Lestrade as he subsided in his nightshirt, why at five o'clock? And why outside *his* window?

Breakfast consisted of toast and black coffee, the milk train having failed to arrive as it was too early for the milk train. Lestrade endeavoured to stay awake. Was this not the man who had hunted the Tammanwool? Who had ridden to hounds with a murderous pack in the *Struwwelpeter* case? Who had flown almost single-handed in a balloon over the Pennines in search of his quarry in the Adair Affair? No, he thought, as he dropped coffee on his tie, probably not.

That morning he would make for Warwickshire again and perhaps revisit Lady Cardigan in the process. The plot, for such the novelists called it, was beginning to thicken, for such was the cliché they used. What would John Watson make of this? And Conan Doyle? Probably rather more money than he would by attempting to solve it.

First, he must drag his weary carcass to the station. The logistics of reaching Tysoe were complicated. He even began to toy with hiring a bicycle, but that was too hearty. Better stick to the safety of train and trap.

'Inspector Lestrade.' A voice behind him made him turn.

'Yes.' He was grateful to drop the Gladstone bag, feeling he could not impose on some woebegotten recruit to carry it for him. He saw a slim young man, perhaps twenty, standing before him in the uniform of an officer cadet from the Military College at nearby Sandhurst. The young man clicked his heels and saluted briskly, 'My name is Churchill, sir. Winston Churchill. Would you accept a lift?' And the cadet extended a hand to a waiting trap nearby.

Any port in a storm, thought Lestrade, mixing metaphors and Forces just a little. But as he suspected, there was an ulterior motive. As they lurched off across Laffan's Plain, it became clear.

'Actually, our meeting like this isn't exactly chance.'

Here we go, thought Lestrade.

'You see, I shall be twenty next birthday and I haven't done anything with my life yet. The truth is, I can't decide whether to become a field marshal or Home Secretary. Either way, I shall have to get a medal pretty soon or there'll be no point at all. Some of the chaps around here were saying that you're interested in Colonel Douglas and the Eleventh Hussars.'

'That's right,' said Lestrade.

'Well, look, if I'm going to become Home Secretary, I shall be giving orders to chaps like you, won't I?'

'In theory,' Lestrade agreed.

'So I thought I might tag along with you, sort of find out what you chappies do for a living. All right?'

'No, Mr Churchill, I'm afraid it isn't,' and Lestrade pulled the horse up. 'You see, I am engaged in a murder enquiry. And such things are always confidential.'

'At least, let me buy you a drink. My local is only a few miles up the road. It won't take long.'

'I really ought . . .'

'Nonsense,' and the cadet cracked the whip and sent the horse cantering along the road to Sandhurst. They alighted at the White Swan a little before eleven and Churchill led the way to the tap room. After the merciless heat of Laffan's Plain, the coolness of the deserted inn was joy itself. There was silence apart from the ticking of the grandfather clock and Lestrade took advantage of Churchill's temporary absence to stretch his legs before the gaping darkness of the empty fireplace. Young Churchill's driving was not as immaculate as it might have been and various parts of Lestrade were decidedly numb. The cadet returned with a ruddy-faced man in a white apron, carrying a tray with three pewter mugs, filled to the brim with local ale.

'That'll be eightpence ha'penny, please.' The barman held out his hand to Lestrade.

'I'm sorry, Inspector,' said Churchill. 'My allowance hasn't arrived yet this month. Father is none too well at the moment.'

Reluctantly, Lestrade ferreted in his pocket for the cash. He found ninepence and said magnanimously, 'Keep the change.'

The barman's face registered his undying gratitude, but to Lestrade's slight surprise he sat down and made it obvious who the third jar was for.

'Allow me to introduce Mine Host,' beamed Churchill.

'Mr David Grantham, Inspector Lestrade of Scotland Yard.'

Mine Host mumbled something in his beer.

'Show him your leg, Grantham,' said Churchill.

Lestrade wondered what sort of young man they were taking at Sandhurst nowadays. The publican rolled up his trouser leg to reveal a livid white scar across his shin and ankle. He thought he had detected a limp as he had entered the room.

'Now the wrist.' A similar scar appeared.

'Very nice,' said Lestrade, on whom these obviously very ancient injuries were lost.

'What made those, Grantham?' asked Churchill, as though putting a forward child through its paces, a party-piece for doting grandparents.

'A sabre, sir.'

'And where did you get those scars, Grantham?'

'At Balaclava, sir, a-serving of Her Majesty the Queen.'

'And which regiment were you with, Grantham?' Churchill noted with triumph Lestrade's growing interest.

'The Eleventh Prince Albert's Own Hussars, sir.'

Churchill rested back in his chair, his victory complete. Lestrade flashed him a glance. 'Remind me to have a word with the Queen,' he said, 'about your promotion to Home Secretary. Now, Mr Grantham, how about another drink?'

The story unfolded, haltingly, between beers, while 'the girl' to whom old Grantham constantly referred, manfully served the steady stream of off-duty soldiery in the other bar. Churchill, with what Lestrade soon realised was customary savvy, had placed a makeshift notice on the door saying 'Closed'.

David Grantham had enlisted in the 11th Hussars in 1850. He had served in F Troop for the first three years, biting the tan with the rest of them, and more than once had felt the lash for slipshod appearance, at Hounslow and Brighton. One particular bastard he remembered, Sergeant-Major Loy Smith, a hard man who picked on people for no reason. Grantham had never been more grateful than when he had been transferred to C Troop, out of Loy Smith's clutches. Then he heard the bastard sergeant-major had begun using a Welshman named Hope as his whipping boy. Grantham was circumspect about Dunn. He too remembered Dunn as a handsome man, casual, careless even, but all right for an officer. Of Colonel Douglas he remembered little – fair, courteous, not a hard man by the standard of the times. It was rumoured they didn't get on. But that was of little interest to the common soldier. And it was forty years ago.

'The girl', a pretty slip of a thing who made eyes at young Churchill, brought them the umpteenth beer as Grantham switched his reminiscences to the surgeons of the regiment.

'A right lot they were. Wilkins, Crosse, the others. Did a proper job on my leg. Why, that's why I still limp today. Sabre wounds should have healed better than that. Doctors! They're all the same.'

Lestrade could learn no more. Yes, Grantham had known Jim Hodges, but not well. He had had a reputation of being a joker and ex-private Grantham had no sense of humour whatever. He wasn't sure he'd keep his present job for long. His customers found him morose, he said, taciturn even. He'd probably end his days in the workhouse.

'I'm heartily sorry for you,' said Lestrade with feeling.

It was on his way out that one of those ludicrous accidents that seemed only to happen to Sholto Lestrade happened. As he reached the door of the White Swan, a passing sergeant dropped his swagger-stick. It rolled under Lestrade's feet and for a moment the inspector teetered on it like an acrobat at the circus. Then he collapsed backwards, jarring his back as he did so, spilling the contents of a spittoon over his jacket. Churchill, suppressing a fit of the giggles as best he could, helped him to his feet.

'Are you all right, Inspector?'

'Thank you, Mr Churchill. By the way, if when you retire at a grand old age from the post of Home Secretary or general or whatever it is you are going to be and you write your memoirs, publish one word about me ending up "head first in a spittoon" and I swear I'll rise up from my grave and haunt you.'

Young Churchill accompanied Lestrade as far as Oxford, whence he alighted among the dreaming spires to make his way home to Blenheim. The conversation had turned on many things. On the possibility that Lord Randolph's debilitating illness was caused by poisoning. And how it would be possible to prove that the murderers – or intended murderers – were a conspiracy of Her Majesty, Mr Gladstone and Lord Salisbury. Or there again, it might be Churchill's old nanny, Mrs Everest. The possibilities were endless. Lestrade remained unmoved. Bearing in mind the stories he had heard about Lord Randolph's liking for the ladies, the debilitating illness of the noble lord had but one source as far as he was concerned – Cupid's measles. But he was not going to let the young man down so heavily.

What of Lizzie Borden? Churchill had also wanted to know. The American case that had recently filled the papers. His mother was American, did Lestrade know that? What was Lestrade's professional opinion? Had she hacked her father and mother to death? Lestrade was non-committal in his answer. After all, no one had committed Lizzie Borden, either.

It was evening before Lestrade sat in the parlour of a neat little house in the village of Tysoe. Thatch, new and clipped, topped the old cottage nestling on the side of the hill as the shadows lengthened. For the second time that day he was alone with a ticking clock, a grandmother made in Coventry. He took in the contents of the room – small windows which let in a little light, two oil lamps steadily burning. A table covered with a cloth of purple velvet and on the sideboard a cluster of faded photographs. Two in particular caught Lestrade's eye. Two rather similar men, one with magnificent flowing dundrearies, popular in the fifties, in the Review Order of the 11th Hussars; the other, taller, younger, neater, a more handsome face, in the uniform of an infantry regiment. The two sides of the triangle, thought Lestrade. And the third side, perhaps the vital clue to all the deaths so far, swept noiselessly into his presence.

'It is not often I am visited by an officer from Scotland Yard, Inspector. Won't you sit down?'

Lestrade eased himself into a tapestry chair, his back, from the day's fall, still causing a certain stiffness. He dared not relax a single muscle – he knew from experience of many such accidents the pain this would cause. At times like these the children of passers-by had been known to comment, 'Mama, there is a man with a coat-hanger still inside his coat.' He carefully laid the metaphorical hook against the antimacassar.

'I will come to the point, ma'am,' Lestrade began as Mrs Douglas rang a tiny silver bell to summon tea. 'The death of your late husband.' Beneath her veil, the widow made no outward sign. She sat, reserved and demure in her black bombazine, a delicate woman of uncertain years. She had once been very beautiful, even the veil and the gathering dusk could not deny her that.

'It has been twenty-two years, Inspector. What possible interest could it be now to Scotland Yard?'

'Ma'am, I appreciate it must be painful for you, even after all this time, but I fear I must persist. What can you tell me about Colonel Douglas?'

'"And darest thou then to beard the lion in his den,
The Douglas in his hall?"'

'Ma'am?'

'Sir Walter Scott, Inspector. His poem, *Marmion*. My husband was descended from the Douglases who waged war on the Marches those long centuries ago. They were ever a fighting family. You have heard of the Black Douglas?'

'Would that be the African branch of the family, ma'am?'

'Oh, Inspector,' chuckled Mrs Douglas. 'You're teasing me.'

Lestrade was about to protest that he wasn't when a maid brought tea, curtsied and left the room.

'John Douglas was a fine man, Inspector. A fine man. Where can I start to tell you about him? His Army career? Well, Hart's List will tell you all that.'

'I do not have a copy with me, ma'am.'

'No, of course not. Sugar?'

Lestrade nodded, but declined the Madeira cake.

'He enlisted as ensign in the Sixty-first Foot in eighteen twenty-nine – my, an eternity ago now, isn't it? Then, let me see, he joined the Seventy-ninth Highlanders. I never really understood why he exchanged into the cavalry. After all, the Highlanders were his own clansmen. It must have been his awful legs. Forgive me, Inspector, but at my age, I am allowed to transcend etiquette. "Lower limbs" are for the young. I call them legs.'

'Quite so, ma'am.'

'Yes, he looked quite dreadful in kilts. When I first received his attentions in a serious way, he was a captain in the Eleventh Light Dragoons. We married after a whirlwind romance – well, three years was a whirlwind in those days. He was tall, handsome, dashing, kind, considerate, everything a girl could wish for. By June eighteen fifty-four he was lieutenant-colonel commanding the regiment. There was only one cloud on the horizon.'

Lestrade braced himself to hear it.

'Lord Cardigan, colonel of the regiment. Ever since that foul old man had been lieutenant-colonel of the Eleventh in the thirties he had regarded it as his pet. Ten thousand pounds a year he spent out of his own pocket to equip his men,' she chuckled. 'I remember a ditty going the rounds in those days – *The London Charivari* coined it – concerning the tightness of the trousers of the Eleventh. It went, let me see, it went,

"Oh pantaloons of cherry,
Oh redder than the berry.
For men to fight in things so tight,
It must be trying, very."'

Lestrade tittered too.

'None of which, of course, had the remotest thing to do with soldiering. God, how John hated that man. Cardigan was a perfect swine to his officers, Inspector. Upbraiding them in public, accusing them of drinking porter at his table. Small wonder there are now Socialists in the world when men with the arrogance of Cardigan strut upon it. The last years were quieter. John became colonel in eighteen fifty-seven and assistant adjutant-general of cavalry after that. He was commanding the Cavalry Brigade at Aldershot when he died. Doubtless you have seen his memorial there, in the garrison church.'

'How did your husband die, Mrs Douglas?'

'In his bed, Inspector.'

'With respect, ma'am, I asked how, not where.'

'What do old men die of, Inspector? My husband was fifteen years my senior.'

'Hence Lieutenant Dunn?' Lestrade rose with difficulty and handled the photograph of the officer in infantry uniform.

Mrs Douglas recovered the slight slip in her composure and poured them both another cup of tea.

'Alex Dunn,' she said with a sigh and gazed into the leafy middle distance of her youth. 'Would you like me to tell you about him, too?'

Lestrade nodded.

'Alex was younger than I, Inspector. Does that shock you? Well, it shocked a good many at the time. He was Canadian by birth. Perhaps it was that initially which made John dislike him. Inspector, the portrait I am painting of my husband is not a flattering one, I fear. He will seem to you petulant, anti-social. He wasn't really. Not really. At least Alex went to Harrow. John and I had been married ten years when Alex joined the Eleventh. He was a young cornet, a dandy, broad shouldered, good looking. I was the colonel's lady. I remember the night he first danced with me. Forgive my memories, Inspector. They cannot be of interest to you.'

'On the contrary, ma'am. Go on.'

'He had booked me for one waltz. And ended up dancing with me all night. Every head in the room turned. You could see all the ladies, the wives of the regiment, fluttering their fans and gossiping. Oh, how I loved it. John was furious.'

'And you became . . . friends?'

'We used the term "lovers" in those days, Inspector. Has it gone out of fashion now?'

'No, ma'am,' smiled Lestrade.

'For two years we met in secret. God, I hated the lies, the deceit. But I was the colonel's lady, Inspector. And it would have broken John's heart. I have all of Alex's letters still. I keep them in the same hat-box I hid them in all those years ago. Then came the Crimea. Alex was awarded the Victoria Cross for valour. He saved the lives of two of his men at Balaclava. Sergeant Bentley I think was one; the other I forget.'

Bill Bentley, thought Lestrade. Somebody saves him from Russian lances so that somebody else can put a pillow over his face. But here at last was a tangible link.

'Alex came home in 'fifty-five,' Mrs Douglas went on. 'I don't know why; perhaps because he had come so close to death out there, so far from home. His attitude had changed.

He was not prepared now to steal the secret moment, to brush my hand as though by accident. He had it out with John. They had a terrible row. I thought they would come to blows. When it was over, I could not stay with John any more. When Alex went to his estates in Toronto, I went with him.'

'And then?'

Mrs Douglas let out a long sigh. 'I knew Alex's army days weren't over. We were blissfully happy, Inspector, for the rest of his life. He became colonel of the Thirty-third Foot in 'sixty-four. We travelled first to Poona, then to Abyssinia, his last posting. He died in a hunting accident on the twenty-fifth of January eighteen sixty-eight.'

The same year as Cardigan, Lestrade reminded himself. 'How did it happen, Mrs Douglas?' he asked.

'A party of officers were hunting buck on the plains near Senafe. They say his rifle jammed and he was checking it when . . . when it blew up. It's funny, I still have the clothes he wore that day.'

'May I see them, ma'am?'

Mrs Douglas looked a little taken aback, but nodded and rang the bell.

'Fetch Colonel Dunn's things.' She sent the maid scurrying into the bowels of the cottage.

'And after Colonel Dunn's death?' Lestrade persisted.

'Afterwards, I came home. To John. Oh, I know it was feeble. My own family did not want to know me. His still less. But we effected a reconciliation – of a sort. I somehow continued the dutiful wife at Aldershot. I still retained some affection for him, Inspector. Perhaps I even loved him a little.'

She paced the darkening room.

'Was I wrong, Inspector? To run away with a younger man, a subaltern in my husband's regiment? Oh, it's the stuff dreams are made of for silly girls at school, their heads full of poetic nonsense. But in eighteen sixty-eight, I was forty-four years old. And romance had been shattered that day at Senafe.'

The maid brought in, with difficulty, a tin trunk. Lestrade helped her with it and immediately wished he hadn't, because the ladies then had to help him upright. Mrs Douglas took out with loving care the shirt, trousers and duster coat with long white scarf and laid them on the table.

'You had these cleaned of course, Mrs Douglas?'

'Cleaned? No, Inspector, I did not. It is common knowledge that Her Majesty has her late husband's evening clothes laid out on the bed each night at Osborne, as though he were there to wear them. Alex and I lived as man and wife for nearly thirteen years. No, Inspector. I wanted to remember him, his strength, his very smell. Does that seem strange to you?'

Lestrade picked up the coat and shirt.

'You say the rifle jammed and exploded?'

'Yes, Inspector.'

'Then how do you account, ma'am, for this?' and Lestrade placed a finger into the single bullet hole through the back of the coat, caked with the faded dark brown stain of Alex Dunn's blood.

Mrs Douglas lit an oil lamp silently and raised her veil to let the light shine eerily from below, highlighting her once fine features, wrinkled now with age and the breaking of her heart.

'Very well, Inspector.' Her voice was still strong. 'I have loved two men in my life – John Douglas, my husband, and Alex Dunn, my lover. How could I know the one would kill the other?'

'How long have you known this, ma'am?'

'For twenty-two years, Inspector. The night my husband died, he told me. He had been ill a short time only. Days, in fact. That last night, he held my hand and said, "Rosa, I cannot go with a lie on my lips. I shot Alex Dunn at Senafe. I killed him to get you back and I would do it again." I just looked at him. "Don't hate me," he said, "I couldn't bear that. My dearest Rosa," and he slipped away.'

Lestrade folded the clothes neatly on the table.

'So you have me at last, Inspector. I didn't realise the holes in his clothes were not consistent with the kind of accident reported. I suppose Alex's friends covered up out of loyalty to me. They didn't want me hurt further. Tell me, will I go to prison?'

'Technically, ma'am, you are an accessory after the fact of murder. But since the murderer is dead, I don't suppose . . . And anyway, I have other fish to fry. You mentioned Sergeant Bentley earlier – the man Alex Dunn saved at Balaclava. What about Jim Hodges? Richard Brown? Do these names mean anything to you?'

'I believe there was a Brown in my . . . in Alex's troop in the Eleventh, Inspector. But it is a common enough name.'

'Indeed, ma'am.' Lestrade's face fell.

'But let me give you two more names, Inspector. Men who can help you more than I – Seth Bond and "Poppy" Vansittart. And now . . . leave me alone with my memories.'

'Of course, ma'am. One last thing. Do you own a ship – or a boat – called *Ora Rosa*? Or do you know anyone who does?'

Mrs Douglas shook her head. And Lestrade closed the door.

The black reaper clanked and rattled its way across the hill, moving inexorably from left to right, over the field of gold. There were shouts from the men, black dots in the distance, walking alongside the horses, checking strap and chain. And the dogs wheeled and yapped around the huge machine, driving obliquely against the jut of the hill.

Nearly a mile away, resting on the five-barred gate in the early morning sun, sat Inspector Sholto Lestrade. He was already in his shirt sleeves, for the day promised to be long and hot. He watched the reapers for a while, but every so often would check the road, left and right, for something more important.

Something More Important arrived after a few minutes, in a phaeton, drawn by two lathered horses.

'Bandicoot.' Lestrade took the driver's hand and helped him down. 'Thank you for coming. What news?'

'Well, Letitia is having problems with her dress apparently. And we haven't had all the replies yet.'

'Banders, delighted though I am that your nuptials are drawing on apace, I do have more pressing business.'

'Of course, Sholto, sorry. You asked me to find these two. Seth Bond and Poppy Vansittart. Well it wasn't easy. I don't understand why you can't use the resources of the Yard for this.'

'Let's just say I am rather "persona non regatta" at the moment. I'm on my own, Harry. My sergeant has gone down with something again. So I have to use rather unorthodox measures.'

Rather hurt to be considered an unorthodox measure, Bandicoot quickly recovered nevertheless his sangfroid.

'Seth Bond is no problem. He lives in a village called

Southam, not far from here. Retired labourer was all I could glean. Oh, that's rather good, isn't it? Glean?'

Lestrade ignored the levity. 'And Vansittart?'

'Ah, yes, that's more difficult. He's dead.'

'When?'

Bandicoot, Lestrade was intrigued to notice, was using his old pocket book for the storage of information. Old habits die hard, even to a policeman of Bandicoot's limitations.

'Er . . . fourteenth of April, eighteen eighty-six. In Paris.'

'Paris?' Lestrade threw up his hands in exasperation. 'All right. Bond it is. I'll start with him. Look, Bandicoot, I need hardly say how grateful I am for this information. Especially from a man about to tie the knot. I appreciate it.'

'How will you get to Southam?' asked Bandicoot.

'I'll hitch a ride, I suppose.'

'Nonsense, Sholto. I'm not tying the knot as you put it for ten days yet. Climb up.'

'I thought you'd never offer,' and the phaeton whirred away down the road.

'What have you got?' Bandicoot asked. 'Isn't that how we used to do it? Sound each other out. You, Forbes, Dew, myself.'

Lestrade chuckled. 'What made you leave the Force, Harry? Given time, you'd have made an average copper.'

'Nice of you to say so, Sholto.' The blond man grinned. 'I don't know really. I think it was the *Struwwelpeter* business. When you've killed someone . . . Anyway, I met Letitia and I realised there was more to life than pounding the beat.'

'So they tell me,' said Lestrade.

'Then there's London. I mean, it's marvellous to come up to town for the theatre and so on, but working there day in, day out . . . And in this heat! How do you stand it?'

'At least you're never alone in the Strand,' commented Lestrade. Bandicoot could not argue with that and accepted the inspector's cigar.

'Talking of which – is Dr Watson still writing about you in that journal?'

'Currently, no. But I fear it will only be a matter of time. You asked me what we've got. Well, chew on this.'

Bandicoot removed the cigar from his mouth, expecting

Lestrade to place something between his lips. He realised his error without appearing too much of an idiot and took up the reins again.

'Four murders. All the victims elderly men. Cause of death in three cases, poisoning. Poisons various. Cause of death in the fourth case, suffocation. Two of them formerly soldiers of the Eleventh Hussars; rode in the Charge of the Light Brigade.'

'Gosh,' Bandicoot was impressed.

'No definite enemies. No obvious motive. All I have is the means. There is no geographical pattern. These corpses have turned up all over the place. But the murderer knows his poisons. That much we do know.'

'Why the suffocation in one case?' asked Bandicoot.

Lestrade shrugged. 'Even your Great Detective would be baffled by that one, I suspect.'

Bandicoot snorted. 'I must admit I was impressed by the late Mr Holmes.'

But as Lestrade knew, it didn't take much to impress Bandicoot.

'I've been given no end of leads,' Lestrade went on. 'I've been passed from pillar to post. And so far, nowhere.'

'Except that you've been suspended.'

'How did you know that?' Lestrade was incredulous.

'No, Sholto. I'd like to claim it was a flash of the old Bandicoot inspiration.'

Lestrade racked his brain to think of an earlier instance of this supposed phenomenon. He could not. 'But in fact, I read it in *The Times* this morning.'

Bandicoot fished about in the boot at his feet and produced a crumpled newspaper. Lestrade found it at the bottom of column three, the sixth page.

'*Yard Man Suspended. Suspected Attack on Royal Personage,*' he read aloud, and ploughed on silently through the rest.

'It says here I attacked the Kaiser. *Inspector Sholto Lefade* – I don't know whether to be outraged or relieved they got my name wrong – *was apprehended with his hands around the throat of His Imperial Majesty at Sandringham on the* . . . This is libel, Bandicoot. Not only libel, but sheer bloody nonsense.'

'One thing is certain, Sholto,' said Bandicoot, optimistically. 'Somebody up there doesn't like you. Doesn't it say you're supposed to answer charges?'

'Yes, next month. Why didn't Frost get a message to me? He knows where I am. And what is the matter with Charlo, with all his devotion to duty?'

'I never understood the workings of the Yard, Sholto. Even the plumbing mystified me.'

And the phaeton wheeled into Southam.

They found Seth Bond in the churchyard, dozing against a buttress, his scythe beside him. A stocky man, with white wispy whiskers, battered derby hat and the traditional leggings of the agricultural labourer. His pipe had slipped from his mouth and lay quietly burning a hole in his waistcoat as he snored. Lestrade kicked him with just enough force to impress upon him the need for urgency in stamping out the minor conflagration growing on his chest.

'Thank'ee, sir. Everything's so tinder dry, it is. We'll have some bad fires this year, I shouldn't wonder.'

'Inspector Athelney Jones of Scotland Yard,' Lestrade said by way of introduction and stamped hard on Bandicoot's foot as the younger man called out in surprise at the lie he had just heard. 'This is Constable Bandicoot.'

Bond looked up at the golden-headed man blotting out the sun. 'You're a fair cop, guv,' he said and allowed the policemen to help him to his feet. 'You don't mind if I carry on? The vicar wants this churchyard cleared by night. Says yer can't see the stones proper. Besides, I shall be lyin' 'ere meself one of these days. I 'ope as 'ow somebody'll be doin' this for me. 'Ow can I 'elp you gentlemen?'

'Cast your mind back,' said Lestrade, 'to your days with the Eleventh Hussars.'

'Ah, great days, they was,' beamed Bond, 'if yer didn't mind the cholera and the flies,' and he swung with extraordinary gusto for a man of his age into the yellowed churchyard grass. Lestrade sneezed several times in quick succession. Townie, thought Bond, and carried on swinging.

'When did you join the regiment?' managed Lestrade.

'Oh, it must have been ... yes, eighteen-forty. The year the old Queen married.'

'Which troop?'

'F Troop. 'Til I was promoted sergeant-major of C Troop.' He straightened himself with the pride of it. 'That was after the Charge, of course.'

'Balaclava?' Lestrade checked.

'That's right, sir. Now there was a battle! I remember old Bill Lamb ...'

'Who?' Lestrade snapped.

'Bill Lamb,' Bond repeated, somewhat taken aback. 'Funny, 'e were a shepherd before 'e enlisted. And became one again, I believe. I thought 'e'd lost 'is eyes in the Valley of Death, to be sure.'

Lestrade held the scythe arm. 'His eyes?'

Bond nodded.

'Did your Bill Lamb have a cut across his forehead, narrowly missing both eyes?'

''E did, sir. A damned Roosian did that for him. So much blood on 'is face, yer couldn't see. Neither could Bill. 'E was stumblin' around the field, calling out "Englishman, Englishman." Must have been a bit light headed.'

Lestrade let the scythe arm go, and looked at Bandicoot. He spun to Bond again. 'What about these names – Joseph Towers?'

Bond grinned. 'Yes, 'e were with us. I remember old Joe.'

'Bill Bentley?'

'Sergeant, 'e were. Family man. Always talkin' about his wife and kid.'

'Richard Brown?'

'Oh, yes, A do-gooder 'e was. Always lickin' around the officers. 'E were the colonel's orderly. I never liked 'im.'

'Jim Hodges?'

'Hodges? Oh, ar, I remember now. Wild man 'e was. Always given to jokes and that. 'E once crep' into the tent of one of the officers an' spent all night sewing the legs of his overalls together. 'Course, 'e was put on a charge for that.'

'The Charge of the Light Brigade?' chimed in Bandicoot. Bond and Lestrade looked at him.

'Mr Bond, you have made my day.' Lestrade shook the

labourer's hand. 'Take care of yourself. Come on, Bandicoot,' and the ex-constable dashed after the pending ex-
inspector.

'It's falling into place, Bandicoot,' Lestrade said as they
reached the lychgate. 'There's the common pattern. Not *two*
former members of the Eleventh, but all five of them.'

'A sort of red-trousered league?' mused Bandicoot. Lestrade ignored him.

'The question is, why? And why did Nimrod Frost send
me to Mawnan to find the corpse of Bill Lamb? Come on,
Bandicoot. You can go to the theatre and I'm going home.
It's time Assistant Commissioner Frost came a little cleaner
than he is at the moment.'

Hot town. Summer in the city. Lestrade and Bandicoot got
off the train at Paddington and made their way to the Yard.
While Bandicoot waited in the hansom, the inspector entered
the building by the back stairs under the shadow of the
gateway.

'I'm sorry, Inspector.' Sergeant Dixon was firmer than
Lestrade had ever known him. 'Mr Frost won't see you, sir. I
'ave my orders. Now, you're not goin' to make a try for the
lift are you, sir?' You see, in this 'eat, I'd 'ate to 'ave to give
chase. Cruel, ain't it. And as for that bleedin' river! I
remember the Great Stink of 'fifty-eight but it couldn't 'old a
candle to this. Them archaeologists blokes keep findin' bits of
old iron in the mud at low tide and doin' their nuts about 'em.
Reckon they're from the Bronze Age, or something. . . .'

'You're changing the subject, Dixon. I have to see His
Nims *now*.'

'Inspector Lestrade. Look at it from my position, sir. I'm a
married man, four kids, two years orf me pension. I shouldn't
even be talking to you, sir. Not at the moment. You know
'ow it is.'

Lestrade stood back from the desk. 'Yes, Sergeant, I know
how it is,' and he strode to the door.

'Thank you, sir. And mind 'ow you go.'

Bandicoot had bought a morning paper from a street
vendor and was eagerly perusing the shares and city news
page when Lestrade returned.

'No joy?' he asked. Lestrade shook his head. He was about to climb into the hansom when the headline caught his eye. *Goron In London. Head of Sûreté On Flying Visit.*

'Bandicoot. It's a long shot, but it could pay off. Where do you stay when you're in town?'

'The Grand, of course.'

'Of course. Well, get me a room too. Don't worry, I'll charge it to expenses. And use the name Athelney Jones. I'd like to see his face when Frost queries *that* bill! I'll join you there later. There's another question I have for Sergeant Dixon.'

As he rounded the corner, a hoarse whisper crackled in his ear. It was Hector Charlo in the shadows, beckoning to Lestrade to join him.

'I'm extraordinarily glad to see you, Sergeant.' Lestrade shook his hand. Charlo whisked him behind a plane tree. 'What the hell's going on? When I saw Frost a few days ago he was all for reinstating me. Now I find I cannot even get to see him. And that fanatical nonsense of Gregson's is all over the papers.'

'I don't know, sir.' Charlo scanned the upper storey windows of the Yard for signs of life. 'All I know is, I've been ordered off the case. I've been told,' he edged carefully round the tree, 'that if I have any dealings with you whatsoever, I'll lose my job.'

Lestrade fumed. 'You got this from Frost?'

'Himself,' nodded Charlo.

'Well, that's it,' shrugged Lestrade. 'Good luck, Sergeant. I'll see you around perhaps, one day.'

'Inspector,' Charlo stopped him, 'if I can get over this damned pleurisy, I'll stay in touch. Where can I reach you?'

'Sergeant, you are putting your head on the block. You realise that?'

'I've been called a chip off the old block before, sir.' It was the first time Lestrade had seen Charlo smile. Lestrade slapped his arm in gratitude, a little too heartily as it transpired, for Charlo winced with pain.

'The Grand Hotel. Under the name of one Athelney Jones, Inspector of River Police.'

Charlo positively beamed.

'Listen. I understand that Monsieur Goron, Head of the Sûreté is visiting the Yard. Any idea of his movements?'

'It's common knowledge where he goes of an evening, sir. Fatima's.'

'Does he now?'

'Why do you want him?' Charlo was puzzled.

'I'm not really sure, Charlo. Take care of yourself.' And he vanished again.

The lamplighter was doing his rounds in the Haymarket when Lestrade and Bandicoot found their quarry. A squat, iron-grey man with untypical pince-nez bustled through the doorway and the knot of evening strollers.

'Well, well, well.' Lestrade clicked his tongue.

'What is it, Sholto?'

'You never did find your way round town, did you? In a professional way, I mean. That establishment is Fatima Charrington's, the best-known bordello in London.'

'Fatima's?' Bandicoot was impressed.

'The logical successor to Kate Hamilton's,' said Lestrade.

'But what would a man of Goron's reputation be doing in there?'

Lestrade looked with faint surprise at his ex-and-acting-constable. 'Bandicoot, before you and Letitia go through with your ceremony, remind me to have a word with you,' and he dashed away across the street.

Bandicoot had not seen the inside of a bordello before, but on the surface it was no different from the hundred or so music halls that littered the West End. Waiters scuttled here and there with trays of champagne. Customers lounged around, laughing and eating grapes proffered by attractive young ladies. On the stage, garishly lit with sulphur, a painted woman sang 'The First Shove is the Sweetest', to a rather discordant accompaniment by a female quartet. Here and there, heavies stood in key positions; one near the bar, another at the door, two more by the stage. The air was thick with smoke and the fumes of alcohol, all of it very expensive.

'Can I help you, gentlemen?' An enormous lady with a blonde wig piled high and cascading over one bare shoulder about the width of Bandicoot's chest barred the way.

'Miss Charrington, I presume?' ventured Lestrade.

Fatima curtseyed, her breasts wobbling like so much whale meat.

'Athelney Jones, Scotland Yard. This is Constable Bandicoot.' And as if to forestall her complaint, 'Don't worry. This is not an official visit. We are here at the request of Monsieur Goron. May we see him?'

'In person or through the spy hole, dearie?' Fatima asked.

Lestrade chuckled. 'In person, please.'

'This way. Now, dearie, what can we interest you in? A chambermaid, is it? Vicar's daughter? Perhaps – yes, I see it. An Amazon?' She was fondling Bandicoot's arm, gazing into his rather crossed blue eyes and running her toad-like tongue over her thick lips.

'Madame, please. I think you have misunderstood . . .'

'Oh, I see,' and she dropped her fatal charm. 'You want Bertram's across the road. Errand boys. Barnardo brats. More cottage loaves in there than a bakery.'

Bandicoot's mouth opened in silent protest.

'Monsieur Goron,' Lestrade reminded Fatima, and she took them up the velvet stairway to an upstairs room, past chandeliers tinkling and dazzling in their myriad brilliance. 'Keep your hand on your wallet, Bandicoot – and leave the talking to me.'

Monsieur Goron sat in an elegant parlour, reclining on a chaise longue of immense proportions. He looked vaguely comical in his pink underwear and top hat, which he now tipped to the newcomers and raised a glass of vintage champagne. The Sûreté certainly do themselves proud, thought Lestrade.

'Who are zees gentlemen?' he asked Fatima. 'I distinctly ordered two *ladies*. And besides, zees two are both white.'

'I fear there will be a slight delay, Monsieur,' she fawned, in what Lestrade would have sworn was a telephone voice had she had such a piece of apparatus in her hand. 'Celeste and Angeline are not yet ready. They are making themselves *extra* beautiful for you. In the meantime, these gentlemen would like to join you.'

'Oh, I see. You wish to see 'ow 'an expert operates, uh? Well, I 'ad no idea zat ma reputation 'ad spread so far.'

'It has, Monsieur Goron, but it is not your prowess in the boudoir we wish to assess.'

'Non? Perhaps eet ees a matter of length?'

'Good God!' Bandicoot was beside himself with indignation.

'No, this is professional business,' insisted Lestrade. 'My name is Athelney Jones, Inspector of Scotland Yard. This is Constable Bandicoot.'

'*Ah, Inspecteur. Enchanté. Enchanté.* You know I am studying La Yarde Ecosse for a few days. You are in charge of the River Police, non?'

'Er, yes,' lied Lestrade.

'Bon. And do you find ze Londres underworld ees particularly prone to ply the river?'

'Er, no more I am sure than their counterparts in Paris ply the Loire.'

'Seine,' said Bandicoot.

Lestrade wondered momentarily whether this was Bandicoot's summation of Goron's state of mental health. It was not particularly helpful or relevant.

'Whenever I come to Londres, I like to spend my first night at Fatima's,' and he kissed the chubby, bejewelled hand of the lady as she swept past in search of Celeste and Angeline. 'I particularly like two girls at once.' Bandicoot was surprised he had the stamina. 'One white, ze other black. It adds to ze zest of the thing, don't you think?'

Lestrade did.

'Uh, Bain-de-Coute, what ees your preference? Non, don't tell me. Beeg, uh? Blonde, like yourself? Probably ze older woman? I know, eet ees ze thighs you go for, locked around your back, uh? I can tell you are a leg man.'

Lestrade sensed the 'constable' tensing at his side. He realised that Goron's description fitted Letitia Lawrenson exactly, although he couldn't really speak for the thighs. His cry of 'Not this one, Bandicoot,' was drowned as the young man snapped at the supposed insult to his lady's honour and, snarling, flung himself at the prone Goron. Lestrade need not have worried, at least not about the little Head of Sûreté. The Frenchman deftly rolled off the chaise longue and brought his shin up smartly into Bandicoot's groin. Another second and

Goron was upright, the twin barrels of a vest pocket pistol nudging Bandicoot's ear. It had appeared so fast Lestrade had no inkling where it had come from.

'Ees thees 'ow you London bobbies treat visiting dignitaries from abroad?' snapped Goron.

'Er . . . a test,' Lestrade was suddenly inspired; 'we have of course heard of your legendary command of self-defence.'

'Ah, oui, the *Système Goron*.'

'Quite so, and Assistant Commissioner Frost has given orders that various constables should learn all they can from you.'

'The hard way,' Bandicoot mumbled into the silk of the chaise longue.

'Personally, I would like to know more of your Cookshop.'

'What?' Bandicoot struggled upright as Goron uncocked the hammers of his pistol and equally skilfully secreted it God-knows-where about his person.

'Quiet, Bandicoot. The grown-ups are talking,' said Lestrade.

'Goron's Cookshop, young man. A suite of rooms at the Sûreté where I interrogate prisoners. Of course, in this sophisticated age, this *fin de siècle*, such things should not be necessary. But you know, both of you, what scum stalks ze earth. I can do things with a leather thong that would make your eyes water – literally.'

'There is one case you can help me with, sir,' said Lestrade. 'Poppy Vansittart.'

'Ah,' said Goron, adjusting himself on the sofa once more and pouring more champagne. 'An Englishman in Paris.'

'You knew him?' Lestrade asked.

'Oh, yes, quite well. Aahh,' and he rose as Fatima returned with an ingratiating smile. 'Celeste and Angeline.' Fatima beckoned with a pudgy finger. He whispered as he passed Lestrade's ear, 'Actually, their names are Gertrude and May and they are both from Glasgow, but Monsieur, the grip . . . Shall we talk as I perform?'

'Thank you, no, Monsieur,' Lestrade declined. 'That is not quite the British way. We will wait for you here.'

Goron shrugged and left the room, unbuttoning his flies.

'Bon appetit,' Lestrade called after him.

What a tasteless remark, thought Bandicoot, but he was still recovering from the kick in the groin and thought he would let it pass.

For a while, they waited, helping themselves to Goron's champagne, then Lestrade slowly leaned forward and put his glass on the table.

'Bandicoot,' he murmured, 'I want you to say nothing. Anything you do say may well be taken down and conceivably used against you. You see, we are about to be raided by the police.' Even as they made for the door, the whole building shook with crashing glass and the scream of police whistles. Truncheons rained through the air as blue helmets appeared at every window. Naked girls ran everywhere, screaming and crying. Equally naked gentlemen, tugging on recalcitrant combinations and grabbing somebody else's hats, canes and scarves, hurtled along the corridors and tumbled down the stairs. In an instant, the place was in uproar.

'What will Letitia say if this gets out?' Bandicoot wailed.

''Not half as much as if *we* don't get out. Come on. Remind me you were an Eton boxing champion,' and he dashed off along the corridor.

''Ere, I want a word with you,' called a uniformed constable. Bandicoot planted a straight left on his nose and the constable crumpled. A second sprang at him, truncheon raised. Bandicoot ducked aside, threw the constable against a wall and tripped up a third.

'That's the way,' shouted Lestrade. 'Not bad for a beginner,' and began to check the rooms one by one while Bandicoot, like a latter-day Horatius, kept the landing so well. The first two rooms were empty, but the third caught the attention of the hastening Lestrade for longer than he intended. A tall, distinguished-looking gentleman was sitting, fully clothed, talking on the telephone. It was obvious he was wearing a false beard and his conversation was not of the ordinary.

'And then what would you do, Fifi?' His voice was strained and his eyes bulging. Lestrade noted that the wires ran through a hole in the wall, presumably to an adjacent room.

'Fifi, what then? I am desperate.'

A semi-naked girl wearing headphones rushed past Lestrade.

'I believe your telephonist has gone,' said Lestrade. The tall man dropped the apparatus and leapt to his feet. In doing so, his beard fell off at his feet.

'Why, Mr Chamberlain,' smiled Lestrade, 'I didn't recognise you without your monocle,' and the tall man swept past him into the battle-ground below.

'Hurry, Lestrade. Er . . . I mean Inspector Jones. Er . . . I mean . . . oh, God?' Bandicoot was valiantly fending off punch, kick and club alike. He could not hold out for ever. One of his wrists was handcuffed already. At the end of the passage, the lights had gone out, but Lestrade recognised the accent in the eighth room he tried.

'*Ah, chéries. Vous êtes merveilleuse. Merci, mes petites. A bientôt,*' and the Head of the Sûreté backed into Lestrade. In a flash, the pistol was against the inspector's nose, or what was left of it.

'Oh, Jones. Eet ees you. Not your idea of un petit joke this, uh?'

'Certainly not,' said Lestrade. 'If my memory serves me correctly, there is a fire escape here somewhere. I would like to talk further with you, Monsieur Goron. Will you wait in the street below while I bail out our friend?'

Goron tugged on his evening jacket and with an agility astonishing in a man his age, and bearing in mind his activities for the last few minutes, leapt out of the fire escape. Celeste and Angeline emerged, staggering uncertainly from the darkened room.

'Eh, hinnie, he's one hell of a goer, that one.'

'Aye, chuck. You can say that again. They're a' the same, these bloody coppers!'

Lestrade realised the odds at the end of the corridor were lengthening, so he searched around frantically for assistance. If only he hadn't left his trusty knuckle-duster and switchblade in his room at the Grand. He ought to have known better, going to Fatima's of a Saturday night. What came to hand, however, was every bit as useful – a chamberpot. He threw the contents at the first constable and clanged a second across the head with it.

'Come on, Bandicoot. Anybody would think you were enjoying yourself. Get out of it, lad,' and he kicked another attacker in the pit of the stomach. For a split second, he recognised the plain-clothes figure making up the stairs through the jostling mass of bodies – Edgar Bradstreet, Gregson's man. What was he doing in a routine raid by the Metropolitan Police? Bradstreet had time too to recognise Lestrade as the inspector flung the chamberpot, pretty with pink flowers, and followed Bandicoot into the darkness of the fire escape and the night.

Lestrade's superlative knowledge of the streets enabled the three respectable fugitives to dodge the crowds of ladies of ill repute, shame-faced clients busily waving bundles of notes at policemen and the scattering Saturday-night crowds, drawn like flies to a corpse to the noise and scandal of the Haymarket. The name of Fatima would resound in many a magistrates' court on Monday morning and would meet the furious gaze of many a wife across the breakfast table from a nervous, sweating husband. It was the way of the world. It was what made the nineties naughty. As dawn broke, pearly and hot as ever over the sleeping city, three policemen, one foreign, one suspended, one retired, sat in the rooms of the Grand Hotel, sipping champagne. It had been Goron's first request as he arrived with the exhausted Bandicoot and Lestrade at their rooms. Now, as they recovered, the Frenchman once again produced his pocket pistol and held it generally at Lestrade's head.

'Now all ze shouting is over,' he said, 'why don't you tell me who you *really* are?'

Lestrade held up a calming hand to prevent Bandicoot repeating his calamitous attempt of earlier in the evening.

'I told you,' Lestrade stuck to his story, 'I am Inspector Athelney Jones of Scotland Yard.'

'You are not, M'sieur, unless of course you have lost five or six stones and had your face radically altered – since yesterday.'

Lestrade and Bandicoot exchanged glances.

'You see, I met Athelney Jones yesterday. Indeed, I met all Nimrod Frost's inspecteurs – expect one. And now I believe I have met him too.'

'Has Nimrod Frost offered you a job at the Yard yet?' Lestrade asked, bemused. 'I think we have need of you.'

'Ha, ha.' Goron once again put up his pistol, this time in the more conventional holster of his waistcoat pocket. 'You would not approve of my methods. Mind you, having seen you in action wiz a chambre pot as I left Fatima's last night, there is 'ope for you British bobbies yet. Now, Inspecteur Le Strade, as one Frenchman to annuzzer, what do you wish to know about Puppy?'

'Puppy?' repeated Bandicoot, wondering if they were talking about a missing pet.

'Coleraine Robert Vansittart; Puppy to his friends.'

'A curious nickname,' commented Lestrade.

'Not if you 'ad seem 'im, Le Strade. He was long and thin wiz a red–gold beard. 'E was a crack shot, a founder member of the *Tir au Pigeon*. 'E was greatly respected in Parisian society. A personal friend of Prince Achille Murat and,' he leaned closer, confidential, 'Napoléon III.'

'His death?'

'Natural causes. He died in bed, in his rooms in La Rue Vernet. Spacious, comfort. It comes to us all, mon vieux.'

'But to some of us earlier than others,' was Lestrade's comment.

'Puppy 'ad a full life. Funny 'e never married.'

'You mean . . . ?'

'*Un pédéraste? Non*, there was nothing odd about Vansittart. But . . .'

'Yes?'

'There was something strange about 'im. I 'ad a feeling 'e was on ze – how do you say it – fringe of something.'

'Something?' echoed Lestrade.

'Ah, non, Inspecteur. You and I are too old hands to deal in speculation. Let's just say 'e was a . . . uh . . . deep one.'

'Do you know anything of his early life? In the British Army?'

'I believe 'e 'ad been a lieutenant in the Elevent' Huzzards.'

His country seat was in le département ... er ... county of Berkshire, but I believe 'e 'ad no family of which to speak.'

Lestrade slumped in the chair.

'A wall of bricks, Inspecteur?'

Lestrade nodded.

'Je regrets. But now, you can do something for me. Jews. Do you have a problem wiz zem 'ere?'

'Not unduly,' said Lestrade. 'There were those who thought Jack the Ripper was a Jew – a slaughterman.'

'Ah, oui. The apron of leather.'

'You are remarkably well informed,' said Lestrade. 'That case was five years ago.'

'Ah, but what a case. I also know a great deal about your Adelaide Bartlett ...'

Don't you mean *your* Adelaide Bartlett? thought Lestrade.

'And your Charles Hurrah.'

Lestrade frowned for a moment. Bandicoot was completely out of his depth. 'I think that's Bravo,' the inspector corrected him.

'Oh, no, it is nothing really,' Goron swaggered. 'But we 'ave ze serious Jewish problem. Ze army, in particular. There id one little Yeed I am after. An insignificant captain of artillerie named Dreyfus. What about scientists? Do you trust zem?'

'Well, I ...'

'Oh, don't misunderstand me. Some of the best gadgets in my Cookshop have been invented by scientists. Madame Guillotine, of course, so preferable to your English drop. And the father of forensic science is a Frenchman, Bertillon. But there are others I do not trust. Anarchists. Socialists. ...'

Lestrade had heard this somewhere else.

'I 'ave my eyes on les frères Curie of the Sorbonne. Now, there is a 'otbed of anarchie if ever there was one. Do you 'ave a similar place?'

'The House of Commons,' said Lestrade, and finished his champagne.

Lestrade was entirely grateful that Goron had announced that he would be collecting the bill for breakfast. It, both bill and breakfast in fact, was immense and the policemen, British and foreign, spent over an hour regaling each other with celebrated cases and the problems of the modern police force. There were times when Bandicoot might as well have been the aspidistra in the corner for all he was able to add to the conversation. When it came to the food, however, it was Lestrade's turn to take a back seat. He felt sure that Arthur Sullivan would not have approved of the range of *haute cuisine* before him, little of which Lestrade had seen before, and none of which he could pronounce. The more cosmopolitan Bandicoot sampled with relish – Gentleman's, of course. The only thing Lestrade felt safe with was the coffee and he confined himself to that.

The dining-room clock at the Grand had just struck ten when it happened. Goron's face seemed to turn the colour of the rainbow in the space of seconds. He choked, tugging at his starched collar, and pitched forward, his nose burying itself in the confiture. The buzz of conversation around the room stopped and as Lestrade reached out to help him, Bandicoot slumped sideways from his chair, dragging the tablecloth and most of its clutter to the floor.

'Get an ambulance!' Lestrade roared, desperately lying both men on their backs and loosening their clothing. Ladies were hurried from the room. The *maître d'hôtel* shepherded them to the swing doors and did his best to form a human screen between them and the collapsed men.

'What is it, Inspector Jones?' He scuttled back to the scene.

'Looks like beriberi to me,' a red-faced man pronounced.

'Are you a doctor?' Lestrade snapped at him.

'Well . . . no, but I've spent years in the tropics. I know beri— '

'Thank you, sir. I will wait for an informed opinion.'

Under the snapping fingers of the *maître d'hôtel*, waitresses and waiters swarmed everywhere, beginning to clear the debris. 'Leave it!' commanded Lestrade. 'Nothing is to be touched.'

'Sir,' began the *maître d'hôtel*, 'I hope you don't think . . . That is, the food . . .'

'Gangway! Gangway! Let me through there. I'm a doctor.' A rubicund gentleman, clearly staying at the Grand by virtue of his still being in pyjamas and dressing gown, threw down his professional bag at Bandicoot's side and looked at the casualties. 'Dead?' he asked Lestrade.

'No, but that was the intention, I think.'

The doctor checked pulses and eyeballs. 'Are these gentlemen guests at the hotel?'

Lestrade nodded.

'We must get them to their beds. You men, lend a hand.'

While the doctor supervised with the *maître d'hôtel* the removal of Goron and Bandicoot to Bandicoot's rooms, Lestrade had the remains of the breakfast collected for him and placed in the kitchens. He bombarded the entire staff with questions for nearly twenty minutes, despite the entreaties of the *maître d'hôtel* to allow his people to continue their duties. Luncheon after all was not long away.

'If either of those men dies,' Lestrade rounded on him, 'this hotel will not be serving luncheon or any other meal again. That much I can guarantee.'

Lestrade had just come to the conclusion that nothing else could be wheedled out of the array of cooks and bottle washers, when one of them mentioned a new man. A temporary he was. Filling in for Smithers who had the flutters. I know a policeman with that problem, thought Lestrade. No. He wasn't still there. He had gone. Odd that. Not particularly, thought Lestrade. What had been his duties? Preparing the preserves and confitures.

Lestrade fled the kitchen as if his tail was on fire. Into the ante-room where the breakfast remains still lay. He dipped a tentative finger into the nearest preserve. No taste other than cherries. He tried a second. Then a third. He stopped at the third. The smell of almonds.

'What sort of jam is this?' he asked the *maître d'hôtel*.

'No sort of jam at all, sir.' The *maître d'hôtel* was desperately attempting to regain something of his dignity after the bewildering events of the morning. 'It is apricot preserve.'

'And do you put almonds in your apricot preserve?'

The *maître d'hôtel* looked puzzled and whispered to the chef beside him. The little white-hatted man shook his head. 'No.' The *maître d'hôtel* was authoritative.

'Just apricots and cyanide?'

'Precisely,' and the *maître d'hôtel*'s mouth fell slack at the realisation of his admission. 'Er . . . that is . . . I . . .'

'Don't worry,' said Lestrade. 'Your secret is safe with me.'

He was there when Bandicoot came round, a little before Goron. Both men were a little pale, a little weak, a little prone to making staggering visits to the bathroom to rid themselves of what was left of their breakfast and the doctor's emetic.

'I can only apologise, gentlemen,' said the inspector. 'Your discomfort was caused by cyanide jam. And it was almost certainly intended for me.'

'Scientists. You see what I mean?' Goron reminded him.

'You may be right, Monsieur Goron, but we have a game in England called Hunt the Thimble. One child hides the thimble. The others look for it. When a child approaches the hidden object, the hider calls out "You're getting warm". And that is what this morning proves. I'm getting warm.'

The Back of Beyond

This time Jacob wrote his letter. Family affair or not, the matter was now beyond his control. He wrote it down, all of it. All he knew. The whole black, bloody mess. And he knew this time exactly where the letter must go. He addressed it to Inspector Sholto Lestrade, New Scotland Yard. He would do something now. Now he had the facts, Lestrade would act.

The inspector had been in the back of beyond before. This time it was called Bishop's Castle, in the county of Salop and, having left the comparative civilisation of the Shrewsbury-bound train, he had to resort to pony and trap for the last leg of his journey. Through the flies and cow dung of the late summer hurtled Lestrade. He made enquiries in the town with its steep cobbled streets and taking a chance that the Shropshire Constabulary would not be familiar with the pattern of suspensions at the Yard, used his own name. A family called Hope, he was told, had a farm out Cefn-Einion way, on the lower slopes of Offa's Dyke. Lestrade had to ask for several repetitions of this, because the constable seemed to have a peg jammed on his nose and to talk as though his cheeks were full of cotton-wool – that is when he had finally abandoned his native Welsh for something that Lestrade vaguely understood. Lestrade in turn found himself shouting monosyllables at the constable as though he were the village idiot. It didn't help. And wasn't it just his luck that the Hope farm should be on the Welsh, and not the English side of this border county?
    The first glimpse of a Hope that he caught was a switch flying erratically into the air behind a small herd of Friesians winding their way homeward o'er the lea. Not that they were Friesians to Lestrade. In fact, they closely resembled black and

white cows. The one at the front, with the rolling pink eye
didn't look at all friendly, however. And it wasn't until
Lestrade took in the bulk of the beast, its stamping hoof and
tossing head in the fierce afternoon sun that he became aware
of its sex. Surprisingly for a man who had seen it all and been
everywhere, it was not until the animal had shouldered aside
his flimsy trap that Lestrade was aware of its masculinity,
sweeping nearly to the ground. By that time, he was
wrestling manfully with the reins as his pony bucked and
shied, unaware in its blinkers of the size of the problem.

'You silly ut!' screamed a voice. The switch emerged from
the rear of the milling cattle to reveal at its other end a short
square woman, in drab blouse and apron, hair strained back
in a bun. She swung back a chubby fist and hit the bull firmly
on its ringed nose. The animal snorted and waddled off a little
sheepishly.

'Sorry about that.' The cowherd shielded her eyes from the
sun. She waited for Lestrade, dusty and sweating in his suit
and bowler, to calm the horse.

'I'm looking for the farm of Mr Hope,' said Lestrade.

'Oh, English you are, is it? I'm Mrs Hope. It's Will you've
come to see, is it?'

Lestrade looked blank.

'My husband, Will,' Mrs Hope prompted him.

'No, actually, I was looking for Henry Hope,' he
answered.

Mrs Hope's face fell. 'Duw, I'm afraid you might be too
late. Gransha's at death's door. That's why I'm out yer with
the animals. Will's with his Tâd. What do you want Gransha
for? 'E 'aven't done nothin' wrong, 'ave he?'

'No, Mrs Hope. My name is Lestrade; Inspector Lestrade,
Scotland Yard.'

'Well, I never!' Mrs Hope climbed up beside him, leaving
him to ponder all the way down the hill what it was she never
did.

They reached, in the fullness of time, behind the plodding
cows, a little thatched cottage. The sun dazzled on its
whitewashed walls and the hollyhocks completed the picture
of rustic idyll. Only the flagstone floors betrayed its dampness
and the only sound within it was the rattle of a dying man.

'Gransha,' Mrs Hope called loudly to the bearded old gentleman propped up on his pillows. 'There's a gentleman to see you – a policeman.'

Two younger men, in leather gaiters and bowler hats, sleeves rolled up for the harvest, stepped aside at the word 'policeman', rather than at Lestrade's entrance.

'I am sorry to intrude,' he said to them all, 'but I must ask Mr Hope some questions. It may be a matter of life or death.'

'Aye, his,' one of the men mumbled.

'This is Will,' Mrs Hope said, as though by way of an apology. 'Don't mind him. Ask away. Oh, he's gone again,' and she leaned over, tenderly slapping the old man's cheeks as he lay, pale and silent. 'He goes like this now and again,' she explained; 'the falling sickness, see. 'E've always had it. Aven't he, Will?'

'Aye.' Will was clearly a master of wit and repartee.

'Can we help, Mr Lestrade?' she asked.

But with that, the old man stirred.

'Oh, 'e's back with us,' and she shook him gently, motioning Lestrade forward as she did so.

'This is Inspector Lestrade, Gransha, from Scotland Yard. London, you know. 'E wants to ask you something.'

The old man muttered something incomprehensible, probably in the nasal Welsh dialect of the district which had so thrown Lestrade before.

'I understand you were once in the Eleventh Hussars,' said Lestrade. No response. He repeated himself, talking more loudly.

'No need to shout, I'm not bloody deaf, mun,' growled the elder Hope. 'Yes, I was in the Eleventh Hussars. And I rode the Charge of the Light Brigade.' He struggled upright in his bed at the remembrance of it. 'And the Heavy Brigade too.'

Lestrade looked for confirmation at Mrs Hope.

'Oh, yes, he rode in both Charges, all right. The only one to do it, mind.'

'I was in the guardhouse, see,' Henry Hope wheezed, 'on the mornin' of Balaclava. Well, seein' all the activity goin' on, and no guards about, I just walked out of the hut and grabbed the nearest 'orse. I felt a silly bugger, mind, the only Hussar in all them Heavies – and on a trooper of the Greys, isn't it?

154   M.J. TROW

But I galloped with them into the Russians. Too late to turn
back, see, by then. Of course, when I got back, my boys were
formed up for the ride and old Loy Smith would 'ave 'ad my
guts if I 'adn't been there. Afterwards, Lord Cardigan 'isself
let me off my charge – I was asleep on duty – well, it was the
fits, see,' and he collapsed in a paroxysm of coughing. His
family clucked round him and Lestrade recognised in the
greyness of the face all the tell-tale signs. With less than his
usual respect for death, he persisted.

'Think back to the old days, Henry. To the Crimea.'

'Leave 'im alone, mun!' bellowed Will, reaching the heights
of articulacy.

'Don't call Will on your father!' barked the old man, with
one of those magnificent pieces of Welsh rhetoric utterly lost
on Lestrade. 'I pawned my bloody medal years ago,' old
Henry moaned.

'Do you remember Jim Hodges?' Lestrade knelt beside the
old man, his bowler awry, his hand gripping the old man's.

'Aye.'

'What about Richard Brown? Joe Towers? Bill Bentley?'
Nothing.

'Think, Henry, think,' hissed Lestrade. And, with the
desperation of a drowning man, 'There's not much time.'

Henry Hope looked up at Lestrade. His eyes widened in
realisation of what the younger man meant.

'Aye, I remember them all. All F Troop.'

'They're dead, Henry. Murdered. All of them. So's Bill
Lamb. Do you remember him?'

'Murdered?' The old man tried to sit up. Lestrade cradled
his head.

'Why, Henry, why? Why should all your old messmates
die?'

'Ask Miss Nightingale,' he said. 'The Lady of the Lamp we
called her. She can tell you . . .' He fell back.

'Henry . . .' Lestrade called to him.

'Can't you see he's dying, mun?' Will snarled.

Lestrade ignored him. 'Henry, why? Why Miss Nightingale?'

'Surgeon . . .' gasped Henry.

''E wants a doctor. Where is the old bugger?' Will snapped,

whirling to the tiny window and back.

Henry shook his head. 'Kill ... Cro ... Kill ...' and he faded away.

Lestrade let the cold hand fall and laid it gently across the old man's chest.

Will and the other man loomed over him, threatening, bewildered at his intrusion and their sense of loss. It was Mrs Hope who intervened. 'What's done is done, Will,' she said. 'Twm. Find the doctor. Make yourself useful,' and slowly the other man shambled out. She saw Lestrade to the waiting trap.

'My condolences, ma'am,' said the inspector. There was really nothing else he could say.

'Was it any help, Inspector – what Gransha said?'

'I don't know, Mrs Hope. Perhaps only time will tell us that,' and he drove away from the whitewalled cottage, over the edge of Offa's Dyke and away to the north east.

They met as arranged before the altar in the north west transept. Two gentlemen, enjoying the sun of September and the cold stone of their mediaeval heritage in the double cruciform pile of Canterbury.

'They found Becket's bones in the crypt five years ago,' Charlo informed Lestrade, as though a local antiquary was exhibiting his knowledge for a visiting tourist.

'Foul play, I understand?' Lestrade could not resist treading on professional ground, even when pretending to passers-by to be an innocent abroad.

Shop again, thought Charlo, but to be fair that was exactly why he had come to Canterbury.

'I got the preserve you left with Bandicoot,' Charlo whispered out of the corner of his mouth as they moved towards the crypt.

'I would love to see the Huguenot Chapel,' Lestrade said, for consumption of the passing public. 'And?' His voice fell to a whisper.

'You were right. I had it analysed by a chemist friend of mine. Cyanide.'

'It's high time the Yard had laboratories of its own,' was Lestrade's comment. 'What news of the Establishment?'

'We've been ordered to take you in for questioning, sir, if you don't attend your hearing today.'

'You've got no nearer to Frost, then?'

'You must remember, sir, I'm only a sergeant. I'm afraid the assistant commissioner doesn't take me into his confidence.'

'Point taken. What about Gregson?'

'The gossip is he's still convinced you tried to kill the Kaiser. Do you think he's sane?'

'Gregson or the Kaiser?'

'Take your pick,' said Charlo, as they descended into the crypt. It was dark here and colder than the nave.

'How is Bandicoot?' Lestrade asked.

'Well, when I saw him.'

'And Goron?'

'Gone home. He didn't appear to bear any grudge.'

'Do you know if he said anything to Frost – about me, I mean?'

Charlo shrugged. 'Why did you want me to meet you here, sir?' The sergeant was positively shivering.

'Well, I might have His Grace the Archbishop on my list of suspects, but in fact we have to look up some records. Coming?'

The short-sighted young officer yawned and shook himself. He looked at the date on the calendar – September 26th. He crossed to the litter bin, stumbling over something, and began to sharpen pencils. The something he had tripped over, a floor-coloured Irish wolfhound, growled resignedly.

'Come in.' There was nothing wrong with the officer's hearing and there had definitely been a knock at the door.

'Inspector Athelney Jones, Scotland Yard, to see you, sir.' The corporal saluted briskly. The officer adjusted his thick-lensed glasses and peered around the door, tripping over the dog again on his return to the desk. 'Sorry, Paddy,' he had the courtesy to apologise.

Lestrade entered. 'I was looking for the adjutant of the Eleventh Hussars,' he said.

'You've found him.' The officer extended a hand, missing Lestrade's by several inches. 'Charles Davenport ... the

Honourable.'

'Athelney Jones, the Quite Ordinary. This is Sergeant Charlo.' Lestrade caught the searching hand. Davenport waved vaguely at the wall somewhere in front of which he assumed the sergeant was standing.

'I'm afraid you've missed the others,' he said. 'They're all out.'

'Out?'

'Yes, in India, in fact. We have a skeleton staff here and I'm it. How can I help you?' Davenport squinted through gritted teeth. Lestrade realised he'd have no problem with his subterfuge here. Athelney Jones could have been Davenport's Siamese twin and he wouldn't have recognised him.

'I am making certain enquiries into the deaths of five men who were all formerly members of your regiment. I wonder if I might see your roster books from the eighteen-fifties?'

'The fifties?' The adjutant stroked his chin. He rang a number of items on his desk, first a paperweight, then a bronze statuette and finally a bell. The orderly reappeared.

'Corporal, get me Ledger E5/21a, could you?'

'Er . . .' the corporal began.

'Oh, God, it's green with gold letters, eighteenth from the end, top shelf.'

The corporal left.

'Why they give me secretarial staff who can't read, I'll never know. Cigar?' and Davenport offered Lestrade a pencil.

'No, thanks, I find the lead doesn't agree with me.'

The corporal returned, miraculously, with the relevant book, and the adjutant began flicking through the pages. Perhaps it's in Braille, thought Lestrade.

'Yes, this is the one. May eighteen-fifty to January eighteen-sixty. You should find what you want in there.'

And Lestrade did. John Douglas, Lieutenant-Colonel, Lieutenant Alexander Dunn, with a pencilled VC alongside. But what really interested him was F Troop – Lamb, Bentley, Towers, Brown, Hope, they were all there. So were others, many others. He scribbled down the other names on a notepad.

'Did all these serve in the Crimea?' That, he reasoned, must be the link.

'Those with a "C" by their name,' said Davenport.

That cut down the field a little.

'Do you have any way of knowing whether these are still alive?' asked Lestrade.

'God, no,' replied the adjutant. 'Some of them would have been getting a pension. You'd have to go to the War Office for that.'

And the War Office meant London, where Lestrade would be recognised, checks made, verification in triplicate, and so on. Here in Canterbury a man on the run could still be reasonably safe. He needed the resources of the Yard, above all, its miles of shoe leather for this. And that was precisely where Charlo came in. A sudden thought occurred to him.

'Will you be offended if I make an observation?' he asked.

'My dear fellow ...' said Davenport, obviously inviting him to feel free.

'I couldn't help noticing you were a little ... er ... short-sighted.'

Davenport bridled slightly. 'I wouldn't have said so,' he said, petulantly.

'Well, anyway, I was wondering if you had a spare pair of spectacles. I need them for another case I'm working on.'

'A spectacle case?' – the adjutant wished he hadn't said it – 'Well, yes, I have actually. For close work, you understand. But how could a pair of specs possibly help?'

'I'm afraid I'm not at liberty to tell you that, sir.' It was the sort of phrase Athelney Jones might use, but Lestrade wondered how long he might be at liberty at all.

'Very well,' said Davenport. 'But I will get them back, won't I? Could you sign here for them?'

Lestrade signed the bus ticket Davenport nudged towards him.

'And here?'

And he likewise signed the serviette.

'And finally here.'

The space on the desk between the blotter and ink stand accordingly received Jones's signature. Davenport handed Lestrade a pair of spectacles the inspector assumed had been made from the bottoms of bottles.

'Let me see you to the door,' said Davenport.

'No thanks, I can manage,' said Lestrade and tripped head-long over the wolfhound, which merely raised its head.

'Perhaps you ought to put those on, old chap!' chuckled Davenport. Lestrade smiled weakly and left, Charlo coughing again in his wake.

Lestrade sent a telegram to Mrs Manchester that day from Canterbury. *Stay with friends. Stop. Police watching house. Stop. Trust me. Stop. Sholto. Stop.* Then he shaved off his beloved moustache, combed his hair in the centre and travelled to London. Money was running out. So was time. It was September 26th, the date, Charlo had told him, of his hearing, but he would not be there. He was alarmed to find his face staring back at him from the front page of the *Police Gazette*. But it wasn't a very good likeness and with the changes he had wrought and particularly wearing Davenport's glasses, he ought to be all right. Just keep away from police stations and don't accept sweets from strangers.

He and Charlo parted company at Waterloo. It was not fair to the sergeant to be in Lestrade's company in London. After all, he had been expressly ordered to break with the man. His very career was at stake.

'I can't order you to do this, Hector,' said Lestrade. 'I can't really even ask it . . .'

'Don't worry, sir. I won't be far away,' and the sergeant wrapped his muffler against the September winds and was lost in the crowd.

'Inspector Jones?' asked the old lady in the wheelchair.

'Miss Nightingale.' Lestrade shook the limp, outstretched hand.

'I don't get many visits from Scotland Yard. How can I help you?'

'The Crimea, ma'am.'

'Ah, yes,' she smiled. 'Always the Crimea. Sometimes, Inspector, I can see it still. Even after all these years, the hospital at Scutari. The dirt. The smell. You know, we found a dead horse blocking the drains! And the men, boys, many of them. I still see their faces, too. That's the worst of it.'

'In particular, I wanted to know if you remembered any names. Joe Towers?'

Nothing.

And nothing for the others who had died.

'What about Henry Hope?' Lestrade ventured, since it was he who had mentioned Miss Nightingale in the first place.

'Oh, yes, now I *do* remember him. A simple, passionate Welshman. He had *petit mal*, I believe. He was with us for two months or so, that would have been the spring of 'fifty-five.'

'When he was under your care, particularly when he was delirious, did he say anything . . . odd?'

'When men are delirious, Inspector, they often say odd things. I . . . can't recall anything particular about Hope.'

'What about the regimental surgeons, ma'am, of the Eleventh Hussars, I mean?'

'Regimental surgeons were our greatest obstacle in the Crimea, Inspector Jones. I don't hold with the new feminism of today, but by Jove we needed it in the fifties. What could I, a mere woman, they used to say, know about medicine? How could I help when they could not? It was war and war was bloody. There was no changing that. The Eleventh, no, I don't suppose they were any better or worse than the others. Most regimental surgeons stayed with their regiments. One or two of them crossed to Scutari.'

'The regiment's records do not appear to show all their names,' said Lestrade.

'Ah, Inspector. Something else I learned about men, army men that is, is that then, medical men, chaplains, veterinary officers, all were regarded as inferior. I do remember one surgeon of the Eleventh come to mention it, Henry Wilkin. He was a good doctor, but he longed to be a fighting officer. Regiments didn't even give their surgeon a horse, or a military burial. I have always found that sad. That a man who made passing as easy as he could for a soldier should be denied full membership, as it were, when his turn came.'

'Do you remember other surgeons, ma'am? Perhaps one whose name begins with the letters C-r-o?'

'C-r-o? Why, yes, I believe you must be referring to John

Crosse. And he's not far from us here. For several years now
he has been the medical officer at the Royal Military Asylum,
Chelsea.'

The Rabbi Izzlebit took rooms in Sussex Gardens. He
shuffled as he walked, head bent down, as though to peer
over the thick-lensed glasses that he wore. He was visiting
London from York, or so he told the landlord and anyone else
who cared to ask. His black coat was shabby in the extreme
and his greasy black ringlets hung sparsely over his hunched
shoulders. On the first full day of his stay, he took an
omnibus and train to Croydon, to Sanderstead Road, where
he knocked vigorously on the door of Number 20.

The burly ex-policeman was not pleased to see him.

'Look, I don't want to be unpleasant,' he said, 'but I don't
give money away to charities, least of all yours.'

'But charity begins at home, Beastie, my dear,' lisped the
rabbi.

'Who are you?' Beastie demanded.

'Sholto Lestrade, you idiot. Let me in, for the love of Allah.
Or am I mixing my religions?'

Safe inside the portals of Number 20, Lestrade took off the
broad-brimmed hat and ringlet wig and peeled off the false
beard and moustache. Over a steaming and welcome plate of
tripe and onions, Lestrade told Beeson all – or nearly all – that
had occurred since Joe Towers had lain on the very table off
which they now ate.

'I heard you was on the run, sir. I couldn't believe it.
What's going on?'

'I wish I knew,' said Lestrade. 'Gregson's always been a
fanatic, but I can't understand Frost backing him this way. I'd
got him down for a shrewder man.'

'What happens now?' Beeson asked.

'We work our way through the list. All the members of F
Troop. I want to know everything about them. Right down
to their inside legs.'

'I don't know, sir. It's been forty years.'

'Why didn't you tell me you were with this outfit in the
first place?' Lestrade asked him.

'I told you I'd known Joe Towers in the army. I didn't think it was relevant beyond that. Anyway, sir, how did you think I got the name Beastie?'

'Your surname, I always supposed.'

'Nah,' the ex-sergeant of police drawled. 'I transferred to the Twelfth Lancers after the Crimea. Did a spell in India. "Bhisti" is the Hindoo name for a water-carrier. God knows why it stuck to me, but it did.'

'All right. This is what we've got. The officers . . .'

'I didn't know them all, sir. You just didn't talk to officers in them days. I don't suppose you do now.'

'I've got a sergeant named Charlo from the Yard still willing to speak to me. He got access to the War Office. He waited until lunch-hour, nobody much about, then claimed to be anxious to trace a missing relative. It worked a charm, really. God knows what secrets he might be able to uncover just for the asking. Makes you realise why Gregson is so insane. National security, and all that. Anyway, he came up with a few deaths. There's no way of telling now whether they were natural or odd. Here goes,' Lestrade read off the list, crossing out the deceased as he went, 'Captain Edwin Adolphus Cook, died eighteen seventy-two. Lieutenant Alexander Dunn. Yes, well, I know about him. Died eighteen sixty-eight. Lieutenant Edward Harnett. I didn't know he was in F Troop. Still alive. He's helped on the case already. Lieutenant Roger Palmer. Remember him?'

'Yes, Jowett saved his life in the Charge. Fair man, if I remember right, but you must remember I was only in F Troop for a few weeks.'

'At the time of the Charge?'

'No, I was in D Troop then. What's the importance of F Troop?'

'If I knew that, Beastie, I'd have our man. Palmer is a lieutenant-general now apparently. He's got more property than you've made arrests – Ireland, Wales, Berkshire. I'd need time and the Yard behind me even to track him down. Lieutenant Harrington Trevelyan. Retired. Now residing in Fresno, California.'

'Where's that, sir?'

'West of Pimlico, I think you'll find, sergeant. Ah, now that's interesting.'

'Pimlico?'

'No. "Poppy" isn't here. No mention of Vansittart, so either he wasn't with F Troop or he didn't ride the Charge.'

'That's right, sir.'

'Which?'

'Both. He was in my troop and if I remember, he was at Scutari at the time.'

'Scutari?' Links were forging themselves in Lestrade's addled brain.

'The hospital base, sir. On the Black Sea.'

'Yes, yes. I know. A little east of Pimlico. Was Miss Nightingale there then?'

'I believe so, sir, towards the end of Lieutenant Vansittart's time. He retired soon after, I believe.'

'Funny she didn't mention him. Still, I didn't ask her directly.'

'Funny he never married.'

Lestrade had heard that statement somewhere before.

'Ah, now, two surgeons with F Troop. Henry Wilkin. He rode the Charge.'

'Yes, sir, he did. He left the medical service the year after Balaclava. Always wanted to be a serving soldier.'

'He died two years ago.'

'Brave man. Should have got a VC in Hindia.'

'Do you remember John Crosse?'

'Not really, sir; except he runs the fund now.'

'Fund?'

'Yes, sir, for the survivors of the Light Brigade.'

'Beastie, what a mine of information you are. How much is this fund? Who puts up the money?'

'Well, I don't rightly know, sir, except that Dr Crosse administers it.'

'Have you ever had cause to claim, Beastie?'

Lestrade had touched the old man's pride. 'Love you no, sir. I'd crawl in the gutter first. I've never taken charity in my life. Too old to start now.'

Lestrade was racing ahead. 'Don't you see, Beastie?

Money. Money gives us a motive. The first one I've got, anyway. Surgeon Crosse merits a visit. Let's go on. Sergeant-Major George Loy Smith.'

'Bastard, he was. Tough old soldier. Joe went in mortal fear of him, I remember.'

'From what I've heard, you all did. He died in Bart's, what . . . five years ago.'

'Serves him right. I've never liked beefeaters.'

'Is that what he became?'

'Yers.' Beeson spat his tobacco quid in the grate. 'I seen him once at the Tower when I were on duty. Told me to push off or he'd knock my helmet off with his halberd. He never forgave or forgot anything; his sort never do.'

And so they worked on through the list of the dead, wringing Beeson's memory for all it was worth on the living. It was dark when they had finished.

'What do you think then, sir?'

'We've got somebody who knows poisons. That points to a surgeon. If it's somebody in F Troop, my money is on Crosse. He also holds sums of money, perhaps considerable sums. How he gains financially from the murders, I don't know – yet. We've got somebody who can travel easily around the country, apparently at will. That points to someone with private means or at least no regular employment. But the fact that this somebody can get close to Mrs Lawrenson, slip her poisoned tobacco. Can also get unnoticed into a lighthouse from a foreign ship. Can wander around a country estate and smear poison on bramble hedges. We might just have a—'

'A master of disguise,' Beeson broke in. 'I remember reading a story in the *Strand Magazine* about this man—'

'Professor Moriarty?'

'That's right!' Beeson was amazed. 'How did you know, sir? Have you read the story too?'

'No, I haven't,' sighed Lestrade. 'Just a lucky guess. I don't think we need to stoop to the mythology of the late Mr Holmes.'

'But he could be an actor, sir, couldn't he?'

'Why do you say that?' Lestrade thought he saw a spark of connection flashing round Beeson's head.

'One of the names on your list, sir. William Pennington.'

'What about him?'

'He's an actor now, sir. I have heard him described as Mr Gladstone's favourite tragedian.'

'*That* William Pennington.' Recognition dawned on Lestrade too. 'Now, that is interesting, Beastie. Good man.'

'There's something else, sir. You mentioned a while ago that as he died, Henry Hope said "C-r-o". Well, all right, that's Crosse, obviously. But he also said "Kill". Am I right?'

Lestrade nodded.

'What did you take that to mean, sir?'

'Well, that Crosse, if that's who it is, had something to do with these deaths.' Lestrade couldn't accept that Beeson had slowed up *that* much.

'Right. That's what I took it to mean too. But what if it doesn't? Your list has the name of Corporal John Kilvert. What if Hope was trying to say Kilvert?'

Lestrade sat in silence. Then he grabbed the list. 'He's still alive all right. The Mayor of Wednesbury.'

'Where, sir?'

'That's north of Pimlico, Beastie.'

'We've got three men, sir – Crosse, Kilvert and Pennington. Placing any bets?'

'There are shorter odds on me staying free until the morning. Beastie, I want you to do something for me. Send a telegram, will you? I'll write it down. I should have gone to the wedding of a friend of mine recently, but what with the way things are . . .'

'I'm sure he'll understand, sir. Oh, by the way. You'll laugh at this.'

There wasn't much Lestrade felt like laughing at.

'I've agreed to sit for Lady Butler, the artist who does the military paintings. She's doing one – "Waterloo Roll-call" – and heard I was an ex-soldier. She knows Pennington too.'

'Does she now?' Lestrade was more professionally interested than amused at the prospect of Beastie in theatrical uniform seated on a wooden horse.

'Oh, yes. He was the central figure in her Charge picture. Funny how people suddenly want to know all about the Light Brigade. But there's somebody killing us. Even those who are already dying in workhouses are targets.'

'When do you go for your sitting?'

Beastie consulted the letter. 'Next Thursday, at ten.'

'I'll come with you if I can,' and he slipped on his beard and moustache, glancing at Lady B's address.

'Where will you be in the meantime, sir? Er . . . in case anybody asks, like.'

Lestrade chuckled. 'Wednesbury. It's time I met Mayor Kilvert.'

'You'll meet him soon anyway, if you want to.'

Lestrade frowned.

'The one place you'll find us all together. I don't know why I didn't think of it before – the Annual Reunion Dinner.'

Lestrade dropped his ringlets.

'Beastie, you never cease to amaze me. When is this?'

'The twenty-fifth of October, sir, of course. Balaclava Day. That was a day to remember.'

They made tubes in Wednesbury. And boilers. And iron plates. Lestrade guessed they very probably wouldn't have a very large Jewish community so a rabbi, particularly one who habitually bumped into things, might attract too much attention. On the other hand, the papers now carried the information that Lestrade was posing as Inspector Athelney Jones, so he would be unwise to use that one. He decided instead to go one better. He arrived in Wednesbury as Chief Inspector Abberline, the man who made his name, about the only one who did, in the Ripper case of '88. Sergeant Charlo sent in to the Yard to say he was sick and caught the train with him. Lestrade was impressed by the man's loyalty and the chances he took.

But they had arrived nearly too late.

A manservant told them that the Kilvert family were at church, attending a funeral. Mrs Kilvert had died the previous week. Lestrade and Charlo joined the mourners by the graveside at St Bartholomew's Church. 'Earth to earth, ashes to ashes . . .' How often had Lestrade heard those words? He assessed the mourners. Solid, respectable, middle-class men and women. Dignitaries from the environs. All the brass of the Potteries. Staffordshire's finest. As soon as was decent,

Lestrade buttonholed the man with the mayoral chain, John Ashley Kilvert, formerly 11th Hussars.

'Chief Inspector,' the mayor shook his hand. 'I'd no idea the Yard was to be called in.'

Lestrade did not know what he was talking about.

'Oh, yes,' he said.

'Have you any news, then?'

'No.' Lestrade tried to sound vague at moments like these.

'Shall we talk in my carriage? I've said my goodbyes to my wife already. She'll not miss me for a moment.' The mayor and the inspector strolled towards the black-draped brougham. 'You know, I still can't quite believe it. I can trace my family back to the Conqueror. Nine hundred years. And it all comes down to this in the end.'

Lestrade nodded in sympathy, desperately hoping for a clue from Kilvert.

'I always wanted to be Mayor of Nottingham, you know. I'll have to settle for Wednesbury now, I suppose. It's a shame Alfreda won't be here to share it with me.'

'Alfreda?'

'My wife, Chief Inspector. Surely the chief constable has filled you in?'

'Not exactly.' Here was Lestrade's opening.

'Oh, I see. Well, painful as this is, I suppose it has to be done. It was a week ago yesterday. Alfreda had a restless night. She doesn't . . . didn't sleep too well. Back trouble, you see. Well, it was all those crates of spirits she used to carry. We ran a pub in the old days. I worked for a wine and spirit merchant. Anyway, that day she was up and helped Emily – our maid – with the breakfast. I was about to sit down and eat, when a deputation from the Tube Makers' Union arrived. I am a man of affairs, Chief Inspector – oh, that's municipal, not extra-marital, by the way. Anyway, by the time I returned, Alfreda was complaining of stomach pains. As the morning progressed, they grew worse. She died at lunch-time, as the clock struck twelve.' Kilvert steadied himself against a tree.

'She was poisoned.' Lestrade was after confirmation.

'Nicotine, the coroner said. Her end was very painful.'

And prolonged, thought Lestrade. He knew that nicotine

usually worked very quickly.

'Her face swelled up . . .' Kilvert's voice drained away.

'Mr Kilvert, I have called at a dreadful time for you, but circumstances dictate that I must be quick. Am I right in assuming that you served in F Troop, Eleventh Hussars in the Crimea?'

'Well, yes, but—'

'You knew men like Joe Towers, Bill Bentley, Richard Brown, Jim Hodges, Bill Lamb . . . ?'

'Yes, I did, but—'

'Did you know Henry Hope?'

'Very well. Inspector, what has all this to do with the death of my wife?'

'For the moment, sir, I will ask the questions, if you don't mind.' In his haste, Lestrade was descending to cliché.

'You say your wife and the maid prepared breakfast?'

'Yes, that's right.'

'What was it?'

'Er . . . coffee, eggs, scrambled, I think, on toast.'

'Is that your usual breakfast?'

'It varies . . .'

'Could the coroner say in what part of the breakfast the poison was contained?'

'No, he could not. You must have read the report?'

'Just double checking,' Lestrade lied. 'This maid, Emily, how long has she been with you?'

'Nearly twelve years.'

'Is she trustworthy?'

'Totally. At any rate, she doesn't go around poisoning her employer.'

'Have there been any strangers at your home recently, say, within the last month?'

'Good God, man, I don't know. As I told you, I am a man of affairs. A municipality of this size doesn't run itself, you know.'

'I'm sure not.'

'Chief Inspector, what has all this about the Eleventh to do with my wife's death?'

Lestrade scanned the cemetery. There was no sign of a uniform. And no one he would immediately place in a plain-clothed category either, except Charlo, trying to look like a mourner and keep abreast of his guv'nor's conversation.

'Your wife's death was an accident, Mr Kilvert. Or at least it was by the way.'

'By the way? How dare you, sir!'

'Don't misunderstand me. *You* were the murderer's target, not your wife. Were it not for the timely arrival of the Tube Makers' Union, they would be laying you to rest today as well.'

Kilvert looked astounded. 'Well, I know I have enemies on the Council, But this . . .'

'I don't think this is municipal murder, Mayor. You – or your wife rather, by accident – are but one link in a chain. A chain that runs right back to the Eleventh Hussars and the Crimea. The names I mentioned earlier – Towers, Bentley and the rest. All of them have died violently in the past months. What is the link? You were all in F Troop. You all rode in the Charge of the Light Brigade. Who wants to see you dead? Think!'

Lestrade relaxed his grip on Kilvert's velvet lapel. The mayor was frowning, racking his brain. Then his frown vanished. He straightened. His face turned the colour of the ashes to which the vicar had referred. His eyes assumed a faraway, sightless look. 'The golden dawn,' he whispered. Lestrade searched the sky. It was mid-afternoon. It was drizzling.

'What?'

The mayor turned away, like a man possessed.

'What did you say, Kilvert?' Lestrade now doubted his ears.

'Nothing,' the mayor answered, dumbly. 'Leave me, Chief Inspector Abberline, to mourn my wife.'

Charlo was at Lestrade's side. 'What is it, Inspector?'

'I don't know, Charlo. He said "the golden dawn". What does that mean to you?'

Charlo sought carefully for the right words. 'Nothing,' he said.

The bearskin did nothing for Ben Beeson. He sat on the arm of a sofa, head tilted to one side, hands resting on the rim of an aspidistra pot.

'I know you were a cavalryman,' Lady Butler was saying, 'but I do hope you don't mind posing as a guardsman for this one. Rabbi, do you like it?'

Lestrade had come as a rather unlikely friend of Beeson's and a connoisseur of art. And he was now heartily regretting the whole thing. He pressed his nose against the canvas, the thick glasses delineating only the vaguest of outlines.

'Delightful, delightful.' Lestrade was lisping, hoping Her Ladyship had not had much regular conversation with Jews. Especially art-loving rabbis.

'It's to be called "The Dawn of Waterloo",' Lady Butler glowed, smearing the contents of the yellow ochre the length of her smock. 'Or is this one "Steady the Drums and Fifes"?'

'Foggy, was it?' Lestrade continued, 'the morning of Waterloo?'

'Foggy?' Lady B's tone was a little too brittle to allow Lestrade to think he was still on the straight and narrow. 'Oh, I see. My dear man, no, these are but the preliminary sketches. I shan't use this canvas at all.'

'How long will this take, mum?' Beeson began to feel himself distinctly uncomfortable under the bearskin.

'About three years,' she said confidently. Beeson's eyes crossed and he resigned himself to a long wait.

'When did you begin to paint soldiers, my lady?' Lestrade ingratiated, stopping short of actually rubbing his hands together.

'Oh, let me see.' She flicked charcoal effortlessly over the canvas. 'It must have been eighteen seventy-two. Yes, that was it. I was watching some manoeuvres. General Butler's influence, you see. I do so love the way soldiers move, don't you?'

Lestrade looked over his glasses at Beeson, a particularly unprepossessing sack of potatoes galloping to nowhere on a sofa.

'Quite,' he said.

'Since then I've never really looked back. Don't move!' she suddenly snapped at Beastie, who froze in terror, though his right buttock was totally numb.

'I particularly like your Balaclava paintings,' Lestrade was worming his way to the matter-in-hand.

'Ah, "After the Charge"? Yes, one of my favourites too.'

'Did Beastie – did Benjamin sit for that too?'

'No, no. But a number of the Light Brigade did. Mr Beeson, could you refrain from doing that? Lestrade turned too late to see what it was. 'Mr Pennington, the actor, for instance. He was a lovely sitter.'

'Anyone else?'

'Yes, Poppy Vansittart. I asked if he'd mind appearing as a private soldier rather than an officer. Dear old Poppy. He understood.'

'But he didn't ride the Charge, mum,' Beeson commented.

'Neither were you at Waterloo,' glared Lady Butler, rapidly losing patience with her latest sitter. Then, acidly, 'Were you?'

'Vansittart?' Lestrade brought her back to the subject other than Beastie.

'Yes, that was rather odd, actually.'

'Odd?' Lestrade asked.

'Yes. You see, I also used photographs of survivors of the Charge. When Poppy saw one of them, he tore it up. When I asked him why, he said, "He was never there. He never rode the Charge. You cannot use him. Let's just say it would have been better had he never existed!" Odd.'

'But our mutual friend has just said that Vansittart never rode the Charge either.'

'Quite. And really, it didn't matter that much. I wonder who he was, the man in the photograph he tore up?'

'He was a murderer, ma'am,' said Lestrade, without the accent. And left the room, leaving Beastie to sort that one out.

He opened the letter with Lestrade's paper knife and began to chuckle at the contents. Yes, it was all there.

> *My dear Inspector Lestrade,*
> *It has been some weeks since I wrote to you concerning my brother. I have received no reply and must urge upon you again the need for immediate action. You cannot know how grave is the danger.*

The tale was spelt out, as far as the writer knew it. It was signed 'Jacob'.

His mood darkened for a moment, then he tore up the letter, throwing the pieces carelessly into the nearest waste basket.

'Oh, I'm sorry, sir, I didn't expect to see you in here. Anything for me today?'

He chuckled. 'No, Dew. Nothing today.'

Mad Houses

Conspiracies, thought Lestrade. Everywhere he went. Conspiracies. As Rabbi Izzlebit he wore more make-up than the witches on stage. The thunder roared through the crowded theatre, howling winds screamed round the proscenium. In the savage green-yellow of the lime lights, the weird sisters cavorted and twirled. A drum, a drum. Henry Irving doth come. The audience broke the dramatic impact of the blasted heath by applauding rapturously at the princely appearance of the man. He stood centre-stage, tall and imposing, dragging his leg as he always did on stage, sweeping his cloak around him. He spoke slowly, deliberately, in that strange, weak voice of his. This was the last night of the run. He had delayed his American tour just to appear before his beloved admirers. It was they who packed the house to overflowing and one of them had been reluctant to give up his seat to the culture-hungry rabbi from York, who just had to watch Irving's last night. It had cost him three pounds, leaving a vast hole in Lestrade's pitifully limited funds.

It was not of course Irving that Lestrade had come to see at all. He wondered why people looked at him oddly when, to appear at one with the adulators, he had whistled and stamped and cried 'Author! Author!' Obviously he was overdoing it. That was not how rabbis behaved. He was more restrained during the rest of the play, largely because he was asleep. He remained awake, however, long enough to catch sight of his quarry – King Duncan. It wasn't only the Macbeths who were after him. Lestrade wanted a brief word too. The old king was suitably regal and suitably trusting as he all-unwittingly entered Macbeth's castle. Was the man under the disguise, William Henry Pennington, as naïve as the character he portrayed? Time would tell.

Perhaps it was Lestrade's seventeen years on the Force. Perhaps it was a gut reaction born of instinct and that indefinable sixth sense which makes a great policeman. Perhaps it was the accidental prod in the vitals from the umbrella of the old lady beside him. Whatever it was, something woke him in time to witness Shakespeare's characterisation of murderers. He found his interest growing in spite of himself. They were professionals, paid killers. But they bungled it. Crime never pays, Lestrade reminded himself. Ah, if only that were true. This Shakespeare fellow knew nothing about the criminal classes. As for this witchcraft rubbish. . . .

Lestrade toyed with going backstage as soon as it was apparent that Duncan was dead. Another killing offstage. What were the public paying their money for? But he thought better of it.

Hats and gloves shot into the air and the atmosphere was electric with applause as Macduff rounded off the play. All this and a happy ending too, thought Lestrade. But he still preferred *Mother Goose*. The cast assembled before the velvet curtains in reverse order of importance. Pennington had solid applause, but the most deafening rapture was, of course, reserved for Irving. He stood in the limelight, where he always wanted to be, proud, lonely and self-centred. A ham of hams.

Backstage, the Lyceum was a maze of corridors, doors and fire escapes. A wonderland of tinselled costumes, wooden props and painted backdrops. Lestrade walked into or tripped over most of them in his hurried search for two things. First, a room in which to change his rabbi suit and second, the dressing room of William Pennington. The place was crawling with admirers, dashing hither and thither with autograph books. Stage-hands and theatre attendants were everywhere. Lestrade kept one hand firmly on his wallet, deep in the long pockets of his long coat. The other he clamped permanently on his right temple as the heat of the sulphur lamps and the hot air spouted by Irving had conspired to unhinge his false beard.

Intent as he was on all this, he did not notice the large woman with the huge, ostrich-feathered hat, although

probably the man sitting behind her all night had. She and the
rabbi collapsed in an undignified heap on the floor.

'Letitia, are you all right?'

Lestrade fumbled for his thick-lensed spectacles immediately, but was too late. 'Sholto!'

Well, the name sounds Jewish enough, Lestrade hoped. For
the second time in a few months he was denying any
knowledge of Mr Bandicoot.

'Oh come, Sholto. You can't wriggle out of it this time.'

After what seemed an eternity of Lestrade contorting his
face and flapping his hands in incomprehensible gestures,
Bandicoot lowered his voice. 'What are you doing here?' he
hissed. 'And disguised as a Jehovah's Witness?'

'May I remind you,' Lestrade fumed through clenched
teeth, 'that I am still under suspension. And, indeed, a wanted
man.'

'Wanted?' Mr and Mrs Bandicoot chorused.

Lestrade flattened himself against a stack of halberds, which
instantly crashed noisily to the floor, thereby attracting far
more attention than the Bandicoots' simultaneous outcry.

'From where I'm standing,' hissed Lestrade, 'everybody in
London seems to know I'm a wanted man. Where have you
been, Bandicoot?'

'The south of France,' Bandicoot answered. 'On our
honeymoon, Sholto,' and he pulled the former Mrs Lawrenson closer to him.

Lestrade felt suitably embarrassed. 'I'm sorry,' he said.
'Mrs Bandicoot, please forgive me.'

'There is nothing to forgive, Sholto. We understand. And
we were sorry not to see you at the wedding.'

'Under the circumstances, ma'am, I felt it best to stay
away. Can you imagine the scene? You and Harry poised
before the altar and me being carried away by four burly
coppers? It would have hardly made your day. Are you
recovered, Harry?'

'That's rather indelicate, Sholto,' Bandicoot answered.

'From the cyanide, man!'

Letitia reached out and kissed Lestrade tenderly on the
cheek, her lips smeared now with his running make-up.

'How can we help?' asked Bandicoot.

'You have the knack of turning up at theatres and circuses and such,' grinned Lestrade, remembering the New Year of 1892 at Hengler's. 'Don't tell me you've brought your trusty brace of pistols.'

''Fraid not, Sholto.' Bandicoot actually looked apologetic. 'We were breaking our honeymoon to see Henry before his American tour. Wasn't he marvellous?'

'Er . . .'

'Letitia's known him for years. Haven't you, Letitia?'

'We were going to see him now. That's when we . . . ran into you, so to speak,' the new Mrs Bandicoot added.

'I'm looking for Pennington.'

'Yes, he was good, wasn't he?' beamed Bandicoot.

'Somehow, Harry, I don't think the inspector wants to offer Mr Pennington his congratulations. They'll all be together, Sholto,' said Letitia. 'There are usually parties after a run. Come with us,' and she led the way.

'We could use her on the Force,' Lestrade told Bandicoot as Letitia unerringly found the right door. The actors were still in costume and the air was thick with the roar of the greasepaint and the smell of the crowd. A cigar looked incongruous protruding from the bloody lips of Banquo and the witches were busy downing liquid of a clear, sparkling consistency, far different from the gruel, thick and slab, they had been concocting all night.

'Lettie, darling,' Lady Macbeth hugged Mrs Bandicoot and when introduced to Harry hugged him as well. She declined to follow suit with the unsavoury-looking Jewish gentleman with them, particularly as his beard was peeling off at one side.

'Er . . . this is . . .' Letitia was lost for words.

'Rabbi Izzlebit.' Lestrade nodded and bobbed as he assumed rabbis did when they were introduced to people, but it didn't matter; he couldn't make himself heard above the noise, anyway.

'Lettie, darling.' A moustachioed man in evening suit hugged Mrs Bandicoot too, and shook hands heartily with Harry. He was content to nod to the rabbi.

'May I introduce Bram Stoker?' Letitia said. 'Henry's manager and a very dear friend.'

'Lettie, darling.' Macbeth whirled cloak and arm in a magnificent theatrical gesture. He bowed low, kissed her hand and pulled her to him as though to break into a gallop.

'Mr Henry Irving, my husband, Harry.'

Irving stamped his feet, pirouetted once and took Bandicoot's hand between both of his. 'My dear boy. You are a lucky man. A lucky man.' His voice was as odd and camp offstage as it was on. 'Ah, if only I were fifteen years younger. . . .'

'Twenty-five' corrected Stoker, sipping his champagne with the deadliness of a viper.

'My dear fellow.' Irving tripped across to Lestrade, ignoring his manager entirely. 'Where are you running?'

'I'm sorry . . .' Lestrade lisped, not following the Great Man at all.

'Don't apologise, dear boy. Rushed over here still in make-up to see me. Entirely understandable. Entirely. What did you think? Come now. Candidly. How marvellous was I?'

Lestrade stood there, momentarily lost for words.

'He is momentarily lost for words,' said Letitia. 'Henry, you are off to America tomorrow. We just had to see your last night. A triumph. An utter triumph.'

'Please, my dear. You know how I hate fuss. A simple "incredible" would have done. Not as good as *Becket* though?'

'Better,' said Stoker, without feeling, diving again into his champagne.

'Well, perhaps, perhaps.'

'Speech,' muttered Stoker, and the cry was taken up.

Irving passed a mirror on the way to a table and checked his appearance before mounting the rostrum.

'Friends . . .' He held up his hands in self adoration.

'. . . Romans, countrymen . . .' mumbled Stoker behind him.

'This is so unexpected.'

'Stoker blew bubbles in his glass.

'What I . . . what we have accomplished tonight is little short of . . .'

'Average,' said Stoker.

'. . . magnificent,' Irving went on. 'You heard them out there tonight. I . . . we never faltered. The Bard . . .'

'. . . must be turning in his grave,' said Stoker.

'. . . could not have wished for better.'

While the Lyceum's lion roared his prowess to the howls and delight of his second audience that night, Lestrade edged as close as he could to the late king.

'Mr Pennington?' he lisped.

Without taking his eyes off Irving, the old actor answered, 'If it's elocution lessons you want, I'm fully booked until the end of the year.'

'Not exactly.' Lestrade tried to stay in character.

Undeterred, Pennington soldiered on. 'Well if it's a repeat of my "Little Nell" may I remind you people, chosen though you may be, that I haven't been paid for the last time yet.'

Lestrade could see he'd have difficulty in removing Pennington from the crowd scene. Perhaps a threat of force? He pressed the rim of his spectacles, still in his pocket, into Pennington's regal robes, as close as he could to the small of his back.

'Can you feel that?'

'Yes,' said Pennington.

'Then I suggest you come with me now, quietly and without fuss into an ante-room. Or I'll use it.'

'Very well,' replied Pennington, unruffled. 'But I'd be intrigued to see in what way you would use a pair of spectacles.' And he opened a door behind them.

Suddenly, he paused. 'They're not loaded, are they?'

Both men were pushed into the room. They spun round to see Bram Stoker, pistol in hand, staring hard at Lestrade.

'I think we'd better let this gentleman do the jokes, William. Rabbis with false beards who don't know Shakespeare from their elbow must have a few good one-liners up their sleeves.'

The suave man with the soft Irish brogue was no fool. Gregson would have a field day with him. Obviously, he was Parnell's successor, intent on blowing up the Houses of Parliament and strangling the Queen, while eating his breakfast.

'All right.' Lestrade broke cover, snatching off the hat and wig.

'Hurts like hell, doesn't it?' Pennington sympathised as he tore off what was left of the facial hair.

'I am not Rabbi Izzlebit.'

'Lawks a mussy!' drawled Stoker, feigning shock and horror. He was still pointing the gun.

'I am Chief Inspector Abberline of Scotland Yard.'

'This is better than a play,' chortled Pennington.

'Is it usual for theatrical managers to carry guns, Mr Stoker?'

'Is it usual for chief inspectors to pass themselves off as rabbis, Mr Abberline?' and he holstered his weapon in his coat.

'Point taken. Believe me, I have my reasons. This is a delicate matter, Mr Stoker, and it is between Mr Pennington and myself.'

'Anything which concerns the Lyceum and its staff concerns me too, Chief Inspector. I'm staying.'

Lestrade shrugged and the three men sat down.

'Mr Pennington, how long have you been an actor?'

'It's kind of you to accord me that title, sir.' Pennington smiled. 'Let me see. I first appeared at the New Royalty in 'sixty-two. Good Lord, more than thirty years.'

'And before that?'

'Well, I was a soldier. The Eleventh Hussars. And before that—'

'And you rode in the celebrated Charge of the Light Brigade?'

'One of the proudest moments in my life. Mind you, I was not so brave that day. When my horse was killed under me, I thought, This is it, Penners old boy. You've bought it. It was George Loy Smith who pulled me through. He was a hard man, too hard, but he knew soldiering. A cooler man under fire I've never known. Why the interest in the Light Brigade, Chief Inspector?'

'Perhaps you've been fiddling your pension all these years, William,' said Stoker. The theatricals chuckled.

'Not all the Light Brigade,' said Lestrade, watching

Pennington's every reaction carefully. 'Just the Eleventh Hussars. Just F Troop.'

'F Troop?' said Pennington. 'Why? Most of them must be dead.'

Was this a confession? Lestrade wondered.

'At least four of them have been murdered.'

Pennington and Stoker exchanged glances. 'By whom?' the actor asked.

'By you, Mr Pennington.' Lestrade pushed as far as he could.

Pennington was on his feet in an instant. 'You're mad, sir. I couldn't kill a man. I don't think I killed anybody in the Crimea. I certainly couldn't start now. What's my motive?'

'Calm down, William. I've a feeling the chief inspector is trying you out. Isn't that so, Mr Abberline?'

'Perhaps.' He handed Pennington a piece of paper. 'Here are the names of the dead men. Do you recognise any of them?'

Pennington did. What Lestrade had not divulged was that he had written down the wrong names, including Kilvert's. Again, he watched intently for a reaction, a flicker. There was nothing. Remember, he told himself; this man is an actor. And he was no judge of how good he was. But in the world of murder – and getting away with it – plausibility was everything.

'Well, well,' said Pennington. 'Old Ben Beeson dead. He was a nice fellow. . . . Wait, I thought you said F Troop.'

'That's right,' said Lestrade.

'If my memory serves me correctly, Beeson was in D Troop, at least, while I was with the Brigade.'

'I think the chief inspector is still trying you out,' commented Stoker.

'Come, Chief Inspector. No more games. These men were friends of mine. They shall be missed at the Dinner this year. How can I help you? You have my word as a private and a gentleman that I did not kill them.'

'I know that,' said Lestrade.

'Then why . . . ?' Pennington began.

'I checked at the box office before the show . . . er . . . performance started. Being up there on stage before hundreds of people each night is quite an alibi, Mr Pennington. And I doubt if even you are actor enough to be in two places at once.'

'Well,' sighed Pennington. 'That's a relief!'

'The fact remains,' Lestrade went on, 'that somebody killed those men. If it wasn't you, I must find out who it was.'

Pennington was stumped.

'Does the phrase "golden dawn" mean anything to you?' He clutched at meaningless straws.

Pennington thought for a moment, then shrugged.

'I'm afraid not,' he said. A series of cheers from the adjoining room brought him back to the present. 'Chief Inspector, Henry is leaving for an American tour tomorrow, attempting to take some culture to those woefully callow people. I really must bid him bon voyage.'

'Of course,' Lestrade was no further forward.

'Chief Inspector. Might I have a word?' Stoker closed the door as Pennington left. The manager crossed the floor to the oil lamp. 'I pride myself on being an intelligent man,' he said. 'I have a Master of Arts degree from Trinity College, Dublin. I am Sometime Registrar of Petty Sessions at Dublin Castle. I could forge a soup tureen from my silver medals for History. And I write. Oh, nothing you've read, I don't suppose. *The Snakes' Pass*?'

Lestrade shook his head.

'No, I didn't think so. Well, we writers keep irons in the fire, Chief Inspector. I'm working on various things now. But there is one work, one work of a lifetime which every writer hopes to complete. I have that work in mind now.'

'An historical romance?' Lestrade was proud of that conclusion.

'Not exactly. Are you familiar with Styria?'

'I don't go to the theatre much, Mr Stoker,' Lestrade confessed.

'Styria isn't a play, Chief Inspector,' said Stoker patiently; 'it's a place. Transylvania? Central Europe? Well, I've been there. And I know strange and terrible things.'

Lestrade felt the hairs on the back of his neck crawl. If Stoker wrote as he spoke there would be no doubt of the best-selling qualities of his book.

'No doubt you found Shakespeare's witches tonight a little false. Funny even?'

'Well, I wouldn't have wanted to be the one to say so,' said Lestrade.

'When Shakespeare wrote that he wrote in deadly earnest. Witches were real to him. The powers of darkness were real.'

'But wasn't that . . . some time ago?' Lestrade was hazy on these matters.

'Do you think, Mr Abberline, because we live in the age of the electric light and the horseless carriage – in the age of the train – that those powers are no more? Go to Styria, Chief Inspector. Ask them about Vlad Sepêc, the Impaler. I tell you, Chief Inspector, if we put Macbeth on in Budapest, the people would riot.'

Having seen Irving, I'm surprised they didn't here, thought Lestrade, though it may have been out of place to say so.

'Forgive me, Mr Stoker, but I don't see what this has to do with the murders of members of the Light Brigade.'

Stoker faced Lestrade over the oil lamp, his smooth features suddenly dark, haunted.

'You mentioned "golden dawn" earlier. Why was that?'

'It was a phrase I heard. From another ex-Hussar. Do you know it?'

Stoker hesitated. 'I know of it.'

'What is it?' Lestrade could not bear the silence.

'It is evil, Chief Inspector. Evil incarnate.'

'But . . .'

'Don't press me further.' Stoker's hand shot out. 'I don't know details, man. But this much I do know. If it's the golden dawn you're after, look to yourself.'

The Royal Hospital at Chelsea was one of those buildings with which Lestrade had grown up. Founded in Good King Charles' golden days, the long sweep of its red brick buildings was a familiar sight to all – the office clerks going about their daily business, the Bohemian artists wandering in varying degrees of inspiration up and down the King's Road. Lestrade entered its portals as Chief Inspector Abberline, praying that the real one was not known to the gatekeeper, or anyone else with whom he might come in contact that morning. On his way up the labyrinthine stairs, he passed a number of proud old soldiers, doddering around in their blue winter uniforms. The morning was crisp, with one of the first frosts after the long summer. Even indoors the standards hung stiff and starched, weighty with their battle honours on the old canvas.

The attendant hurried on into the bowels of the building, turning now left, now right. At an ominously padded door he stopped, tapped sharply three times. A grille high in the studded woodwork slid back with a grating sound reminiscent of the portals of Hell. Or at least, the Openshaw Workhouse, Manchester.

'Visitor for Dr Crosse.'

The door swung back and the next attendant took Lestrade into an ante-room. He was asked to wait. He was not alone. Three men sat at points around the room, all of them dressed in disreputable nightshirts. One stared ahead, unblinking. Another rocked backwards and forwards. A third was mumbling to himself.

'What are you here for?' the mumbler suddenly asked Lestrade.

'To see Dr Crosse,' he answered.

The man's eyes widened in terror. 'Him?' he gibbered. The rocker turned in his chair, attempting to climb the wall, sobbing quietly and burying his head in his arms. The starer stared on. He had not moved, not blinked.

'You see how they love me?' A voice brought Lestrade back to reality. In the doorway stood an elderly man in a white coat, for all his years still erect and fit-looking. He motioned Lestrade to enter his office, then quietly shut the door.

'John Burton St Croix Crosse,' he said, extending a hand. On the telephone you said you had to see me urgently.'

'That is correct, Doctor.' Lestrade sat down. 'When I heard you were medical officer of the Royal Military Asylum, I assumed that—'

'That I patched up abrasions and prescribed for gout? No, Chief Inspector, I deal with wounds of the mind. Look at this.'

Crosse dragged a large glass jar into the centre of his desk.

Floating in its semi-opaque contents was a human brain.

'You know what this is?'

'I've seen a few in my time. Or what was left of them,' said Lestrade.

'This particular one is rather special. It belonged to the poisoner, Dr Neil Cream.'

Lestrade was interested. Why should Dr Crosse find a poisoner's brain interesting?

'I knew him,' said Lestrade

Crosse looked at him. 'Alas, poor Yorrick, eh?'

Lestrade didn't follow that.

'Then you will know better than I,' Crosse said, 'that this man was hanged in November last for the murder by strychnine of several prostitutes. Nux vomica, gelatine capsules and some bottles of strychnine were found at his home. Not very careful, was he? I look at this sometimes,' he said, indicating the brain, 'wondering what it is about the brain that makes a man a murderer. There is a theory, of course, that physical deformity deranges men. Oh, I know phrenology is old hat now, but to an old stager like me, it still has its appeal. You will know that some of the most murderous monsters in history have been deformed. Genghis Khan. Richard III. Cream of course was cross-eyed. His optician swore this was the cause of his crimes.'

'Interested in poisons, are you, Doctor?' Lestrade fished.

'No more than the next man.' Crosse shrugged and slid the brain to one side. 'But I digress. What can I do for you?'

'You were once a surgeon with the Eleventh Hussars,' Lestrade asserted.

Crosse chuckled. 'In my dim and distant past,' he said. 'I was born in the year of Waterloo, Chief Inspector. And my memory goes back a long way. Don't tell me someone has stolen the regimental plate?'

'No, sir, someone is killing survivors of the regiment. Or of F Troop to be more exact. Joseph Towers, Bill Bentley, Richard Brown, Jim Hodges. And I have reason to believe that others may yet be targets. I have to work fast to stop this maniac – oh, begging your pardon, Doctor.'

'How did they die?' Crosse asked. 'They must all have been old men.'

'They were,' answered Lestrade; 'but not by natural causes. One was suffocated, the others poisoned.'

Crosse looked at the swimming brain. 'Ah, perhaps it's Cream reaching from the grave?'

'What do you know of aconite, Doctor?'

'Aconite,' Crosse repeated. 'Never heard of it.'

'But you are familiar with strychnine?'

'Of course. Is aconite a poison too?'

Lestrade sensed he could fence all day with this man. Old as he was, his mind was as sharp as a razor, honed no doubt in countless battles of wits with half-wits, whom Lestrade had learned over the years never to underestimate.

'I understand there is a fund for survivors of the Light Brigade,' Lestrade changed tack.

'Indeed there is. I have the honour to be in charge of it.'

'How much money are we talking about?'

'I don't believe I have to tell you that, Chief Inspector.'

'No, sir, you don't. But please believe me when I say it may be fundamental to my enquiries. That only with that information may I prevent more deaths.'

Crosse ruminated for a while, then crossed to a safe tucked in a corner. He pulled out a sheaf of papers and riffled through them.

'At the last count, two hundred and sixteen pounds, sixteen shillings and fourpence,' he said. Hardly a fortune, thought Lestrade. Another wall reared up as he realised financial gain as a motive fluttered out of the window. Surgeon Crosse's pension alone would be worth more than that. Still, he had better leave no stone unturned.

'And where does the money come from?' he asked.

'Oh, various sources. Bequests. Donations from various individuals, ex-officers, mostly. It doesn't go far, I'm afraid. Perhaps one day a philanthropist will come along and really provide for these men. I feel sorry for them. However,' he grew stern, 'there are people who are prepared to go to extraordinary lengths to be deemed eligible for a share.'

'Indeed?' said Lestrade, sniffing a suspect.

'Unprofessional though it is, I shall name names. Robert Davies, formerly sergeant, Eleventh Hussars, now honorary lieutenant-colonel, has had the bare-faced effrontery to ask for a share. I ask you, lieutenant-colonel! The man of course was promoted officer without purchase – no tone at all!'

'Do you remember a soldier in the Eleventh named Hope?'

'Why, yes I do. Epileptic. Interesting condition. Always falling asleep all over the place. Why?'

'He remembers you,' answered Lestrade.

'That's nice.'

'Have you heard the phrase "golden dawn"?' Lestrade tried another new tack.

Crosse looked levelly at Lestrade. 'Yes, Chief Inspector, I have.'

'What does it mean?' Lestrade sensed the electricity in the air.

'I'm not sure,' Crosse said. 'A former patient of mine was obsessed with it.'

'Go on,' said Lestrade.

'Come with me,' said Crosse and led the inspector out of the double windows into a quiet courtyard overhung with ivy and privet. The dew was still on the grass and as they walked beneath an archway, they emerged into a small graveyard. Crosse pointed out a grave, complete with gleaming marble headstone. It read 'In loving memory of Donald Crowley, Surgeon, 11th Hussars 1820–1893'.

'This was the patient to whom I was referring,' said Crosse.

'Did he serve in the Crimea?' asked Lestrade.

'Oh yes. There were five of us. And Gloag, the vet.'

'May I have the names of the others?' Lestrade whipped out his trusty notepad.

'Er . . . oh, God . . . Wilkin. Henry Wilkin.' Lestrade knew he was dead. 'Malcolm Ancell. He died at Kadiköy in 'fifty-five.'

Lestrade wrote the name anyway.

'Ormsby Miller. Funnily enough, I read about him only the other day. He's high sheriff for Galway now.'

Crosse tapped with his rattan cane on the headstone.

'And poor old Crowley here.'

'You said he was a patient of yours . . . .'

'Yes, on and off for nearly twenty years. More or less since I've been here.'

'Did he . . . er . . . live in?'

'Towards the end, yes. He was . . . not fit to be by himself.'

'And the golden dawn?'

'It was some sort of organisation, I think. He always spoke of it in awe, but never in detail. I don't hold with this hypnosis nonsense, Chief Inspector. My patients only tell me what they want to tell me.'

'An organisation,' mused Lestrade. He had sensed conspiracy all along. Every since he had been rattling across Norfolk with Bradstreet after the Bentley investigation. The pieces of the jigsaw were starting to fit.

'The odd thing about Crowley,' Crosse went on, 'was that he rode the Charge of the Light Brigade. So did Wilkin, mind. But *he* longed for action. Wrong temperament for a doctor, really. I never took Crowley for that type, but still. He was captured by the Russians. We thought he was dead. Then, oh, years later, he turned up in England. That would be about eighteen-seventy. He'd lost his memory. With care and the love of a good woman we nursed him back to health.'

'Why is he buried here?'

'This was the nearest he had to a home recently. His wife died some years ago.'

'We were speaking of Henry Hope earlier,' said Lestrade. 'He died last month. I was with him. He said two things I couldn't understand. "Kill" and "Cro . . ." I took "Kill" to mean John Kilvert, also of the Eleventh. And "Cro . . ." I took to be you, but what if I was wrong? What if Hope was referring to Crowley? And why should he want to kill him?'

Crosse's mood changed suddenly. 'Chief Inspector, I have given you all the help I can. As you saw earlier, I have patients to treat. Go through that door. It will take you to the street. Goodbye.'

'One more thing.' Lestrade stopped him. 'The names you mentioned, your fellow surgeons of the Eleventh. I recognised all those names. Except one. Why should someone have removed Crowley's name from the muster-roll?'

'I really couldn't say, Chief Inspector,' and he vanished through the archway.

Lestrade looked down at the grave. He crouched, sifting the marble chippings with his hand. For a while he ruminated on the transient nature of man. Then he opened the door and walked into the street.

Except that it wasn't the street. Instead, he found himself standing in a long dark corridor. After the sun in the courtyard, the darkness was total. He must have taken the wrong door. He turned, but the door was shut tight. He rattled the lock. It did not give. He heard something behind him. A rasping sigh. He was not alone. He turned to face the darkness, feeling the lock in the small of his back. As his eyes accustomed themselves to the dark, he made out figures, rising up from benches on both sides of the corridor. He heard the rattle and slither of chains.

'Who's there?' he called.

A mocking laugh answered him. Then another.

'Nobody here,' a hollow voice said. 'Nobody at all.' He felt hard steel jam into his throat and a powerful force spun him round and down. He was on his knees facing the door, a steel chain round his neck.

A ragged figure with mad, staring eyes appeared before him, giggling hysterically. In the darkness, Lestrade saw his predicament. There were five figures, perhaps six, with enough chain between them to armour all the ironclads in the Navy. The pressure on Lestrade's throat grew greater and in a moment of inspiration – or was it panic? – he fought his way upright and gasped out the opening words of a ditty which might have some effect on these lunatics.

'We're the soldiers of the Queen, my lads . . .'

And one by one, they took up the chorus. A mumble at first, but Lestrade stood to attention, his hands pinned to his sides, unable to reach for his trusty brass knuckles, singing for all he was worth. It wasn't exactly Marie Lloyd; after all, Lestrade's voice had never been trained and he did have iron links wrapped around his throat. The mumble rose to a crescendo and one by one the sad ex-soldiers, stirred by their memories, came to attention and the grip relaxed on his neck.

They were still singing and he was by no means sure how many verses there were to go before they became bored and returned to their previous amusement. As it was, he was already at the 'la, la, la' stage. So he bolted forward, the chain bruising his neck as he lunged and threw himself bodily at the door. It gave under his weight and he rolled into the sunshine. Behind him he was aware of a whip cracking and cries of 'Get back'. By the time he had knelt upright, the door was back in place and all trace of his would-be attackers was gone. Suddenly, he was aware of a pair of blue uniform trousers inches from his head, above a pair of large, black hobnailed boots. He didn't really have to look up to know he was in the presence of a constable of the Metropolitan Police. The voice confirmed it.

Balaclava Revisited

They detained Lestrade for an hour or two at Bow Street where he gave his name as Chief Inspector Abberline. 'I'm sorry, sir,' the constable had said, as though it were quite permissible for chief inspectors of the Yard to be found, bruised and with a dislocated shoulder, on Chelsea pavements. 'I didn't recognise you.'

I'm not surprised, thought Lestrade; but thank God for the lack of observation of the copper on his beat. He had spent a further couple of hours being generally made to feel a lot less comfortable by a doctor and nurses at St Thomas's Hospital. The doctor, it is true, found Lestrade's injuries a trifle inconsistent with being run over by a dray, which was the injured man's story. But then Lestrade reasoned, he had to keep his stories to police and medical authorities the same or awkward questions might be asked. In any case, who would have believed him had he said he had narrowly escaped a beating in a dark corridor full of homicidal lunatics and had damaged himself in a bid to escape? No, the runaway dray it had to be.

'Good God, sir, you look terrible,' was Ben Beeson's comment as Lestrade walked stiffly over his portal. 'How's the other fella?'

'Chained to a wall in Chelsea,' Lestrade croaked, edging to a chair. 'How I got to Croydon, I shall never know.'

'What happened?'

And the whole story came out.

Beeson sat motionless, with his hands clasped around a mug of steaming tea. Lestrade's hands did likewise around his.

'So you've got him,' said Beeson. 'You've avenged Joe Towers.'

'Not yet,' said Lestrade. 'Surgeon Crosse is still at large. Anyway, I don't think it's quite as simple as that.'

'I don't follow you, sir.'

'Whatever the golden dawn is, Beastie, it's made up of more than one man. John Kilvert, Bram Stoker, John Crosse, they all spoke of it as being something evil. Something. Not someone. Actually, John Kilvert didn't talk about it at all, but he *was* a frightened man. The golden dawn isn't just Crowley. Besides, when Joe died, Crowley had been in his grave a week. I checked. What do you remember about him, this Crowley?'

'Not much. He joined the regiment late. We were already at Balaclava, I seem to remember. He kept to hisself, mostly. Then he rode the Charge and didn't answer the roll-call.'

'Crosse thought it odd that he should have ridden in the Charge at all. Why?'

'Well, medical men usually keep to the rear in action, sir, waiting to pick up the pieces afterwards, so to speak. But Surgeon Wilkin rode the Charge. No reason why Crowley shouldn't. Good God!'

'What's the matter?' asked Lestrade.

'Oh, it's nothing probably. Only I've just remembered it. You bringing up Crowley again after all these years. It was the morning of the Charge. I was sitting my horse with old John Buckton. He was in F Troop, come to think of it. Strange you didn't mention him on your list.'

'Somebody got to that list, Beastie. Crowley's name wasn't on it either.'

'Well, anyway, John was going to tell me somethin' about Crowley. Somethin' I'd never have believed, 'e said.'

'What?' Lestrade threatened to dislocate his shoulder all over again.

'I dunno.'

Lestrade flopped back in the chair.

'That's when the galloper came with the orders and we all had to shift.'

'This Buckton. Is he still alive?'

'I dunno. I last saw him at the Annual Dinner three years ago.'

'Will he be at this one, do you think?'

'It's possible. I haven't been since 'ninety.'

'You said you could get me in,' said Lestrade.

The ex-sergeant's face fell. 'I may have been a little hasty there, sir. The dinner is for members of the Light Brigade only.'

Lestrade fell silent. Painfully, he got to his feet and paced the kitchen. The sight of his arm in its sling in the kitchen mirror made him turn.

'Beastie, do you think I resemble, in the remotest sense, Joe Towers?'

Beeson got up and walked over to him. Lestrade saw the old copper's disbelieving face in the mirror.

'Not even in the remotest sense, sir,' he said.

'Come on, Beastie. In a bad light, old men's eyes. Most of them won't have seen him for years, will they?'

'No, I suppose not,' Beeson said. 'In fact, Joe hadn't been to a Dinner since the first, back in 'seventy-five. But you're . . .'

'Yes, I know. Thirty years younger! But with some of this,' he held up a greasy stick, 'I might just get away with it.'

'What's that, sir?'

'A spot of five and nine, Beastie. Theatrical make-up. I used it as Rabbi Izzlebit. And when I was at the Lyceum recently, I liberated a little more. A man never knows when a little discreet make-up is going to come in handy.'

Beeson took the inspector's word for it.

'What's the date?' Lestrade asked.

'Er . . . the twenty-third, I think.'

'That gives us two days before the dinner.'

'That's right, sir. It's the day after tomorrow.'

'Right, Beastie, I've got to get there. To get in amongst your old mess mates of the Light Brigade. To talk to John Buckton, if he's there. The answer's there somewhere, damn it. Mind if I get my head down until then, for old times' sake?'

'Lord love you, sir. You only got into all this on my

account. I owe you that at least.'

Lestrade settled into the chair again, nursing his aching arm. 'Beastie, have a butcher's out of that window, will you? I've had the strangest feeling since I left the Lyceum that I've been followed.'

'Perhaps they want their make-up back,' grunted the ex-copper, flicking aside the nets. 'Wait a minute.' Lestrade struggled upright. 'There is somebody there. Youngish bloke, dark hair, wearing a grey overcoat. . . .'

By the time Lestrade got to the window the figure had vanished.

'Shall I go after him, sir?'

'No, Beastie. Let him go. Whoever it was, I daresay we'll see him again.'

'You're going to the dinner, sir?' Charlo's consumptive croak was worse than ever. 'Is that wise?'

'Good God, man.' Lestrade was past all that. 'There comes a time when wisdom follows other things. Like survival. There's a maniac trying to kill what's left of F Troop, Sergeant.'

'And he's trying to kill you, sir. The breakfast at the Grand? The Chelsea incident? I've got to admit, sir. I wish you'd give it up.'

'But we're so close, Hector. After all these months, we're nearly there. Would you have me stop now?'

Charlo leaned back in his chair. 'I can't help any more, Inspector. My doctor says I must rest. Have a long break. I've seen Frost. He's given me a month's leave.' He extended a hand.

Lestrade rose painfully and took it.

'Hector,' he said. 'You've risked a lot for me. I want you to know – whatever happens – I appreciate it.'

October 25th, a Wednesday, dawned hard and cold.

'What were you doing thirty-nine years ago this morning, Beastie?' Lestrade asked.

Beeson fell silent for a moment, doing some mental arithmetic. Only his frown, his silently moving lips and his wildly twitching fingers bore witness to the exertion it was causing. He smiled at the end of his calculations. 'Shivering,' he said. 'We'd stood to since five o'clock. Saddled and waiting. My fingers were so numb I could barely work the leather. I remember we had no breakfast. Some of the officers had boiled eggs. We didn't even get our rum ration that day. Wait a minute,' and he dashed into another room. Back he came with an old uniform of the 11th Hussars, the colours still bright, the yellow cord still intact on the jacket and the brass buttons shining.

'I gave mine up when I transferred to the lancers,' he said. 'This was Joe's. I don't think he'd mind if you wore it tonight. Not if it helps get his killer, anyhow.'

'Thanks, Ben.' Lestrade smiled.

'Chances are you'll get into it. Oh, and this,' and he pulled out a small box. 'Joe always kept it polished. As I have kept mine,' and he flicked the lid to show a silver medal with a pale blue ribbon and on it the clasps for Sebastopol, Inkerman and Balaclava.

So Lestrade began another subterfuge. In the past weeks he had been Athelney Jones, Chief Inspector Abberline, the Rabbi Izzlebit. He was fast forgetting his real name. And now he was Joseph Towers, deceased, former private, 11th Prince Albert's Own Hussars.

The two men walked slowly into St James's Restaurant a little after seven o'clock. Beeson looked as smart as his police pension would allow in formal grey suit and bowler hat, his Crimean medal sported proudly on his lapel. Lestrade was wearing the braided jacket and crimson overalls of Joe Towers. They were just a *little* snug. His hair, beneath the crimson forage cap, had been clipped short on top and greyed with powder and greasepaint. Lestrade had etched in wrinkles and lines where he could, ignoring Beeson's constant clicks of the tongue and shakings of the head. He would have to do.

The foyer was already full of old men getting plastered. What was still a sacred trust to many of them was also an excuse for a knees-up, although it was very debatable how far up any of these knees would come. Lestrade counted twenty-five, including Beeson. He was one of five in uniform, although he couldn't help noticing that the others had been let out considerably here and there to accommodate advancing years and advancing girths. And patched here and there with the passage of time. Only medals and eyes were bright. And hearts were great.

He was relieved there was nobody else in the 11th uniform. If his limited knowledge served him correctly, one was from the 17th Lancers, two more from the 4th Light Dragoons as they then were and one from the 8th Hussars. It suddenly dawned on him, however, that had any of his co-banqueteers been in his 'old' regimentals Lestrade would have been able to avoid them so as to avert any awkward questions about his miraculous change in appearance. As it was, any one of the bowler- or top-hatted gentlemen might suddenly say 'Who the hell are you?'

'Who the hell are you?' The bombshell burst behind him. He opened his mouth to attempt an answer.

'Ben Beeson, Eleventh Hussars,' his companion answered.

'Of course,' beamed the other man. 'I didn't recognise you. You've put on some weight. Job Allwood, Thirteenth Lights.'

'How are you?' Beeson returned the handshake. 'Er . . . you remember Joe Towers?'

'Yes, of course,' beamed Allwood. 'Good to see you again, Joe. My God, can you still get into your old uniform? The years have been kind.'

Let's hope they go on being so, thought Lestrade.

'Well, well.' Beeson moved on like a shield before the doubly vulnerable Lestrade. 'Jim Glanister. How are you Jim?'

'Not bad,' slurped the other, the left corner of his lip dragging to reveal a row of brown, uneven teeth. 'I can't complain.'

'Remember Joe Towers, F Troop?'

'Oh, yes.' Glanister was having serious salivary problems as he shook Lestrade's hand. 'That's funny, I remembered you being taller.'

'I haven't been well,' ventured Lestrade.

'You don't look well, either,' another man chipped in.

Lestrade turned to face John Kilvert, socially superior as always in his astrakhan collar. Kilvert's smile vanished.

'Haven't we met recently . . . ?' he said. Lestrade glanced at Beeson for support. None was forthcoming.

'Not since the Crimea,' said Lestrade, hoping he had said the right thing.

'Oh,' was Kilvert's limp and dissatisfied rejoinder. And the gong sounded to summon them to dinner. It was a fine spread. Roast goose with all the trimmings. Unfortunately, Lestrade found himself next to Glanister and spent most of the meal watching items of food miss the old man's mouth altogether, slithering down his left arm.

'Pistol ball at point-blank range,' Beeson whispered in Lestrade's other ear, as though to explain Glanister's problems.

'Time heals all wounds,' Glanister said at some point during the conversation. Not very well, thought Lestrade, flicking cream off his sleeve.

'Gentlemen, pray silence for the regimental tunes,' a major-domo barked from a corner. The good-natured banter stopped as one by one the regiments' marches played. As the band struck up, knots of men stood here and there at the sound of their own regiment's calls. Beeson tugged Lestrade to his feet at the commencement of 'Coburg', the slow march of the 11th. Lestrade hoped his delayed reaction was explained by his age and his recent fall.

Across the room from them, away from the 11th men, a figure stood alone while Coburg played. He had arrived late and was not in time to take his place alongside his old messmates.

'John Buckton,' hissed Beeson from the corner of his mouth, nodding in his direction. Something fell from Glanister's mouth too, but Lestrade didn't care to notice what.

When the Tunes of Glory were done and the handkerchieves put away for another year, the major-domo rose again.

'Gentlemen, pray silence for His Excellency the

Quartermaster-General, Sir Evelyn Wood, VC, GCB.'

'And bar!' shouted Sir Evelyn, one of the halest men there, though as old as any of them. 'Which way is it?' The veterans broke into cheers and applause. 'Gentlemen, I will not keep you long. I am here tonight as your guest of honour. Some of you may think me a fraud.' Cries of 'No,' 'Shame,' and 'Resign.' Wood held up his hand. 'But I am here for two reasons. I had the distinction many years ago of sharing quarters in the Sepoy Mutiny with a fine and gallant gentleman, now, alas, deceased, Colonel Morris of the Seventeenth Lancers.' Cheers from the men of the 17th. 'And I am proud to say that I was greatly honoured to serve with him and some of you in that fine regiment. Shortly after the Crimea, I joined the Thirteenth Light Dragoons' – the veterans of that regiment whistled and stamped – 'and no more loyal and impressive body of men could be found anywhere.' Applause.

Get on with it, thought Lestrade. If we are going to have Sir Evelyn's life story, I'll never get across to Buckton.

'Some thirty-nine years ago tonight, gentlemen, I was a midshipman in the Royal Navy. And on my ship I heard of what was described as "a short, sharp, cavalry action".' Guffaws and poundings on the table. Beeson was working things out on his fingers again. 'I think in all my years of service I have never heard of an engagement described with such woeful inadequacy.' More poundings. 'Gentlemen, I can only misquote the late Poet Laureate, Lord Alfred Tennyson, and say to you, men of the Light Brigade, "When can your glory fade?"'

The rapturous applause from so small a group of men promised to bring the chandeliers down. Even Lestrade found himself joining in in full measure, physically painful though it was to him. Toasts to Her Majesty, to Sir Evelyn, to the commanders of the various regiments at Balaclava, all now dead, followed.

Then the major-domo announced 'Coffee and brandy, gentlemen, by courtesy of Sir Evelyn Wood.' Poundings on the tables greeted this not altogether unexpected privilege. Cigars appeared from leather cases. Kilvert, not for the first

time that evening, studied Lestrade closely through wreaths
of smoke. Lestrade himself was about to make a move to
contact Buckton, when there was a resounding crash in the
passageway leading to the banqueting room. A white-coated
waiter burst in, rushing in Buckton's direction. 'Don't drink
the coffee!' he screamed as the man had the cup poised at his
lips. Even as he reached Buckton, a shot rang out and a scarlet
gash appeared in the centre of the waiter's back. In the
seconds of panic that followed, a figure stood in the shadows,
aiming his pistol first at Buckton, who ducked under the
table, then at the knot of 11th men around Lestrade. The first
bullet whistled past Beeson's head. A second shattered the
coffee cup between Lestrade and Glanister. The latter
crumpled, though unhit, clutching his jaw and moaning,
'Not again!'

Lestrade wasn't waiting for the next shot. Needs must
when the devil drives and he stood up, hurling over the table.
He and Beeson clambered over it as the others crouched,
bewildered and confused, in the smoke.

'Our friend isn't much of a shot, thank God,' said Lestrade.
He reached the fallen waiter and turned him over. 'Good
God,' he said, recognising under the slicked-down hair the
mournful, haunted face of the Bounder, with whom he had
absconded from Openshaw Workhouse, an eternity ago.
'He's still alive, Beeson. Look after him.'

'I'm coming with you, sir.' All pretence at his being Joe
Towers had gone.

'No, no. This one's mine,' and Lestrade dashed for the
door. 'Sir Evelyn, I wonder if I might use your sword for a
moment?'

The general, who had not moved from his seat during all
the shooting now stood up and drew the ivory-hilted weapon
from its scabbard. 'My dear fellow, be my guest,' and called
after him, 'Remember the "Rear Protect", private,' as
Lestrade disappeared down the darkened corridor.

'Was it the Russians?' asked Glanister, emerging from the
tablecloth. Someone patted him calmingly on the head.

Lestrade dashed, as fast as his bruises would permit, past

the milling waiters and servants, through the kitchen swarming with hysterical cooks.

'That way,' somebody shouted at him, pointing to the
open back door.

'Who was it?' he yelled.

'One of the waiters,' came the reply. You can't get decent
staff these days, thought Lestrade. But that was what he
wanted to know. He had not seen the figure who fired the
shots at all closely. Now he knew his target wore a white
jacket and shouldn't be difficult to see in the dark. He edged
into the yard. Empty, save for a couple of dogs tethered and
barking. Behind him, the noise and lights died away. He was
aware of men coming out of the doors and windows being
opened overhead. But no one followed him.

He took stock, as he moved, of his situation. He was
carrying a general officer's mameluke sabre. A beautiful,
ornate weapon, but it gave no protection for the hand. In a
fight, he would have reach, but his adversary, whoever he
was, had a gun. All right, he was no great shot, but he could
get luckier. And Lestrade couldn't move as he usually could.
He turned into an alleyway. Ahead, a brick wall, the
intangible counterpart of which had risen before him so often
in this case. He stood still, panting with the effort of having
run this far. No other sound, except somewhere a distant
train whistle and the snort of a hackney horse.

He slithered round the corner into a second yard. It had
been raining and the cobbles glistened wet in the green
gaslight. A white jacket lay at his feet. The would-be
murderer's disguise had gone, but it didn't matter. Lestrade
knew where to find his man, if he had left the yard. He
advanced slowly, sword arm extended. To each side were
piles of timber and sacking. Good hiding places for a
desperate man. His lips were dry. He licked them, tugging
open the Hussar jacket for a bit more air, a bit more freedom
of movement. His breath was visible on the air before him.
And then he heard it. A tapping on the cobbles. Footsteps. He
threw himself against the wall, trying to melt into the
shadows.

A thick-set man in a Donegal and bowler stood squarely in the light from the gaslamp. He had a revolver gripped firmly in his right hand, raised at shoulder height.

'I know you're there, Lestrade,' the killer spoke. 'Come out, come out, wherever you are.'

Silence.

'I'm not a patient man.'

Lestrade lurched forward from the wall, some yards away from the man with the gun.

'Hello, Gregson,' he said.

The Head of the Special Irish Branch brought his pistol hand down on his left wrist to steady the gun for the recoil.

'So, it was you all along?' said Lestrade.

'Me? You mean that bungled shooting tonight? You're upsetting me, Sholto. You know I wouldn't miss.'

'The murders, then. The poisonings.'

'My God, you really haven't a clue, have you? I took you for a better policeman than that.'

He clicked back the hammer. Once. Twice.

'I tried to make it easy for you. That trumped-up charge of mine about attacking the Kaiser. But you went on, didn't you? Worrying it. Teasing it. You wouldn't leave it alone. Well, you've only yourself to blame, Lestrade. For what follows. Only yourself to blame.'

For a long second, Lestrade stood there, expecting Bandicoot's cased pistols to blast out or the Abo's silent arrows to hiss through the air. In the event, all he heard was the roar of Gregson's revolver. Too far away to reach his man, he spun round, attempting God Knows What. Perhaps just to be spared the bullet in his face. Perhaps it mattered how you died. As he turned, the sword came up behind his right shoulder, roughly in the position of 'Rear Protect' and the bullet clanged off the blade and ricochetted across the cobbles.

Lestrade continued his turn as Gregson recocked the weapon, cursing his luck, and threw the general's sword for all he was worth. The tip sliced deep into Gregson's stomach and the second shot went wide. In disbelief, Tobias Gregson staggered backwards, the gun gone from his grasp, Wood's blade gleaming from his stomach in the lamplight, blood trickling over his fingers. He looked uncomprehendingly at Lestrade, reached out as if to drag him to Hell with him and pitched forward, driving the blade right through his body, so that the crimson tip protruded steaming through the folds of his Donegal. Lestrade eased himself down on one knee, and checked his pulse. Weakening. Gone. Police whistles were sounding from nowhere. He kicked Gregson's body over and wrenched out the sword, wiping the blade clean on his coat. Then he stumbled back to the restaurant.

Beeson was cradling the fallen waiter in his arms. As Lestrade arrived, he looked up and shook his head. Lestrade took the Bounder's face in his hands. 'Can you hear me?' he asked.

The Bounder opened his eyes and flickered into liveliness. 'Did you . . . get him?'

'Who?' asked Lestrade.

'Oliver.'

'No, I got Tobias Gregson.' Beeson's eyes nearly popped out of his head. Had Lestrade gone mad?

'Oliver . . . Oliver's the one you want. You must get him,' and he began to cough up blood.

'I will. I think I know where he is. Listen, you haven't got long.' There was no time for niceties. 'Who are you?'

'Jacob Crowley,' the Bounder/waiter answered. 'I wrote to you. Twice. Three times. I can't remember. Why didn't you answer my letters or at least *do* something?'

'I received no letters. Beastie, get these men away from here.' Lestrade waved an arm in the direction of the stunned bystanders.

'Come along now.' Beeson the old copper was in charge again. 'There's nothin' to see. Move along, now. Move along.'

'And Donald Crowley . . . ?' Lestrade turned to the Bounder again.

'My father. Oliver is my brother. They're both mad, Inspector. Quite mad,' and he coughed again.

'Beeson, water,' snapped Lestrade.

The Bounder waved it aside. 'I've got to tell you. Got to explain,' he mumbled.

'Why the murders?' Lestrade tried to simplify things for the dying man. 'The men of F Troop. Why?'

'My father joined a religious sect called the Order of the Golden Dawn when he was a . . . young man.' His speech was slurring now. Lestrade knew he would lose him soon. 'They are Satanists, Inspector. They worship the Devil,' and the pain took him again. He writhed, then lay still. Lestrade mopped his sweating forehead until he recovered. 'The night before Balaclava, F Troop were on patrol. A few of them got separated from the rest and in the hills above Kadiköy they found my father carrying out his rites.'

'Rites?' Lestrade checked he had not misheard.

'Sacrifice, Inspector. Human sacrifice. My father was a neophyte then. He . . . had to attain a higher level within the Order. The only way was to . . . kill and devour a human being.'

Lestrade sat upright. In all his seventeen years on the Force he had heard of nothing like that.

'He was . . . in the act of eating a Turkish boy when some of F Troop found him. He did his best to get himself killed. The . . . next day . . . he rode the Charge . . . expecting a bullet or a cannon ball to end it all. He reached the guns. He was taken prisoner by the Russians. . . . His life for the next sixteen years is a closed book to me. What he did in Russia, how he lived, I cannot imagine. But . . . the Golden Dawn is an international sect, Inspector. The Russian Golden Dawn may have found him, rescued him from the threat of suicide.'

'So, that's why he rode the Charge,' Lestrade said.

The Bounder nodded. 'When he came back to England, and I never knew why he came back, he feigned . . . loss of memory. But my brother Oliver was brought up in the foul traditions of the Golden Dawn. And he is as mad as Father.'

'Go on, if you can,' said Lestrade.

It was becoming increasingly difficult. 'Who can understand a madman?' the Bounder asked. 'Father had remembered the names and faces of those men who had seen him that dreadful night before Balaclava. Perhaps he knew he was dying. Perhaps the Golden Dawn demanded it. Anyway, he killed the first one. William Lamb.'

'Lamb?' Lestrade broke in. 'But he was killed by an animal. A Tasmanian wolf.'

The Bounder managed a chuckle. 'Yes, I read the newspaper reports at the time,' he said. 'I'm sorry, Inspector. That poor dumb beast may have killed sheep, but it did not kill a man. Father was carrying out his murder in the old ritualistic way.'

'He was trying to eat Lamb?' Lestrade asked, incredulous.

The Bounder nodded. 'And then he died. Merciful heaven released him.'

Lestrade thought quickly. The hairs from the thylacine which he found on the body must have got there *after* Lamb died. The smell of blood would certainly have attracted it.

'And the poisonings?'

'Oliver. He too trained as a doctor. For some years he served with the Army Medical Corps. He knew a great deal about poisons . . . .'

'And had access to them,' Lestrade added.

The Bounder coughed his agreement.

'And when we met at Openshaw?' prompted Lestrade.

'I was trying to stop him. All along, I've been . . . one step behind Oliver, one step ahead of you. He was the medical officer who was the locum before you arrived. He used the name . . . Corfield, Inspector. A pun. A taunting, arrogant pun. The Latin for the crow family is *corvus*. And another name for ley is field. Corfield and Crowley were one and the same. He gave the poisoned tobacco to Mrs Lawrenson.'

'And it's you who has been following me since the Lyceum?'

'And before. I should . . . have confided in you earlier, Inspector, but . . . I was trying to save Oliver from himself. From his insane desire to carry out Father's wishes; and all the time I thought you had received my letters telling you all this.' He tensed, and tremors shook his whole body. 'Lestrade,' he clutched convulsively at the policeman's sleeve, 'stop him. And look after cousin Aleister. I'm afraid he's going the same way.'

'I will, and we'll watch out for cousin Aleister.'

And the Bounder died in Lestrade's arms.

'Beastie.' Lestrade folded the man's arms across his chest and closed his lids. 'The police will be here any minute. Inspector Gregson's body is a few yards from here. Tell them what you know. And tell them that I shall be calling in to the Yard as soon as I can. General, thank you for your sword.'

And he handed it back.

'Glad it was of service, Private ... er ... Inspector,' said Wood.

'Sir,' Beeson joined Lestrade, 'I wish you'd let me come with you.'

'No, Beastie. There's only room for one in that corridor.'

'I thought you might say that, sir, so,' and he produced an obsolete pistol, Lancer pattern, 1842. 'This belonged to George Loy Smith,' he said. 'The old bastard was hard enough on F Troop while he was alive. Let him strike a blow for them now he's dead.'

Lestrade took the weapon.

'And remember,' said Beeson, 'that's cap and ball. You've got one shot in the breech already. Miss with that and you're a dead man.'

'This is a devil of a time to call, Bradstreet.' Nimrod Frost was less than chipper. 'God, man, it's the early hours.' He looked like Wee Willie Winkie, well, Willie Winkie anyway, standing in his hall in nightshirt and cap, holding aloft a candle. 'Go to bed, Richards. It's only one of my officers with a bad sense of timing. You're out of breath, man,' he rounded on Bradstreet, 'and you know I don't like calls at home at any time. Go to bed, Wilhelmina,' he roared to the apparition on the stairs. 'There's nothing wrong.' He ushered Bradstreet into the study. 'Or is there?'

'It's Inspector Gregson, sir. He's dead.'

'Good God.' Frost sat down heavily on the chesterfield.

'But that's not the worse of it. Lestrade killed him.'

'Lestrade?' Frost was on his feet again.

'I knew the man was suspended from duty, sir, but frankly ...'

'Yes?'

'Well, I worked with him, sir. Frankly, I thought Inspector

Gregson was overhasty. . . . It's not my place to say, sir.'

Frost whirled round the furniture, brain and fingers fidgeting wildly. He stopped before Bradstreet's tie-knot.

'What's your view of conspiracies, Bradstreet?'

'Life is one big conspiracy in the Special Branch, sir.'

'Yes.' Frost scrutinised him closely. 'Yes, I suppose it is. You were Gregson's right-hand man, weren't you?'

'I worked with him, sir, yes.' Bradstreet was beginning to smell a rat. It was not every day that inspectors of the Yard tried to kill each other.

'Well, get back to the scene of the crime, Bradstreet. I'm going to the Yard. I'll want a full report tomorrow. Er . . . later this morning.'

Bradstreet departed. Frost saw him to the door and summoned a figure from the shadows.

'Follow him, Constable. I want to know exactly where he goes.'

Lestrade took a hansom in the street, dodging the coppers running to the scene of Gregson's death and swarming into St James's Restaurant. He'd given the cabbie strict instructions and with cries of 'I'll lose me licence for sure,' he hurtled through the makeshift cordon of policemen who, as Lestrade knew they would, broke at the last minute to avoid impact.

The Royal Hospital was in darkness and silent. The inmates were in their beds now. Except one. Lestrade crossed the frontage, past the Chilianwalla Memorial, past the silent cannon, mouths gaping to the night sky. His hand rested on the pistol butt, jutting awkwardly from his barrelsash. The front door was locked. Never mind, always worth a try. He circled the main block, trying first one door, then another. At last one gave under his weight and he was inside. A faint light flickered on the wall at the far side of a large hall. He recognised this. He had been taken this way on his last visit. For a man in cavalry boots, he moved like a cat. But when he began to count his lives, he decided to leave that analogy alone.

Up the twisting staircase, past the dormitories of snoring soldiers. The sky, blue against the blackness of the window-frames, lit his movements. Now and then the moon scudded into view, to vanish again in her shyness. Perhaps there were lovers out there somewhere, arm in arm and heart in heart, Lestrade thought. Then, reaching for the studded door, he remembered, and dashed back to the window. It wasn't a *full* moon, was it?

The padded door opened noiselessly. There was no one at this time of night to work the grille. Across another moonlit hall, below the silent standards. Past Crosse's door.

Lestrade stopped. There was a light in his office. Faint. An oil lamp, he guessed, trying to remember whether there was one on the desk or not. He cocked the pistol. Well, Sergeant-Major Loy Smith, let's hope you kept your gun in good order. And let's hope Beastie has since. And Lestrade crashed through the door, flinging it wide on its hinges. Crosse leapt upright behind the desk, rattan cane poised in his hand.

'Put it down, Doctor.' Lestrade's voice was firm, the pistol aimed at the old man's head. 'Or I'll kill you where you stand.'

'Abberline.' Crosse threw the cane onto the desk. 'I hoped it might be you.'

'Not Abberline, Doctor. Lestrade. Inspector Sholto Lestrade.' He tugged off the forage cap. He had all but forgotten it was still on his head.

'I . . . don't understand,' said Crosse.

'Never mind that. Where is he?'

'Who?'

'Doctor, I was nearly beaten to death by your maniacs, almost given poisoned coffee to drink, and shot at, all in the space of three days. I am not at my best at the moment. Now, once again and for the last time, where is Oliver Crowley?'

'Upstairs. Second door on the left. Lestrade, he's armed. . . .'

'And dangerous. Yes, I know that, Doctor.'

'Lestrade.' Crosse crumpled into his chair. 'Let me explain. I owe you that much at least. Don't worry, he's not going anywhere. He's waiting for you. Up there.'

'Quick then, man.'

'I panicked the other day. I have been working in this living hell for twenty years, Inspector. Twenty years of trying to give men back their sanity while somehow hanging onto mine. In that time, in all that lonely time, I made one mistake. I let a man escape. A dangerous man. Oliver Crowley. He was my patient too, like his father. I didn't tell you that. As a boy he seemed normal; oh, a little quiet, perhaps, a little solitary; not like Jacob, the younger brother. Oliver was born shortly after Donald had sailed for the Crimea. He wanted to go in for medicine and to join the army, just like his father. Well, why not? Perfectly laudable profession. But he began to take after his father in other ways. He joined the Golden Dawn – and as God is my judge I know no more about that. He became moody, unpredictable. The same curse that fell on his father also fell on him. I tried to persuade his mother, while she was alive, to talk him into coming here, as an in-patient. He wouldn't do that, but he did visit his father now and again, sometimes staying for days at a time. Occasionally, he would talk to me. It was working; we were getting somewhere. And then . . .'

'Then?'

'His father died. He became inconsolable. Irrational. He had to be admitted as an in-patient after all. But he said he had things to do. His father's work, he said. One night, he overpowered his orderly and fled.'

'And you did nothing?'

'If you mean did I report it? No. I paid the orderly to keep his mouth shut. Crowley had a private room. Few people saw him anyway. It was easy.'

'And the killings? Did you know about them?'

'No.' Crosse buried his head in his hands. 'God in heaven, no. But I couldn't find him. He had vanished without trace. I knew Jacob was looking, but it seemed hopeless. When you came, three days ago, pressing me about the Golden Dawn, I knew it was all over. Unless . . . unless I could silence you somehow. I didn't mean those inmates to kill you. Just rough you up a little. Frighten you . . . .' A pause. 'What happens now?'

'Now I'm going upstairs. Whether I come down or not

remains to be seen. Either way, Doctor, you can reckon on a well-earned retirement. Where you spend it depends on me, doesn't it?'

Crosse slumped head down on the desk, a broken man, as Lestrade turned for the stairs. The second door, Crosse had said, on the left. Lestrade steadied the pistol in his hand. He had no idea what lay behind that door, but he knew that if the room was in darkness, he would present a perfect target silhouetted against the faint light in the hallway. He could of course wait for daylight, but by that time Crowley could be down the drainpipe and away.

He dithered for an instant, then threw his less painful shoulder at the door. It swung open, crashed back, the noise simultaneous with two pistol shots. Plaster rained down on his head. The room was in darkness as he kicked the door shut again. Crowley's eyes were more acclimatised to the total blackness than his, but unless the man were totally blind, the angle of the shots which had hit the plaster meant he was on the floor. That was where Lestrade was too, face down behind a sofa. He still held the horse pistol, still cherished his single shot. He had to make it a good one.

'Hello, Inspector.' The voice was hollow, mocking, unreal. 'I wondered when it would come to this.'

'Give yourself up, Oliver. You haven't a chance.'

'Oh, but you're wrong, Inspector. You see, I haven't finished my holy mission yet. John Kilvert. John Buckton. When they're dead, all those my father cursed will be gone. The prophesy of the Golden Dawn will be fulfilled.'

'You know I can't let you do that, Oliver.' Lestrade was working his way on knees and elbows to the right of the sofa. Two more flashes and crashes. The wood from the sofa splintered in Lestrade's cheek. Either that was luck, or Crowley's aim was improving.

'I know exactly where you are, Inspector,' the mocking voice went on, 'and don't bother to count the shots. I have an arsenal with me here. And you have one bullet.'

The Devil, thought Lestrade. How did he know that?

'You have violated the Golden Dawn, Inspector.' Crowley's voice was rising. 'For that you must die.'

'Gregson's dead.' Lestrade tried to rattle Crowley, distract him just for long enough to squeeze off a shot.

'He knew the risks. As we all do. But the Power, Lestrade. It is worth daring all for the Power.'

Lestrade bobbed up, trying to bring his right arm with him. Crowley blasted again, once, and the bullet hit the wall an inch or so above the inspector's head.

'Gregson kept me informed about your enquiries and unwittingly poor Jacob did too, in stumbling so ineptly about all over the country. But the best informant of course was . . . Hector Charlo.' The voice was transformed at the mention of the name into an asthmatic rattle. There was a livid flash of light as Crowley lit a torch above his head. Lestrade fired widly, the ball lodging somewhere in the ceiling.

'Charlo,' the inspector repeated dumbly. Before him in the flickering flame light was the sergeant of the same name, sitting cross-legged on the floor, dangling with magician's robes and wearing the horns of a goat.

'Crowley,' the magician roared in reply. 'And you didn't have a clue, Lestrade, did you? As feeble, loyal Charlo tramped around with you, following when you thought he was flat on his back. You fed all the information I needed. You poor bastard.' Crowley's pistol was pointing at Lestrade's head.

The inspector tried desperately to keep the conversation going.

'So it was your ship at Cromer lighthouse?'

'Yes. That fisherman nearly did for me, there. Only he didn't get the name quite right. *Aurora Aurosus* – Latin for the Golden Dawn. If he'd remembered it correctly and if you'd checked it, you'd have solved this months ago.'

'Or you'd have killed me months ago?' Lestrade was scanning the room, trying to find something to use as a weapon. He still held Loy Smith's empty pistol in his hand, but knew he couldn't throw it faster than Crowley's bullet. Nor would he be as lucky again as he had been with Gregson.

'And that's why you wore the muffler at Ladybower? In case those labourers recognised you?'

'I'd been there the day before. But you know what these clods are, Lestrade. They wouldn't have recognised me again if I'd been wearing these robes in broad daylight. Yes, it was risky to smear those hedges. But I'd watched Hodges for days. It was likely he'd scratch himself on them at some point. It's a wonder no one else did.'

'What if someone else had?'

'Do you suppose the Golden Dawn cares for human life, Lestrade? Any life? Yours will come as cheap as the rest.' The flames crackled and spat on the pole gripped in Crowley's right hand.

'Clever of you to get into the workhouse like that.' Lestrade tried the old ploy of flattery, as he slowly uncoiled himself into a position to try something at least. 'But you made one mistake.'

'Not the disguise. Letitia Lawrenson was as unnoticing as the rest.'

'No, not the disguise. The name. Oh, Corfield is a clever enough pun. But you'd already used it, hadn't you? You see, I'd heard it before. I told you I had. Only I couldn't remember where. Now I do. When we first met, when you were unable to go with me to Cromer – unable because you had sailed there ahead of me and didn't want to risk being recognised – you sent me a doctor's note. It was forged, of course. Written by yourself, as a doctor. And you signed it Corfield.'

Crowley's eyes blazed. He laughed, deep, booming. 'Yes, that was stupid. But it doesn't really matter now, does it?'

Lestrade saw him cock the pistol.

'But to kill your own brother . . .' Lestrade blurted.

'Yes, poor Jacob. The silly meddling boy kept writing you letters. I, of course, as the devoted, efficient Charlo, kept intercepting them. It was all too easy. You see, poor Jacob did not know about my other existence at the Yard. And there are higher loyalties, Lestrade. I have many brothers in the Golden Dawn. But you got one thing wrong, Inspector, when you suspected way back that the solution might lie with the Dunn–Douglas ménage. You were wrong about the shape. It wasn't a triangle, Inspector, eternal or otherwise. It was . . . a pentangle.'

Crowley plunged the torch downwards to reveal for a split

second a five-pointed star marked on the floor with black powder. The star exploded into a sheet of livid flame, and in its centre Crowley rose up like a great beast, arms outstretched. The flames engulfed him, shattering the windows with the blast and Lestrade was somersaulted to the door. Desperately, he tried to reach Crowley, but the magician had gone, disintegrating in the terrible heat and dense acrid smoke.

Lestrade somehow found the door handle and fell out into the corridor. He reached the stairs as he heard the alarm bells ring and a terrible, half-human, half-beast – 'Ipsissimus.' Nothing more.

There were odder sights on that sunny October morning than an 11th Hussar in obsolete uniform, jacket open, overalls torn, face and hair scorched and blackened with fire, walking purposefully towards Scotland Yard, but one would have been hard put to it to find one.

But something nearly as odd was walking towards Lestrade as he neared the river.

'Lestrade – Good God, not another commissioner's fancy dress ball?'

Lestrade's heart sank. Of all the people to meet on one's way to twenty years in Pentonville – Dr John Watson, sometime of Baker Street.

'Good morning, Doctor. I really can't stop.'

'One moment, one moment, I must tell you this. I met a young chap called Friese-Greene the other day.'

'A refrigerator manufacturer?' asked Lestrade.

'No, no, a film maker. He's just taken out a patent on what he calls stereoscopic cinematography. It's rather like the wheel of wonder, only better.'

'Fascinating.' Lestrade passed on.

'But the best part is,' Watson continued, 'he says he can make moving pictures of one of my books . . . well, mine and Conan Doyle's. Can you imagine it? – Moving pictures of the great Sherlock Holmes himself!'

'Who in their right minds would pay money to witness such a spectacle?' sighed Lestrade. 'Or do you pay them?'

'Why, anyone would be delighted, delighted.'

By now quite a crowd had gathered around the oddly scorched soldier and the gesticulating general practitioner.

'And actors will be queueing up for the honour and privilege of portraying him on the cinematograph. Pennington. Irving, even.'

'Madam.' Lestrade buttonholed a curious lady with husband and child. 'May I ask, how old is your lovely boy?'

'He's thirteen months,' she answered in a clipped, unusual accent.

'My family and I are here on holiday,' said the father, 'from Johannesburg.'

'Here you are then, Watson. Someone with just the right mental skills to play the Great Detective.'

'That child?' said Watson disparagingly.

'Basil is a very bright baby.' His mother was on the defensive.

'Oh, er . . . of course. I had no intention of giving offence, Mrs . . . er . . .'

'Rathbone.'

Watson tipped his hat.

'You see, Lestrade . . .' but Lestrade had gone.

There was to be no pussy-footing around this time. No sneaking in the back way. Straight up the steps and into the front door of the Yard marched Lestrade.

'Morning, sir,' Sergeant Dixon greeted him, as though it were perfectly natural for a suspended inspector, wanted for the murder of another inspector, and for attacking a Foreign Important Dignitary, to saunter in to work done up like a nigger minstrel.

'Got you . . . sir,' said Dew, leaping forward with one hand on Lestrade's collar, the other on his wrist.

'Not now, constable,' Nimrod Frost bellowed from the cloakroom door. 'Got it at last, have you, Dew, your great collar? Yes, I can see the book title now – *I Caught Lestrade*. Except he hasn't done anything. Now be a good chap and put the inspector down, there's a good lad.'

'Sorry, Walter,' grinned Lestrade. 'Better luck next time, eh?'

'Yes, sir . . . er . . . no hard feelings, sir?'

'A cup of tea, Dew. I'll be down for it later.'

'Yes, sir,' and the crestfallen constable scuttled off to do what he did best.

'I'm glad you've lost some weight, Lestrade,' said Frost 'or I doubt we'd both get in this lift.'

They travelled in silence to the first floor.

'There's some sorting out to be done, Inspector. But first, there are two gentlemen who'd like a word with you.'

Frost kicked open his office door to reveal a tall, dandyfied gentleman with a gardenia in his buttonhole.

'Chief Inspector Abberline.' Lestrade grinned through gritted teeth. The man with him, shorter, stouter, wearing the black patrol jacket of the River Police.

'Athelney Jones,' said Lestrade.

'You've been taking our names in vain, Lestrade.' Abberline pompously rocked on his heels, then broke into a broad grin. 'But I suppose it was in a good cause,' and he nodded to Frost as he bade him good day.

'Good to have you back, Lestrade.' Jones slapped him heartily on the shoulder as he left the office.

'Now then, you'd better sit down and tell me all about it,' said Frost.

'It's difficult to know where to begin, sir.'

'How about with the Golden Dawn?'

'Ah, Beeson told you about that?'

'Beeson? Good God, no. I don't listen to retired coppers, Lestrade. They can get you into all sorts of trouble. No, I've known about the Golden Dawn all along. We grocers' kids from Grantham are nobody's fools, you know.'

Well, thought Lestrade, I've arrived. He'll be offering me a cigar next.

'Have a cigar, Lestrade.'

'You've known about the Golden Dawn all along?'

'Yes, why do you think I sent you to Mawnan all those months ago? We got a tip-off. Anonymous, of course. Aren't they all? It simply said that a shepherd was going to be killed. When you found that hyena thing, I assumed that was it, but the killings went on.'

'I suspect your tip-off was from a hapless young man named Jacob Crowley. I assumed William Lamb had no connection with the other deaths. Why was a warrant put out for my arrest?'

'To trap Gregson. I'd had my suspicions about him from the start. Too fanatical. Too suspicious. Of everything. Everybody. That sort of man has something to hide. That's why I sent you undercover to Manchester. Official enquiries, great feet, anything like that would have frightened him off. I wanted him to dig himself in deep. He was a neophyte, a novice if you like, in the Order of Golden Dawn.'

'Are you seriously expecting me to believe, sir, that Tobias Gregson worshipped the Devil?'

'No, Lestrade, he worshipped the pound note. Or to be more precise, lots of them. As far as we know, the Golden Dawn is a society of cranks, like the Flat Earth Society. Only occasionally, along comes a maniacal family like the Crowleys and all hell breaks loose. For most of the Golden Dawn, it is a matter of power, politics, big business. Things you and I don't understand, Lestrade.'

'So you knew about the Crowleys too?'

'No, not in detail. Until I had a visit not an hour ago from a Doctor Crosse. I believe you've met him?'

'And who paid Gregson?'

'Ah, there you have me. Whoever paid him wanted you out of the way. Off the case entirely. Hence this trumped-up nonsense about the Kaiser and hence my need to play along with it. Mind you, you kept out of my constables' way fairly effectively. Calling yourself Abberline at Bow Street took some nerve.'

'So the Golden Dawn still exists?'

'Yes, it does. We only found the tip of the iceberg here, Lestrade. Most of it is in the murky depths somewhere, but we do what we can.'

'And in those depths you didn't suspect Charlo?'

'Charlo?' Frost's composure was rattled. 'What has he to do with this?'

'You will find his charred body in whatever's left of the

wing at Chelsea Hospital, sir.'

Frost blinked as realisation dawned. 'You mean, he and Crowley . . . ?'

'. . . were the same man. Yes, sir.'

Frost's lower lip threatened to disappear below his cravat for a moment. 'I must confess, Lestrade, I never gave him a thought. Oh, I found his chronic absences suspect and I began to doubt my judgement. But I just assumed he was work-shy, a hypochondriac. Charlo, a neophyte of the Golden Dawn! No wonder he didn't look well. To be candid, Lestrade, I had my doubts about Bradstreet, but this . . . And I gave him to you as your go-between with me. My dear chap, I could have been the death of you.'

Lestrade was just about magnanimous enough to wave that aside. 'What does Ipsissimus mean?'

'Ah, Ipsissimus. As I said, I don't know much about the Dawn, but Ipsissimus is the Top Dog, the leader of the whole stinking lot. They aren't all madmen, they aren't all Satanists, but they play a dirty game and they are probably everywhere.'

'Sort of Freemasons?' ventured Lestrade.

'If I'm right, the members of the Golden Dawn would make the Masons look like choirboys. Which reminds me, when is my next Lodge meeting?' Frost consulted his diary. 'You know the definition of Ipsissimus, Lestrade? Evil beyond all comprehension. That frightens me, Lestrade. That frightens me.'

'I've an idea you know who Ipsissimus is, sir,' said the inspector.

'I was talking to the commissioner the other day. He had been talking to the Home Secretary—'

'Mr Churchill?' interjected Lestrade.

Frost ignored him. 'Let's just say I have a few ideas.'

'May I hear them, sir? After all, I have been through rather a lot on this case. You see, there is one thing I don't understand. Donald Crowley came back to England in eighteen-seventy, but it was twenty-three years before he began to kill, before Lamb's death. Why the delay? Why did he wait to carry out "the prophesy of the Golden Dawn"?'

Frost looked at him hard. He opened the door and checked the corridor outside. 'Let's just say this, Lestrade. You breathe one word of this to a living soul and I'll have you off the Force, I swear it. All I have is conjecture. Circumstance. Absolutely nothing that would stand up in a court of law. Ipsissimus is not one man, Lestrade. At least, he is a man who changes with another post, simultaneously held by the incumbent. I am not going to tell you what that post is, Inspector. Suffice to say that the residence that goes with it is Number Ten in a certain street by the river.'

'You mean . . .'

'As that office changes, so does Ipsissimus. It has been so since the days of Walpole.'

'I still don't see, sir.'

'Only one man in that post has refused to assume the title and role of Ipsissimus, Lestrade. The man who currently holds it. Educated at Eton and Oxford, one of the ablest lieutenants of the late Mr Peel; he has a perfectly hideous wife and spends a great deal of his time chopping down trees.'

'The GOM' said the inspector.

'Lestrade!' Frost clapped an hysterical hand over his subordinate's mouth, eyes swivelling manically round the room. Then, in a whisper, 'He's on his way out, Lestrade. The man who has held the position by the river four times this century. He probably knows as much about the Dawn as any of its members and you know what a confounded Christian he is? Well, it's my belief that before he goes – and he has said he will not stand again – it's my belief he'll speak out. Denounce the Dawn and all its members.'

'Then he is in danger?'

'Yes. Don't worry. I'm working on that one.'

'And Ipsissimus?'

'Take your pick. The title must have been transferred. I'm sure your knowledge of the current political situation is as good as mine. They'll bring the' – again the whisper – 'GOM down soon. Ireland. The Naval Estimates. It won't matter what. They're preparing for that day, Lestrade. Whoever the new Ipsissimus is, he's a new broom, sweeping clean. Donald Crowley represented a cobweb. There were men alive – the men of F Troop – who had knowledge which could, in the right hands, draw attention to the Dawn and all its machinations. These men had to be silenced. And madmen like the Crowleys were the very ones to do it.'

'The irony was,' said Lestrade, 'F Troop had forgotten. The Charge on the following day had pushed what they had seen at Kadiköy out of their minds. And what did they see? On patrol in a hostile land? Far from home? And at night? None of these deaths need have happened at all.'

'Lestrade,' said Frost, 'I have said more than enough. You've been playing chief inspectors for too long. Now go and get your tea.'

Lestrade turned to go.

'Oh, and Sholto,' said Frost softly; 'apart from the GOM, you are the first, as far as I know, to break the Dawn's defences. We may both be marked men, you and I. Mind how you go.'

'Oh, Sholto, all I heard from you was "Stay with relatives. Stop. Away for some time. Stop." I wasn't there when you needed me.'

Lestrade reached over to the lovely warm body of the woman beside him.

'You are now, Sarah. That's the important thing. And God, I need you now.'

He kissed her cascading blonde hair where it tumbled over her bare shoulders and full breasts.

'Mrs Manchester, I think it's time I made an honest woman of you.'

'What, Inspector Lestrade, you mean you're going to pay me the back rent you owe me?'

'Sshh!' whispered Lestrade. 'You're supposed to be my housekeeper, not my landlady. The shame of it.'

'Sholto.' She was suddenly serious. 'You won't . . . won't go away again, will you?'

'No, Sarah, I won't go away again.' Do you hear that,

Constance? Do you hear that, Daisy? He vowed to the night, I won't go away again.

'You know the funniest part of all this?' Lestrade turned to the voluptuous Mrs Manchester again. 'Nimrod Frost thinks you're sixty-one.'

And they laughed together in the darkness . . . .

Lestrade
and the
Hallowed House

Volume III in the Sholto Lestrade Mystery Series

M.J. Trow

A Gateway Mystery

REGNERY
PUBLISHING, INC.
Since 1947 • An Eagle Publishing Company

To the Bills

'Not a mouse
Shall disturb this hallow'd house:
I am sent with broom before,
To sweep the dust behind the door.'

A Midsummer Night's Dream Act V sci

Contents

Chapter One

A Scandal in Belgravia

The Great Queen was dead. All the years of tribulation – and the trials – over at last. The century had barely begun before the great heart had given up the ghost. And peace came. So much for Oscar Wilde.

Within three months, at Osborne in the Isle of Wight, Victoria, Queen Empress by the Grace of God, also shuffled off the mortal coil. Her passing went more noticed than Oscar's. After all, she had not outraged society during one of its periodic bouts of morality. Neither had she called the Marquis of Queensberry a libeller. And she remained strangely unmoved by errand boys. All in all, most people said, a very pointful life. Under her auspices, Britain had become truly great. And the Empire had been created on which the Sun Never Set. It was a gilded age of cliché and pomposity. But most people, while looking back with more than a hint of *fin de siècle*, looked forward too. A king again after sixty-four years! Only the feminist coterie around Mrs Pankhurst failed to stand and cheer for that. It was a brave new world, a new century. And if the tiresome Boers insisted on dragging their petty problems into that century, well, rest assured that Bobs and this new fellow – what was his name? – Kitchener? They would soon put that right.

Walter Dew stood in the changing room in the basement of Scotland Yard. He carefully macassared his hair for the second time that morning and admired again the metaphorical stripes on his sleeve. Not bad, he thought to himself. Fifteen years in the Force and a sergeant at last. He was just burnishing the new tiepin in the spotted green of the mirror when a face appeared over his shoulder.

'Very nice, Dew. Very nice.'

'Oh, good morning sir.' Dew snapped to attention as the Donegal and bowler hat hit him in the chest.

'Vanity,' the newcomer clicked his tongue, 'all is vanity.'

'Well sir, it's just . . . my new position sir.'

The newcomer wondered if it was the translation of that naughty Indian book by Sir Richard Burton which was currently doing the rounds at the Yard that prompted the new sergeant's remark, but he dismissed it. Dew didn't have the intellect.

'Tell me, Sergeant, between polishing your stripes and your hair, have you had a chance to read the Orders of the Day?'

Dew racked his newly promoted brain. 'Quantity of ping-pong balls stolen, sir. And the Egyptian Ambassador has reported people calling him a damned fuzzy-wuzzy again.'

'Forgive me, Dew,' the newcomer checked his half-hunter, 'I was under the impression this was H Division. I'm sure Superintendent Abberline can handle serious crime of the ping-pong variety. As for the Egyptian gentleman, I don't think we need trouble Special Branch, do you? Especially since the last person I heard refer to His Potentateness as that was the Commissioner of the Metropolitan Police!' He tried again, 'Anything for me?'

'Ah, yes sir. His Nims would like to see you, sir. Matter of the utmost urgency, he said.'

The newcomer nodded with a tired look on the narrow, parchment-coloured face. He checked his moustaches in the mirror momentarily, careful not to let the sergeant see, and made for the stairs. Dew reached for the telephone on the wall. It clicked and vibrated and a whistle answered.

'Mr Frost sir, this is Sergeant Dew.'

A silence ensued.

'Sergeant·Walter Dew, sir. H Division.'

'Well?' an unreasoning crackle snapped back at him.

'Inspector Lestrade is on his way up, sir.'

'Well, you'd better hang up his hat and coat, hadn't you?' And the whistle sounded in his ear. He was still standing there, open-mouthed, wondering how Nimrod Frost knew he was holding Lestrade's accoutrements, when the inspector reached the lift.

He missed old Dixon on the front desk. There was a blue-eyed boy there now – whose, he wasn't sure. But certainly it was true what they said. When policemen started looking younger than you, it was time to hang up your truncheon.

'Come!' the voice bellowed through the ornate glass-fronted door. Why was it, Lestrade wondered, that Heads of the Criminal Investigation Department never said 'in' at the end of that sentence?

'Good morning, sir.' The inspector beamed.

'Lestrade, you look terrible. Have a cigar.' Frost shoved a cheroot into the inspector's lips. He rang a bell, which summoned a demure, middle-aged lady with iron-grey locks and a face to match.

'Miss Featherstonehaugh, tea, please.'

'Lemon?' she asked.

'No. Cream and sugar.'

'It's not good for you, Mr Frost. Your arteries.'

'My arteries,' Frost heaved himself upright to his full five foot six and his complete nineteen stone, 'are the least of my problems this morning. Inspector Lestrade always looks worse than I do.'

Miss Featherstonehaugh smiled coyly at the inspector, then reached up and tweaked his cheek, chuckling as she did so. 'Never,' she sighed, her matronly bosom heaving with lust or the discomfort of her stays, 'you gorgeous boy,' and she swept from the room. Lestrade wished again that the ground had opened up for him.

'She'll have to go,' grunted Frost, accepting Lestrade's

proffered Lucifer. 'You wouldn't think a woman of her age and marital status would harbour such indecent thoughts, would you?'

'I prefer not to think about it, sir. I'm a funny age myself.'

'How old now, Lestrade? Not long to retirement, eh?' The Head of the Criminal Investigation Department blew smoke rings to the ceiling.

'Forty-eight, sir. I have given it some thought.'

Frost grinned. 'I can't see you growing petunias in Peckham, Lestrade. Not for a while yet at least. Which is just as well.' His face darkened. To business thought Lestrade. 'What do you know about Ralph Childers?'

'Nothing, sir.'

Frost was checked, momentarily. 'Come, come, Lestrade. You are a man of affairs . . .'

For a second, Lestrade's heart skipped a beat. Who had been talking?

'I happen to know you read the *Sun*. News, man. Parliament. You know, that collection of misfits and pederasts who presume to run the country.'

A little strong, Lestrade thought, for the Head of the Criminal Investigation Department, but it wasn't his place to say so.

'Ah,' he volunteered, 'Ralph Childers the MP.'

'Ex-MP.' Frost corrected him.

'XMP, sir?' Clearly the *Sun* had let Lestrade down. He hadn't met those initials before.

'His body was found early this morning, Lestrade. At his home in Belgravia.'

'And you suspect—'

'Everyone.' Frost nodded.

Miss Featherstonehaugh scuttled in, fussing round Lestrade with the cream and sugar and leaving Frost to help himself.

'When you've finished,' bellowed Frost, more loudly than he intended, 'helping the inspector, Miss Featherstonehaugh,' mellower now, 'perhaps you could leave us?'

She snorted indignantly and drew up her skirts, sweeping

noiselessly from the room.

'You'll find the local boys on hand of course,' Frost went on, applying his blubbery lips to the porcelain. Lestrade enjoyed the luxury of a cup with a handle. So superior to the mugs in his own office on the floor below. Frost leaned forward. 'But this is a delicate one, Lestrade. There are rumours . . .'

'Rumours, sir?'

Frost looked around him, checking particularly that the horizon was free of Featherstonehaughs.

'Let's just say,' he whispered, 'that the late Mr Childers' favourite reading, apart from Private Members' Bills, was the Marquis de Sade.'

Lestrade was sure there was a joke there somewhere about the bills of private members, but he let it go. What did Frost mean? Was there a French connection?

'Any leads, sir?'

Frost slurped his second cup, having doled in his usual three sugars.

'None. Apparently, the body hasn't been moved. The coroner will take over when you've finished.'

Frost looked up. Lestrade knew the interview was at an end. He left what remained of his tea and took his leave. 'Oh, and Lestrade,' Frost stopped him, 'let's be careful, shall we? It's a jungle out there.'

Lestrade collected his accoutrements from his sergeant. For a moment, he toyed with taking Dew with him. He could see the mental anguish on the man's face as he screwed his courage to the sticking place and sharpened a pencil prior to tackling the morning's paperwork. But no, Frost had implied the matter was delicate. And Dew would be no use in this case. He could barely read English, let alone French. The inspector caught a hansom and hurried west.

He alighted within the hour – the new Underground *would* have been quicker, he now realised – and looked up at the Corinthian columns of 102 Eaton Square, an imposing edifice, Georgian and opulent. Lestrade didn't like it. Wealth on this scale both annoyed and unnerved him. Two burly constables saluted as he leapt up the steps between them and turned not a hair as the inspector somersaulted gracefully over the top step and caught himself a sharp one on the brass jaws of the lion knocker. Another constable opened the door, by which time Lestrade had recovered his composure and wiped the tears from his eyes.

'Who are you?' a voice from the aspidistra grove in the far corner demanded.

'Inspector Lestrade, Scotland Yard,' he answered.

'Oh, I'm Smellie.' A man appeared from the foliage.

Probably, thought Lestrade.

'Pimlico.'

'Inspector?' asked Lestrade.

'Nine years tomorrow.'

'Doesn't time fly?'

Lestrade had worked with bobbies outside the Yard before. To a man they resented him. The Yard. The very Force itself. No point in being polite to them. As you walked away, you felt the knife between your shoulder blades.

'He's in here.' The uniformed inspector led the way into a vast library, wall to wall in red leather. Chairs, lamps, books by the hundred. It was a veritable British Museum. But there was no body. In answer to Lestrade's silent enquiry, Smellie pressed the spine of a rather out of place Mrs Beeton and the entire wall swung away to reveal a passage, dark and bare.

'After you, Inspector.'

And although that sounded uncomfortably like a sentiment of Miss Featherstonehaugh's, Lestrade complied.

For a man with Lestrade's problem, to lead the way in a darkened space, especially a confined one, was not the safest of moves. Still, he wasn't about to embarrass himself in the presence of this lesser mortal from the Metropolitan Police. Lestrade had his pride. It was the Smellies of this world who brought it out. Even so, he was grateful for the glow of light as he turned the corner.

'We're going west under the servants' quarters, now,' Smellie informed him. Lestrade turned in the gloom to look for the compass. There wasn't one. Perhaps Inspector Smellie had a naval background.

The glow was coming from a single oil lamp which threw long shadows on the red walls of another room, smaller than the one upstairs and almost directly under it. The passage must have wound back on itself in a tight angle. But there were no books. Lestrade saw a second lamp, a third, a fourth, until he realised he was surrounded by mirrors and it was the same lamp. Even on the ceiling, though the ascending smoke there had darkened the glass and spoiled the effect. The blood red around the mirrors burned back from every side, plush and sickening.

A study in scarlet, mused Lestrade until something more prosaic caught his attention. Smellie moved to turn up the lamp.

'Gloves, man.' Lestrade checked him.

Smellie complied, cursing himself that the Yard man had caught him out in an elementary slip.

The full light rose on the late Mr Ralph Childers. Or what was left of him. He was hanging upside down from a chain pulled taut from the centre of the ceiling. He was naked, his hands manacled together and wrenched behind his back. From them the chain ran back to his ankles and joined the single links from the beams. His back and buttocks were scarred. Old ones, new ones. Some still sticky with blood. Others livid white in the flickering lamplight. Lestrade pulled Smellie's arm closer. There was no sound but the quiet click of the chains as the former Member of Parliament swung gently in the draught. The odour in the room was sweet – a sickly combination of sandalwood and cedarwood – and lurking there, in the experienced nostrils of Lestrade, the familiar smell of death.

As Lestrade urged Smellie's arm lower, the local man paused, 'It's not a pretty sight down . . . there.'

Lestrade glanced at the deceased's private parts. Not the prettiest he'd seen, but he felt Smellie was over-reacting. Then he realised it was the head to which his colleague referred. The hair swept the ground. It had been grey; now it was matted with blood and the head above it was split open, like the water melons Lestrade had seen at the Albert Dock when he'd been a Bluebottle in the days of his youth, catching villains at Wapping and wading up to his armpits in cold, brackish water at Shadwell Stair. One bulging eye, sightless and dull, gleamed white as the body twirled. Carefully, Lestrade parted the unkempt beard to reveal the iron collar with its spike driven deep into the throat.

'Is he dead?' Smellie asked.

Lestrade straightened. 'I thought you'd checked all this,' he said.

'No, I only just came on duty. My constables told me it was a messy one. I've never seen anything like this.'

Lestrade noticed how the colour had drained from Smellie's face. 'Come on,' he said, 'let's get some fresh air. Then I want more light down here. And no one,' he paused and took Smellie's sleeve, 'no one gets in here until I say so.'

'There is a coroner upstairs.'

'Let him wait. The last thing we want is his great feet sloshing about down here. Who found the body?'

The policemen reached ground level. 'Beales. His man.'

'How many other servants?'

'Eight. The others are at the weekend retreat in Berkshire. A house called "Draughts".'

Lestrade gave explicit instructions to Smellie, who vanished with his constables to carry them out. At least, thought Lestrade, the man isn't going to be obstructive. Whatever private thoughts he harbours about the arrogance of the Yard, he's keeping them to himself.

It was nearly lunchtime before the inspector sat down at Mr Childers' magnificent desk in the library. He had gone back to the weirdly scented little room below. This time he had gone alone. Years of 'the sights' had taught Lestrade that he operated best on his own. He was surer of his emotions – and his stomach – that way. He flicked open the notepad to make sure he hadn't overlooked anything. Cause of death? A blunt instrument to the back and top of the head, he would guess. Or perhaps the collar had been snapped shut first so that the iron spike had penetrated windpipe and spinal cord. So was he dead when he was hauled upside down so cruelly near the floor? And what about the whipmarks on the body? Or was 'whipmark' too much of an assumption? Lestrade had learned a long time ago to keep an open mind, almost as open, he mused in one of his more grisly moments, as that of the late lamented who had been twirling below stairs. Childers had been taken away through the tradesmens' entrance, of course, but even there a crowd of fascinated sightseers had slowed his undignified journey to the waiting Maria. Lestrade had watched from an upstairs window. Errand boys and shop lads nattering like fishwives over the handlebars of their Raleighs; the servants of neighbours who 'happened-to-be-passing', and as Lestrade's eyes shot up to the nearest windows on his own level, the neighbours themselves, curious behind the shivering nets. Smellie's constables elbowed the gathering crowd aside and Lestrade heard the familiar cry, 'Move along there, move along.' He noticed one or two young men scrabble nearer than the rest, prying under the grey, regulation blankets and then break away, scattering in different directions, ahead of the more idly curious. He recognised the gait and the lean and hungry look – newshounds from Fleet Street. So much for Nimrod Frost's 'delicate one'. It would be all over London by nightfall – the *Standard* would see to that.

'You found the body?' Lestrade looked up from his notepad.

Beales, the gentleman's gentleman, nodded. Lestrade looked at him hard. Every gesture, every move was ordered and precise. He mentally crossed the man off his list of suspects. Here was a man who did not like to soil his hands or spoil his routine. A little Goddards for the silver cleaning, the odd funeral of a maiden aunt in Cheltenham, but not a waistcoat drenched in his master's blood and not the appalling physical and emotional wrench of smashing in a skull. Where was the economy of word and manner in that? But Lestrade was leaping howitzers. He had already envisaged a frenzied attack – the work of a deranged

maniac. As for the bloodsoaked waistcoat, the murderer had
been as naked as his victim . . . But all this was surmise. Facts, he
told himself. What of the facts? And this careful, calm, studied
man before him. He at least knew something of his former
master's habits. Lestrade slowly produced a cigar and it shook
him a little as Beales leapt upright to light it for him. The
gentleman's gentleman's nostrils quivered disapprovingly as he
inhaled the smoke. He found himself looking Lestrade up and
down. A man of middle years – forty-five, forty-six. Five foot
nine or ten. Appalling dress sense. No one wore Donegals any
more. He looked like a coachman.

'You found the body?' Lestrade's question ended the valet's
rambling assessment of his interrogator.

'Yes sir.' Beales thought perhaps a vocal answer would satisfy
the man. A nod clearly hadn't worked.

'Tell me about it.' Lestrade began to circle the room, glancing
occasionally at Beales, occasionally fingering a book on a shelf.
To Beales' domestic brain, it appeared as though the inspector
was looking for dust.

'It was six thir—' Beales was unnerved by the whirling
policeman. He turned one way, then the other, trying to fix him
with his eyes. All his training had taught him to look a man in
the eyes, except of course when receiving a gratuity or when
one's master, believing himself to be alone, began to pick his
nose.

'You are very precise,' Lestrade cut in.

'I am a gentleman's gentleman, sir. Precision is my trade.'

Lestrade stopped. 'Go on.'

'My late master was also a creature of habit. I had strict
instructions to wake him at six thirty each morning. He
invariably bathed and took a ride along the Row before lunching
at his club or going to the House.'

'His club?'

'The Diogenes.'

'The House?'

Beales looked up, his look of amazement turning to contempt. 'Of Commons, sir,' he said acidly.

'Just checking,' said Lestrade. 'Go on.'

'Mr Childers was not in his room. I brought the tea here, thinking he might be working on some papers. He was not.'

'So you went downstairs?'

'Not immediately. I checked the dining room and the breakfast room, although I knew his breakfast was only then being prepared. I was about to try the stables in the mews. Sometimes Mr Childers could not sleep and had been known to saddle his horse himself.'

God, thought Lestrade, the versatility of the landed classes.

'I don't know what made me go to the Cell.'

'The Cell?' repeated Lestrade.

'The room in the basement, Inspector. Where your constables found the . . . Mr Childers.'

'You said Cell. Do you mean cellar?'

'No sir . . . Perhaps I had better explain. After all,' Beales began to twitch his fingers a little, the first sign of a slipping composure, 'I am anxious to help all I can. It's just that a gentleman's gentleman must be loyal. And discreet.'

Lestrade played the moment as it came. He supposed, at that moment, that Beales was everything he appeared to be. The inspector placed an avuncular hand on his shoulder. 'It's a little bit late to be loyal, Mr Beales. And discretion isn't going to help me catch his murderer, now, is it?'

Beales breathed in tortuously and nodded. 'Have you heard of the Hell Fire Club, Inspector?'

'Is that the little one in Cleveland Street?'

Again, amazement swept briefly over Beales' face. This time it was not followed by contempt.

'No sir. It was organised by Sir Francis Dashwood a hundred and fifty years ago. It was composed of gentlemen – bloods or rakes I suppose they would have been called – who were known as the Monks of Medmenham. They practised every vice known to man. Not to mention woman.'

'Women?'

'Please,' Beales started in the seat, 'I asked you not to mention women. Mr Childers was a bachelor, sir. He never officially entertained ladies. Nor was he seen in their company. Without wishing to be unkind to my staff, he chose the plainest of females for his household. His misogyny was well known.'

Lestrade had no answer to that, but his straying hand came fortuitously across a dictionary and he riffled through its pages. After what seemed to both men an eternity, Lestrade snapped shut the book triumphantly.

'So he didn't like women?'

'No, sir.' Contempt had returned to the gentleman's gentleman. 'However, when the fit was on him, sir, he . . .' Beales was uncomfortable, 'he occasionally gave way to . . . excesses.'

'You interest me strangely,' said Lestrade, stubbing the cigar on an ashtray as he alighted again in Childers' chair.

'He would put rough clothes on and slip out at night.'

'And?'

'He would find an unfortunate, a lady of the streets, and bring her back here. There is a door your men will not have found, Inspector. It leads directly to the Cell. There, Mr Childers would don his monk's robes and indulge in . . .'

Lestrade remembered the whips and thongs that lined the scarlet walls below. And the iron shackles. And the chains. And the mirrors for a better view.

'Hunnish practices?' he asked.

'The English Vice,' nodded Beales, as though it were a loyal toast.

'Tell me, was Mr Childers the only member of this reincarnated club?'

'No sir. On high days, the Cell was a hive of activity.'

'Beales,' Lestrade was perambulating again, 'I pride myself on being abreast of current affairs.' He hoped Frost couldn't hear him. 'How is it that I have never heard a whisper in what Fleet Street have been known to call their "newspapers" of Mr Childers' habits?'

'I clean them myself sir. Oh . . .' And for once it was the

gentleman's gentleman's turn to misunderstand. 'There are laws of libel as I am sure you are aware, Inspector Lestrade. In any case, Mr Childers was the soul of discretion. The Cell is carefully padded so that no sound escapes. That is why I would have heard nothing of this dreadful deed in the night. Only I – until today – knew of the room's existence. No one else – not the staff, not the master's colleagues – knew that he ... er ... entertained. He used to say ...' Beales stopped.

'Yes?' Lestrade chipped in.

'He used to say that when his back and buttocks hurt him after a debauch, he would find the seats in the House very uncomfortable. And at those moments, he swore that the Grand Old Man was watching him.'

'You mean Gladstone?' Lestrade asked.

'When the old gentleman was alive.' Beales assented.

'Didn't the late Prime Minister have similar habits?' the inspector ventured.

'I'm sure I don't know, sir. But you must remember, Mr Gladstone was a Liberal.' To Beales that explained it all.

'When you said earlier,' Lestrade flicked aside the nets to look at the mews in the watery afternoon sun, 'that no one but you knew of the Cell, you were not, of course, including the other members.'

'Members?'

'Of the Hell Fire Club, man,' beamed Lestrade. 'Those latter-day bloods and rakes who joined your dear departed master in his interesting habits.'

'They of course knew of the room, sir.'

'Tell me, was 102 Eaton Square the headquarters of the club?'

'As far as I am aware, sir.'

Lestrade dropped the joviality. 'I want their names.'

Beales leapt to his feet. 'Sir, I am a gentleman's gentleman. Loyalty and discretion are my watchwords. Nothing will drag that information from me.'

'Beales,' Lestrade leaned towards him, 'I am an Inspector of the Metropolitan Police. I don't have any watchwords at all.

And I can get you fifteen years for obstructing a police officer in the pursuance of his duty. I think Pentonville will drag any information out of you.'

For a moment, the two men looked at each other. Then Beales summoned what dignity he could. 'If you go to Mr Childers' country house in Berkshire,' he said, 'you will find a red leather box in the centre drawer of his study desk. This,' he produced it deftly from his pocket, 'is the key to that box. I think its contents will give you the answers you need.'

'And why should you have a key to such a Pandora's delight?' It was the only bit of mythology that had stayed with Lestrade since Blackheath crammer days.

'I was to destroy the box, sir. In the event of Mr Childers losing an election. But now that he has lost his life . . .'

Lestrade took the key. 'What will you do now, Beales?' he asked.

The gentleman's gentleman shook himself from the new realisation of his master's death. 'Mr Joseph Chamberlain has often hinted to me that I would be most welcome in his service, sir.'

'Well, then.' Lestrade patted the valet's shoulder.

'Oh, no, sir,' Beales looked horrified, 'Mr Chamberlain *was* a Liberal!'

And that again seemed to say it all.

On his way through the hall, Lestrade met Smellie.

'I'll leave the other servants to you,' he said, 'they may be able to add something. Send your report to the Yard, will you? Oh, and Smellie . . .'

The inspector looked up.

'With your compass-like sense of geography, where is Berkshire?'

Smellie thought hard. 'On the map, it's the bit on the left-hand side. Turn right out of the door.'

Lestrade took the train to Hungerford and a carrier's cart to Ogbourne Maizey. Smellie's geography may not have been what it once was, but he had elicited the name of the village of which the great house of 'Draughts' was the manor. It was sunset when the cart crunched on the gravel outside the mellow, yellow entrance porch. The dying sun threw long shadows of the twisted chimneys across the lawns. Lestrade tipped the carrier, making a mental note to charge it to expenses and pulled the doorbell. He heard the answering ring down the hall and waited as the bolts slid back. A sour-faced housekeeper appeared. She had heard the news from Mr Beales via the telephone. Yes, the house had all the modern conveniences. There was a shower, if the gentleman cared to use it. Lestrade wondered if his armpits had betrayed him; but he stoically declined the offer and was shown into the study.

It was scarlet again, a copy, if the inspector's memory served him aright, of the one in Eaton Square. Around the walls hung a number of framed Spy cartoons, characters of today and yesterday, colleagues of the former back-bencher. There was even one of Nimrod Frost, looking stones lighter than he actually was. Was one of them, Lestrade wondered, the murderer of Ralph Childers? He'd always thought the Archbishop of Canterbury looked a bit shifty, but the man was eighty if he was a day. How many octogenarians were capable of hoisting a dead weight of twelve or thirteen stone off the floor with chains? No, Cantuar could sleep easy in his bed. Lestrade unlocked the drawer and placed the walnut burred box on the desk. It was inlaid with the initials of the late lamented, and a series of incomprehensible hieroglyphics. The inspector inserted the key and the lid flipped open. Nothing. The box was perfectly empty. So Beales had sent him here on a wild goose chase. Lestrade fumed at the waste of his time. He fumed still further at being taken for such an idiot. In an uncharacteristic gesture he slammed the box down hard on the red leather of the desk only to see a drawer at its base slide open. 'Ah,' he smiled, 'the old secret-drawer ploy.'

In it lay a book, in plain black leather and its pages were filled with notes in Childers' handwriting. Lestrade had seen examples of it at Eaton Square. The book appeared to be a diary and the inspector read until darkness drew over the house. The sour-faced housekeeper solemnly lit the lamps around Lestrade.

'Mrs . . . er . . .' The inspector stopped her.

'Smith,' said the housekeeper.

A likely story, thought Lestrade. 'Tell me, does – did – Mr Childers entertain?'

'Now and again, sir. But he didn't come here often. Most of his friends were Members of Parliament, sir, like himself. He didn't bring many of them here.'

'And has he had any condolences?'

'The vicar, sir. Nobody else. His colleagues would use his London address.'

'Mrs Smith, is there lodging in the village?'

'There's an inn, sir, but it's not the best. I had instructions from Mr Beales to accommodate you here. There's plenty of room now the master's gone.'

And so it was that Lestrade spent the night at 'Draughts'. He couldn't sleep. It was probably the pork and pickles of the melancholy Mrs Smith. Or the changeable weather of the early spring. He'd seen no other servants, only a couple of gardeners pruning the privet, glimpsed from the study window. There was no life in this house. It was obvious that Childers used it infrequently. Everywhere druggets were pulled over the furniture, giving each room a ghostly appearance in the gloom of the April evening.

A little before midnight, showers beat on the leaded panes of Lestrade's window. He disliked four posters. They made him feel claustrophobic. And he'd never really recovered from being seduced in one. So he sat in the deep recess below the window, and ploughed on through the diary he had found. What was it Beales had said? The contents of the box would give him the answers he needed. But most of it was cryptic nonsense. A series of jumbled letters, spaces and dots. Perhaps the cypher department at the Yard could make something of it. Certainly Lestrade could not.

The inspector wandered with his oil lamp through the upper reaches of the house. The modern conveniences of which Mrs Smith had spoken did not extend to electricity and by the morning Lestrade had hammer toes to prove it, where he had tripped over the wainscotting in the long, dark shadows.

Breakfast was as unadventurous as his supper of the night before and he was glad to be aboard the Western Region again, rattling towards the City, with his book and his problem. He turned to his own face in the window. Who would kill a Member of Parliament? Six hundred odd other Members of Parliament? But no, this was not political. It was sexual. Whatever torrid events went on in the Cell at Eaton Square, there was one person who was sure to know. And it was on her door that Lestrade was knocking by mid-morning.

The grille in the little door in Greek Street slid back. A heavy black face shone through. 'Yes?' it asked. Lestrade fanned the air with a roll in the time-honoured manner.

'Miss Labedoyere.' He made a brave stab at the French.

The shining pink eyes in the shining black face didn't blink. 'Who sent you?'

Lestrade gambled on the inhabitants of Greek Street bordellos not reading newspapers. 'Ralph Childers,' he answered.

The grille slammed shut. Had he said the wrong thing? Given the wrong password? Perhaps if he'd said, 'The boy I love sits up in the gallery'? Still, it was too late now. He heard the bolts jar and clank. The way was opened by a huge negro, in loud check suit and silk shirt. The black man snatched Lestrade's money and locked the door behind him.

'Miss Labedoyere don't really receive guests at this hour.'

Lestrade tried to place the accent. Caribbean with a hint of Seven Dials.

'I'm sure in my case she'll make an exception.'

'Wait here.'

Lestrade was shown into an anteroom, hung with plush velvet and heavy flock wallpaper. Everywhere was the smell of cedarwood and sandalwood. It was the Cell at Eaton Square. He sensed he was on the right track. The beaded curtain swished and rattled behind him and a powerful woman strode into the room wearing a basque bodice bedecked with bows, and a vast plume of ostrich feathers in her hair.

'Mr . . . er . . . ?'

'Lister.' Lestrade used his favourite alias.

'I am Fifi Labedoyere.'

No, mused Lestrade.

'What can I do for you, for' – she riffled the notes in her hand – 'five pounds?' She swirled around Lestrade, studying him carefully. 'A bit of brown?' She laughed. 'No, silly of me. A handsome, full-blooded man like you,' she swept off his bowler hat, 'will want a bit of red.' She pushed him back onto a *chaise-longue* with a tap which could break a swan's wing. 'Now . . .' She tickled his moustache with her tapering, pointed finger nails.

You're a man of the world, Lestrade told himself. Don't sneeze.

'There is Charlotte. Fresh from the country. A virgin, Mr Lister. Only fourteen years old.'

Yes, Lestrade could imagine. A raddled bag of forty done up in ringlets and rouge.

'Ah, but no. I have Celeste. A nymph of the Orient. With skin like a ripe peach. She has ways of driving a man mad.'

Some dragon from Chinatown, without a tooth in her head, Lestrade imagined.

'I . . . er . . . was hoping for something a little . . . stricter,' he ventured.

'Ah,' Fifi's eyes lit up, 'you require Tamara. She is Bavarian. I have seen her reduce men to putty under her tawse.'

'Miss Labedoyere, forgive me,' smiled Lestrade, 'but I was hoping for your own exquisite services.'

Fifi laughed so that her bosoms, threatening and wide, wobbled above their whale-bone cages. 'For five pounds, dearie? I'm not that good natured.'

'A pity,' Lestrade was trying to keep the madam's fingers

away from his groin. 'Ralph Childers highly recommended you. What was it he said? "The iron of a gauntlet and the velvet of a glove."' Lestrade flattered himself on that one. Look to your laurels, Alfred Austin!

'And how is dear Ralph?' Fifi had expertly undone three of Lestrade's buttons and was whisking aside his shirt flaps.

'Dead.' Lestrade stood up, hastily adjusting his dress.

Fifi was alongside him. 'Dead?' she repeated. And realisation dawned. 'I smell copper.' The soft French had become harsh Bermondsey.

'Very astute, ma'am,' answered Lestrade.

'Bert!' the madam bawled and the Caribbean gentleman blocked the doorway. 'It's the Bill,' she snarled in a confusion of Christian names, 'he's leaving.'

Lestrade had to think fast. The bouncer was four or five stone heavier than he was and if the inspector had stood behind him, he wouldn't have been visible at all. And he appeared to have muscles like a steam hammer. Lestrade fumbled in his pocket for the brass knuckles he kept there but when he pulled his hand free, he was only holding a pair of spectacles. They helped with the mild disguise. Men called Lister always wore glasses. The negro paused momentarily, one hand on Lestrade's lapel, the other in mid-air, lining up the copper's jaw with all the science of an ex-prize fighter.

'You wouldn't hit a man with glasses?' Lestrade whined, gripping the useless rims in both hands.

'No, I'd use my bloody fist,' the negro snarled.

But Lestrade was faster. For years, the bouncer had been used to cringing middle-aged men and had learned to take his time. This time, the pause was nearly fatal. Lestrade jabbed upwards with both hands, the spectacle arms ramming painfully into the bigger man's nostrils. As the black buckled, clutching a bleeding nose, Lestrade's knee came up. Simultaneously he found the knuckles in his other pocket and brought them down with both hands on the bouncer's skull. There was a dull thud and a gurgle and the building shook as he hit the floor.

'Now then, Miss Labedoyere.' Lestrade turned to the madam. Fifi spat contemptuously, although she was a little nonplussed at seeing the unstoppable Bert lying in such an ungainly heap. She backed away, uncoiling a whip which Lestrade had not noticed dangling from her wrist.

'Nice of you to offer,' said Lestrade, 'but I'm afraid I told you a teensy fib. Mr Childers did not recommend you. His tastes and mine scarcely coincide at all.'

'You flatfoot bastard!' Fifi shrieked, her breasts slapping from side to side as she let fly with the rawhide thong. It ripped across Lestrade's nose and cheeks, drawing a crimson line the width of his face. He spun round, bouncing off the wall and stumbling over the prostrate Bert. Can't win them all, he mused as his tear-filled eyes attempted to focus on Miss Labedoyere. The lady in question was snaking back her arm for another lash, when Lestrade rolled backwards, tugging hard on the beaded curtain. It ripped away from the wall, a shower of beads clattering and bouncing on the floor. Lestrade was already down and within seconds, Miss Labedoyere had joined him, floored by the rolling beads. She cursed and swore until Lestrade wrapped the whip around her neck and sat back against the wall with the quivering heap trussed in his lap.

'Here's a new position for you, Gertie,' he hissed, trying to catch his breath. A man on the brink of his fifties shouldn't be doing this. Time to leave it to the younger coppers.

'Who?' Fifi snapped.

'Gertie Clinker,' said Lestrade, 'late of Wapping and all points east. You know, you and I are getting a bit old for this sort of game, aren't we?'

'You speak for yourself, copper!' she bellowed.

'Shame on you, Gertie. You didn't know me, did you? And me the only boy in blue who ever gave you the time of day.'

'Blimey,' she muttered, 'Sergeant Lestrade!'

'Well, that dates you, dearie,' Lestrade said. 'I've been an inspector for sixteen years.'

Gertie giggled, despite the ligature around her neck, 'Course you 'ad a nose then. Where d'you get all them cuts?'

'Well, at least one of them I got from a madam of a bordello in Greek Street.'

Gertie giggled again, 'Sorry, lover. Me eyes ain't what they used to be.'

'Are you sitting comfortably? Or shall I go on talking to the back of your head?'

'I won't give you no more trouble, Mr Lestrade. Onest. I'll come quiet. Make a change for me.' And she giggled again. Lestrade uncrossed his hands. He was glad because Gertie was a big girl and his knuckles had long ago turned white.

'Without wishing to offend, Gertie,' he said, uncrumpling his Donegal and skating warily to the corridor, 'it's not you I'm after.' He mechanically checked the bouncer. Broken jaw, he guessed. 'You will, however, need a new fancy man.'

'Well, after today's performance, I should think I do,' agreed Gertie.

'Ralph Childers,' Lestrade came back to the point.

'Oh yeah, you said.' Gertie poured them both a sizeable slug of gin. 'Here's mud in your eye, Mr Lestrade.' And she downed hers in one.

'You know I can't drink on duty.' The inspector toasted the madam and sipped the clear liquid. It affected his focus again.

'Come on dearie. Let me put something on that face.' And she ferreted in a cupboard and began dabbing away the blood. Between Lestrade's jerking and inward gasps, Miss Clinker took up his line of enquiry.

'Did I hear you say Mr Childers was dead?'

'As a doornail, Gertie.'

'Well, I'm not surprised. Did 'e overdo it a bit?'

'It?'

'E took and gave, 'e did. A right one. My arm would ache for days after one of his visits.'

'Could he have overdone to death, Gertie?'

She looked at him, pausing from her ministrations. 'In all my years in the business, Mr Lestrade, I've never known it.

Everybody has a point when enough is enough. Course if 'is ticker was dicky—

'I don't think it was his heart that took the punishment, Gertie. When did you see him last?'

'Oohh, three, maybe four months ago. 'Ere, you ain't suggestin . . . ?'

'Did you ever pay Mr Childers a house call?'

'I don't do house calls, Mr Lestrade. Mr Childers may have had floozies at his place, but for a professional service, 'e always came here.'

'Did he have any friends with him on any occasion? Or was anyone introduced to you by him? Someone with similar tastes, perhaps?'

Gertie racked what passed for a brain.

'There was one bloke. In politics 'e was, like Mr Childers. Name of . . . cor, luv a duck. What was it now? Cor, brain like a sieve, Mr Lestrade, I always 'ad.'

Lestrade reached wearily into his pocket and produced another handful of notes. 'This is the second roll, Gertie, and the last.' He placed it in her hand. She smiled triumphantly, squeezing the money into the infinitesimal space that formed the edge of one breast and the beginning of another.

'Holmes,' she said. 'Tall bloke. Thin face. Smoked a pipe.'

Lestrade was halfway down the corridor before the bewildered Gertie called him.

'One roll deserves another, dearie,' she said, standing with legs apart and hands on hips, 'for old times' sake.'

Lestrade glanced back as he reached the door.

'Gertie, I couldn't afford you,' he said.

Like what you've read so far?

Then turn the page for a special offer...

A STEAL OF A DEAL

LIKE WHAT YOU'VE READ SO FAR?

Then order this third volume in the Lestrade Mystery Series direct from the publisher. Just fill out the form on the opposite page or call our operators.

Get *Lestrade and the Hallowed House* sent directly to your home for a steal of a price. Follow the Inspector as he investigates a series of bizarre and brutal killings in the wake of Queen Victoria's death.

Volume III in the Lestrade Mystery Series will be sent from the publisher — <u>via free expedited shipping</u> — directly to your home at a cost to you of <u>only $15.95</u>.

That's a savings of nearly $10 over the actual retail price of the book and normal shipping and handling charges.

ALERT SCOTLAND YARD. IT'S A STEAL!

Call 1-888-219-4747, and tell our operators you want the
<u>Lestrade Steal of a Deal</u>!

Or fill out the form to the right and send it in.